"You will not pay me for helping your daughter. I..."

The rest of her words were muffled by Michael's fingers. "You didn't let me finish, Kate."

Shock held her immobile at the feel of those fingers, large, yet curiously gentle, pressed against her mouth. When he moved them, his fingers left a lingering warmth in their wake.

"Will you have dinner with me?"

Kate blinked at him, trying to still the foolish leap of her heart that his words had elicited. She shook her head. It had been surprisingly difficult to work with him around. But now that she was finished, there was little reason for the two of them to see each other.

Sternly Kate told herself it was for the best. What could the most mind-numbingly, knee-shakingly sexy man she'd ever had the occasion to meet want with her?

She was almost afraid to think about it....

Dear Reader,

It's month two of our special fifteenth anniversary celebration, and that means more great reading for you. Just look what's in store.

Amnesia! It's one of the most popular plot twists around, and well it should be. All of us have probably wished, just for a minute, that we could start over again, be somebody else…fall in love all over again as if it were the first time. For three of our heroines this month, whether they want it or not, the chance is theirs. Start with Sharon Sala's *Roman's Heart*, the latest in her fabulous trilogy, THE JUSTICE WAY. Then check out *The Mercenary and the Marriage Vow* by Doreen Roberts. This book carries our new TRY TO REMEMBER flash—just so you won't forget about it! And then, sporting our MEN IN BLUE flash (because the hero's the kind of cop we could all fall in love with), there's *While She Was Sleeping* by Diane Pershing.

Of course, we have three other great books this month, too. Be sure to pick up Beverly Barton's *Emily and the Stranger*, and don't worry. Though this book isn't one of them, Beverly's extremely popular heroes, THE PROTECTORS, will be coming your way again soon. Kylie Brant is back with *Friday's Child*, a FAMILIES ARE FOREVER title. Not only will the hero and heroine win your heart, wait 'til you meet little Chloe. Finally, welcome new author Sharon Mignerey, who makes her debut with *Cassidy's Courtship*.

And, of course, don't forget to come back next month for more of the best and most excitingly romantic reading around, right here in Silhouette Intimate Moments.

Leslie Wainger
Senior Editor and Editorial Coordinator

Please address questions and book requests to:
Silhouette Reader Service
U.S.: 3010 Walden Ave., P.O. Box 1325, Buffalo, NY 14269
Canadian: P.O. Box 609, Fort Erie, Ont. L2A 5X3

FRIDAY'S CHILD

KYLIE BRANT

Published by Silhouette Books

America's Publisher of Contemporary Romance

SILHOUETTE BOOKS

ISBN 0-373-07862-5

FRIDAY'S CHILD

Copyright © 1998 by Kimberly Bahnsen

This edition published by arrangement with Harlequin Books S.A.

® and TM are trademarks of Harlequin Books S.A., used under license. Trademarks indicated with ® are registered in the United States Patent and Trademark Office, the Canadian Trade Marks Office and in other countries.

Printed in U.S.A.

Books by Kylie Brant

Silhouette Intimate Moments

McLain's Law #528
Rancher's Choice #552
An Irresistible Man #622
Guarding Raine #693
Bringing Benjy Home #735
Friday's Child #862

KYLIE BRANT

married her high school sweetheart sixteen years ago, and they are raising their five children in Iowa. She spends her days teaching learning-disabled students, and many nights find her attending her sons' sporting events.

Always an avid reader, Kylie enjoys stories of love, mystery and suspense—and insists on happy endings! When her youngest children, a set of twins, turned four, she decided to try her hand at writing. Now most weekends and all summer she can be found at her computer, spinning her own tales of romance and happily-ever-afters.

Kylie invites readers to write to her at P.O. Box 231, Charles City, IA 50616.

For Jim and Marge,
who have been more than in-laws

Chapter 1

"**Y**ou need a wife, not a secretary."

Michael Friday's eyes never left the computer screen in front of him. He'd been working on solving the glitch in this program for two days, and he wasn't in the mood for interruptions. At any rate, he'd grown used to the nagging and was immune to the disapproving tone.

"Applying for the job, Bernie?"

He heard a sudden huff as his secretary drew in an outraged breath, and this time he did look up. He never missed the opportunity to watch Bernie engage in a full-blown snit. Right now her stern face was turning bright pink, her hands were perched on ample hips, and her generous bosom was quivering.

"I can assure you, I wouldn't consider it a promotion."

He nodded with mock seriousness. "Just as well. You'd be damn hard to replace. It would be pretty tough to find a secretary who actually knows how to use the intercom to buzz her boss before interrupting him."

"It would be difficult to buzz you, *sir,* since you turned off your intercom. Again."

"Some people might interpret that action," he said in a politely instructing tone, "as indicating a desire for privacy." With great deliberation he propped his long legs up on his highly polished walnut desk, crossing them at the ankles. The action could always be depended on to send his secretary into near apoplexy. The desk was the same highly polished walnut one his predecessor had used, and she regarded it with a reverence usually reserved for an altar.

The sight of his scuffed, size-thirteen running shoes on the sacred desk sent instant flags of color to her cheeks. Michael grinned. She'd never made any bones about her disapproval of his often casual attire, or about her disapproval of *him*, period. He'd gone to great lengths when he'd taken over the company three years ago to soothe employee fears. He'd kept on all workers interested in continuing, retired those employees of age with generous pensions and offered better benefits and flexible working hours to the others. The result had been instant devotion from his employees, with the notable exception of one. He couldn't buy her, he couldn't charm her, and it seemed he couldn't impress her. But she was entertaining.

"You missed another appointment yesterday afternoon," she said through clenched teeth. It was plain to see that she considered his error a blot on her own record. "I don't know how I'm expected to keep track of your meetings when you don't bother to keep me informed of all of them. I was wrong earlier. You don't need a wife, you need a keeper."

She turned and stomped back through the door connecting their two offices, but her voice drifted behind her. "After all, what woman in her right mind would shackle herself to the Beltway Raider?"

He winced at her use of the nickname that appeared with increasing regularity in the *Post*. "Shut the door on your way out," he bellowed.

But the woman who appeared in his doorway midbellow was a far cry from Maxine Bernwood. This woman's face was a perfect oval, with a small, full mouth placed precisely above her rounded chin. Curly brown hair was piled on top of her head, accentuating the curved line of her jaw. And then he saw her eyes, and thought deserted him completely. They were a pure shade of blue, the color of an Indian summer sky.

All his hormones went on red alert. With more speed than grace he dropped his feet to the floor and rose. He smiled disarmingly as he approached the woman, who was watching him with the wary fascination people usually reserved for rabid dogs. "Sorry. I didn't realize I had a visitor. Please come in," he invited, holding out his hand to her. "I'm Michael Friday, and you're in luck. I happen to have some time free this afternoon, Miss..." His tone tapered off hopefully.

"Katherine Rose." The woman supplied her name faintly as her hand was engulfed in his much larger one. He drew her inside his office and closed the door on his secretary, who was pointedly ignoring the fact that she'd failed to announce the woman's arrival.

"Please, sit down," he said, indicating chairs grouped around a long table in the middle of the room.

She shifted the bag she was carrying and then, after a brief hesitation, chose a chair. He sank into the one next to hers and grinned engagingly. "I have to admit, I'm not much for surprises, but your visit is the first thing that's gone right in two days."

"I see."

He couldn't tell by what act of nature her hair stayed up in that gravity-defying hairdo. It wasn't a bun, it was too loose, but it was secured nonetheless. He decided that he would die happy if he could just once see that glorious hair spilling in a riot of curls down her narrow back. Her narrow, *naked* back, he amended. He'd always believed that if one was going to set a goal, one should aim high.

"Katherine," he said, savoring the syllables. "Is that what your friends call you? Not Kathy, Katie?"

Surprise layered over the nerves mirrored in those incredible blue eyes. "No. That is...my friends call me Kate."

"Kate." He tasted the name, liked its flavor. "Why don't you tell me why you've come." Then he glanced at the watch on his wrist. "Better yet, you can tell me over dinner."

Her eyebrows rose. "It's barely four-thirty."

"I'm a slow driver," he said solemnly.

She gave him a considering look. "You don't know who I am, do you?"

He shook his head. "But I'd like to. Very much."

"Katherine Rose," she repeated, watching his face for a flicker of recognition. When none came, she added helpfully, "Chloe's teacher."

"Chloe's teach—" His disbelief colored his voice. "*You're* Miss Rose?" He shouldn't be so surprised. Chloe had never mentioned her teacher's age, not that it would have mattered. Anybody over the age of ten was old to his daughter. She had, however, in her usual descriptive fashion, told him many times that Miss Rose's eyes looked like they had pieces of sky in them.

"Yes," Kate said crisply. "I am. After you missed our conference yesterday, I decided to take a chance on catching you here."

"I missed our conference?" Michael got up and strode to his desk, flipping the page of his daily planner to yesterday's appointments. There, scrawled in his own handwriting, was the message, "Miss Rose 3:30." The missed appointment Bernie had been referring to. His eyes slid shut in chagrin. Yesterday at three-thirty he'd been deeply embroiled in a strategy session for yet another takeover bid, this time for a small computer company that manufactured a progressive microchip he wanted. The meeting had lasted until well after midnight.

He returned to his chair. "Miss Rose, you have my sincerest, most embarrassed apologies. I've mastered the art of writing down messages but clearly need work on reading them later."

"It's all right, Mr. Friday. Your absence wasn't totally unexpected." Her voice held a note of cool reproof. "You've missed our last five scheduled conferences."

He winced. The lady had him dead to rights and, for all her youth, made him feel as guilty as a mischievous boy in the principal's office. He held his hands up in surrender.

"Again, I plead guilty. But I did send my man, Trask, in my place to two of them. He takes care of my home, and of Chloe, while I'm away or working. And he faithfully repeated your messages about her progress in first grade." Telling her how busy he'd been for the last several months would seem like a lame excuse, so he didn't bother.

He was facing the problem common to divorced parents—balancing a career with quality family time. His company, Security Systems and Software, was leading the competition in software designed to protect computer programs. He'd marketed a variety of products suitable for the private sector, and the profits he'd reaped had taken his company to multi-million-dollar status. He'd recently been awarded a highly competitive government contract. The project, dubbed FORAY, was a new design to protect NASA's most sensitive high-tech computer research files. If he'd had greater fore-warning that Chloe would be coming to live with him, maybe he'd have been a bit more settled, both with the company and in the home he'd recently bought in Great Falls, Virginia. He sometimes felt like a juggler with too many balls in the air, and the missed appointments she referred to didn't fail to register a stab of guilt.

"Yes, I spoke with Mr. Trask," Kate agreed. "But the school year is almost over. I've met with all my other students' parents at least three times by now. I thought it was necessary for the two of us to get together."

He leaned forward, his hazel eyes intent. "You're absolutely right. About us getting together, I mean."

She eyed him carefully. "To discuss Chloe."

"Of course."

Michael watched with amusement as she edged her chair a little away from his, even as she busied herself taking Chloe's portfolio out of her bag. Her posture was ramrod straight and she kept her gaze focused firmly on the folder in front of her. He didn't mind her show of nerves. There were plenty of other emotions he'd like to elicit from her of course, but nerves were a start. At least it proved she was aware of him.

She took out a packet of papers and passed a painting over

to him. "One of Chloe's favorite activities is art class. She's a very creative little girl."

Michael studied the painting of a horse with a small figure, presumably Chloe, riding it. "Yeah, she is," he said indulgently. He waved his hand to the line of paintings and drawings that hung from the front of his desk.

Kate looked at them and smiled. "I recognize her style."

He felt an involuntary reaction in his loins. It was going to be damn hard to concentrate if the woman continued to smile like that. As a matter of fact, it was going to be damn hard to concentrate just sitting this close to her. He continued to listen, attending as much to her pleasantly husky voice as to her words. Interspersed with his interest in hearing how bright his little girl was, and how kind she was to others, was a parallel interest in the woman sitting beside him.

He wondered if she was as young as she looked. Surely not. Even a beginning teacher would have to be around twenty-two. And then he wondered if she'd scooped her hair up like that to make herself appear older. Dressed as she was in a casual denim jumper, colored T-shirt and brightly colored wooden necklace, she could pass for a teenager. He hoped she was a great deal older than that. He hated to think he was lusting after a woman half his age.

His eyes hooded, he leaned back, listening to her talk animatedly about Chloe's progress with a half smile on his face. He concentrated at least as much on the sound of her voice as her words. This had to be the best conference *he'd* ever been a party to.

The day was definitely looking up.

"Just what the hell are you saying?"

Kate met Michael's gaze unflinchingly but swallowed hard at the mask of severity that had descended over his expression. The look of half-amused indulgence had vanished from his thick-lashed hazel eyes. They were narrowed at her now, as if daring her to repeat herself.

"As I said, Chloe has a great deal of difficulty listening and following directions, as well as an abundance of energy."

"She's in *first grade*," he stressed mockingly. "If you're going to teach at that level, you have to be prepared for the activity level of the kids. My God, having Chloe and two of her friends around is enough to keep our house rocking for a week afterward."

"I've taught first grade for five years, Mr. Friday," Kate said evenly. "One of the things I love most about my job is the energy and enthusiasm of six- and seven-year-old students. What I'm suggesting is that Chloe's activity level is not totally caused by her age or grade level."

"And what, in your infinite experience and wisdom, do you believe it is caused by?"

Kate's lips compressed at his sarcasm, but she trod carefully, ready to parry the next explosion. "Her excessive activity would not be so unusual by itself, given her age. But coupled as it is with her distractibility and short attention span, I'm suggesting that there may be a medical factor involved."

Temper flashed in his eyes, dangerously close to the surface. "You're saying there's something wrong with my daughter?"

Swallowing a sigh, she wondered at exactly what point she'd lost control of this conversation. She'd documented her concerns and anecdotal data very carefully for the past few months and had tried to arrange several opportunities to share it with Chloe's father. After her many frustrated attempts to meet with the man, she'd determined to approach him at his office. She hadn't been prepared for his anger, although defensiveness wasn't all that unusual a reaction.

Her voice remained level. "I try to organize my classroom in such a way that there is ample opportunity for activity throughout the day. Little people need that, and I've found it beneficial to offer it to them. What I usually find is that by this time of year, the students have settled into a routine, are more accepting of structure and are better equipped to handle those times when seat work is required. Chloe has not made that transition, and it isn't because she is consciously choosing not to. When she's supposed to be doing her work, she might be crawling under her desk, visiting with others or walking about the room.''

His scowl succeeded in wiping away the memory of how his earlier good humor had lightened his expression. Now his face, with its high cheekbones, blade of a nose and square chin, seemed all brutal lines and harsh angles. "So you're saying you can't handle one six-year-old girl?"

"I'm suggesting that it may be appropriate for you to explore medical reasons for Chloe's attention problems. As I've said, she's an extraordinarily bright little girl. But I have to sit with her one-on-one to keep her focused enough to complete her work.

"Mr. Friday—" Kate leaned toward him, her voice earnest "—I'm not qualified to judge the exact nature of Chloe's attention problems. That would take a medical doctor. All I'm suggesting is that you take Chloe to her pediatrician, explain the problems she's having in school and—"

"It seems to me that Chloe's *problem*," he said bitingly, "is school. Or rather, her teacher. I gave a great deal of thought to her placement before deciding on the Children's Academy. I'd hoped that a private school would offer her the benefits that a public one couldn't."

Kate nodded. "The academy is a wonderful institution—"

"It appears I was wrong." His tone was icy. "If the school was as wonderful as you say, they'd employ teachers with more knowledge and experience." He rose in an abrupt movement to tower over her. "I'll continue this discussion with your principal."

Kate stood to face him. "If we could just discuss this further—" She was interrupted by a whirlwind coming through the door.

"Daddy, Daddy, Daddy, guess what? Me 'n Trask have a sa-prise for you." A small blond girl sped across the room and launched herself at Michael. He caught her in his arms.

Belatedly, the intercom sounded, and Bernie announced, "Your daughter is here, Mr. Friday."

A huge man ducked into the office, visibly embarrassed. "Chloe, I told you to wait." Kate recognized him at once. It was hard to forget someone as big as a redwood and nearly as taciturn. Trask, Mr. Friday's employee.

"Trask said we can have a popcorn party tonight, Daddy, 'cuz I didn't have any holes in my mouth."

"No cavities," Trask muttered. His gaze landed on, then slid by Kate to fix with what seemed to be great interest on the far wall.

Chloe bounced excitedly. "And you get to come to our party, Daddy, even if you have holes in your mouth, you still get to come. So you gotta come home early or you'll miss our party."

Michael's face softened as he looked at his daughter. "That's super, munchkin. You must have had a really good visit with the dentist."

She nodded her head with enthusiasm. "I got a ring, because I sat still. Kinda still," she amended honestly. "And I looked for a ring for you, too, but they didn't have any big ones. But you can share the popcorn party with me."

He gave her a hug. "I wouldn't miss it. I'll be home in time, I promise. But right now I'm in the middle of a conference with your teacher."

Chloe's head jerked around, and for the first time she noticed Kate in the room. "Miss Rose!" she squealed. Wiggling down from her father's arms, she gave Kate a hug. "I didn't know you were gonna talk to my daddy today."

Kate smiled. The child's exuberance was infectious. "Hi there, Chloe."

But Chloe had already whirled away. "Daddy," she said solemnly, "be sure you have your listening ears on when Miss Rose is talking to you. If you don't, you might have to go to the thinking chair." She turned back to her teacher for corroboration. "Isn't that right, Miss Rose?"

The flush that Kate felt scalding her cheekbones was the curse of fair skin. She concentrated on Chloe, not daring a glance at Michael. "I don't think your father needs to worry about that."

"'Cuz he's listening good?"

"Listening well," Kate corrected. And not exactly, she answered silently. "Adults don't need a thinking chair." Stemming the question she sensed poised on Chloe's lips, she added, "Adults can do their thinking wherever they are. They don't need a special place."

That seemed to satisfy the little girl. "Oh."

"I'm glad you came to tell me about your dentist appointment." Michael's words drew Chloe's attention. "You go on home with Trask and have your dinner, and I promise to be home by six-thirty. How's that?"

"That's good, Daddy. That's re-e-al good. I'll know if you're late, because I can tell time. Can't I, Miss Rose?"

Kate smiled down into Chloe's wide hazel eyes. "You certainly can. And very well, too."

Satisfied, Chloe beamed, then dashed across the room to Trask. "C'mon, Trask, let's go home so we can time Daddy."

Trask took the little hand placed entrustingly in his huge paw and muttered, "See you at home, Michael." His gaze flitted past Kate. "Miss Rose." Then he and his small charge left the office.

"Whew." Kate shot Michael a laughing look. "I'm guessing she keeps you on your toes."

A corner of his mouth kicked up. "You know it. You'd never believe what she did last weekend when we…" He stopped, and the humor abruptly vanished from his face. He reverted back to the stern, cold stranger he'd become before Chloe's visit with the ease of a chameleon changing colors. "I'm afraid that's all the time I have today, Miss Rose."

Kate had never been a quitter, and there was nothing she wouldn't do for one of her students. Although the dark expression on his face had nerves skittering up her spine, she said, "Mr. Friday, if you would just consider—"

"I'm out of time," he repeated flatly. "I'll be talking to your principal soon." He walked to the door and opened it, a silent invitation for her to exit.

Kate studied him for a moment, at a loss. Nothing more was going to be accomplished today, that was apparent. She picked up her bag, the portfolio she'd been sharing with him, and walked to the door. "You may keep this file of Chloe's things," she said, offering it to him.

Slowly his hand came up to take it from hers.

She tilted her head, newly aware that, even standing, she had to look up a good six inches to meet his eyes. His narrowed regard was unflinching. Except for the muscle twitching in his cheek, his face could have been etched from granite. Shaking her head, she murmured, "Thank you for seeing me today, Mr. Friday."

He watched through hooded eyes as she walked swiftly into the outer office, collected her coat and went out the door, all without a backward glance. It wasn't until he noticed Bernie taking in the whole scene with avid interest that he backed into his office, slamming the door. His nostrils flared at the elusive scent Kate had left in her wake. It was something light and inherently feminine. It stirred a dormant, visceral response, which merely deepened his anger. He didn't want to respond to her, not on any level.

He strode back to his desk and propped his hips against one corner. Far from his first, hormone-driven assumption, Katherine Rose's visit fit perfectly into the trouble he'd been having the last two days. But his struggles with a pesky programming bug paled in comparison with what she'd had to say. Though he hadn't been listening very well when it had become obvious she was suggesting that his little girl had...

A problem. The thought caused acidic snakes to churn in his gut. He didn't know how his first impression of the woman could have been so wrong, but his opinion of his daughter's teacher had changed drastically since she'd walked into his office. Of course, he hadn't been thinking with his head when he'd first seen her.

He glowered in the direction of the door. Her suggestion that Chloe wasn't normal had all his paternal protective instincts rushing to the forefront. He'd never been around kids much, not when he was growing up, nor later, when he was busy scrabbling for his first million. But he'd been ecstatic when Deanna had gotten pregnant. A house, three cars, a wife

and now a child. The picture, one he'd formed in his mind
when he'd been only a child himself, had been complete.
This, then, would be a real family, one suitable for those
goofy, picture-perfect Christmas cards.

He'd been totally unprepared for the tidal wave of emotion
he'd experienced the first time the nurse had put Chloe into
his arms. He'd gazed down into his daughter's scrunched-up
red face and recognized the scowl she'd regarded him with
as a miniature of his own. He'd since realized that the accompanying turbulence of feelings had stemmed from the
emotional equivalent of having his six-foot, four-inch, two-
hundred-ten-pound body wrapped around a baby's pinky. His
baby.

Chloe had been the sole reason he'd battled so hard to save
his marriage. Once Deanna had walked out, however, it
hadn't been his wife's cool blond beauty he'd found himself
missing; it had been the sight of his daughter's heartbreaking
grin. He'd battled valiantly in court but had learned firsthand
that many judges still favored the mother with primary custody. He'd been faced with the prospect of visits two nights
a week and every other weekend.

When Deanna had broached the subject of reversing the
arrangement last summer, he'd been stunned but had quickly
agreed. He hadn't inquired very deeply into her reasons. He'd
been overjoyed at the prospect of having a real home and a
life with Chloe.

Though their life together lacked the June and Ward
Cleaver stamp of approval, he thought they were doing well
enough. Despite the appearance given by the missed appointments with Miss Rose, making time for his daughter was his
top priority. Trask would be nobody's idea of a nanny, but
he doted on Chloe almost as much as her father did. In fact,
Michael was ashamed to admit that Trask was actually a better disciplinarian. Whatever Chloe's transgression, the sight
of her tears had the ability to turn Michael into a quaking
mass.

As he remembered the teacher's words, anger flared like a
gasoline-soaked match. He'd be the first to admit that Chloe

had enough energy to fuel a rocket. Their home echoed with her laughter and her running footsteps. She had the bright, inquisitive nature of a normal, healthy almost-seven-year-old, and he fiercely resented the suggestion that she was anything but.

His brooding was interrupted by a knock on his office door. At Michael's growled invitation, his vice president, Derek Latham, entered, stopping short when he caught sight of Michael's expression. Raising both hands in the air, he said placatingly, "Ms. Bernwood said I should come in."

"She would," Michael muttered, surveying his vice president. Bernie didn't look on anybody in the company with favor, but Derek elicited a little less than her usual level of hostility. It was probably his looks. The silvery blond hair was always professionally styled, and it would be safe to say that, unlike Michael, Derek would never think of giving himself a trim with the kitchen scissors. The man had lavish tastes in clothes, cars and women. There had been a time, in the year after Michael's divorce, when the competition between the two men had spread to women. Or, more specifically, to see who could romance the largest number of them in the shortest amount of time. After long months of meaningless encounters, Michael had come to his senses. Derek, however, showed no signs of slowing down.

He had no more desire to speak to his vice president than he had for another visit from Miss Rose. His brows lowered farther. She was probably on her way to a conference with some other poor sap of a parent. Maybe she had a quota of days to ruin.

"I wanted you to know that I've just about wrapped up work on that new software protection package."

"Good," Michael said, still scowling at the door. "That's good." He searched his memory, but he couldn't remember Chloe speaking of Miss Rose in anything but glowing terms. Somehow he'd imagined the teacher as a grandmotherly figure, somewhere around Bernie's age, only with a better sense of fashion. He sure as hell hadn't expected a woman who looked to be barely out of her teens, one who hadn't been teaching long enough to know the difference between normal first-grade energy and some imaginary *problem*.

Derek arched a brow at his boss's lack of enthusiasm. "Actually, it's damn near brilliant." He slipped his hands into his pockets, being careful not to disturb the crease in his trousers, and strolled past Michael. With an eye on his boss, he continued, "So brilliant, in fact, that I deserve a ten percent bonus for my work."

"Whatever." Maybe that was the whole problem, he mused. Miss Rose didn't belong in front of a classroom, she belonged back in one as a student. She had a lot to learn about children. Maybe after a few more years of classes she'd know better than to falsely alarm parents with a bunch of psychobabble garbage.

"Perhaps now would be a good time to ask for a better parking space, as well. Your spot would do nicely." Cool amusement laced Derek's voice.

"What?" Michael jerked his head around to glare at his vice president. "What the hell are you talking about?"

Derek tsked. "Your priorities, Michael, are deplorable. Talk of money goes right by you, but your attention is snared by parking spaces." He shook his head sadly. "Doesn't speak well for the future of this company."

Michael walked around his desk and dropped into his chair. "The future of this company never looked brighter. And I was paying attention the whole time. You've got the software security package completed."

"Just about," Derek repeated patiently. "As a matter of fact, a few more hours will do it. I was going to stay and finish it up. I can go over it with you later this evening, if you like. Are you staying?"

"No, I promised Chloe I'd come home early. Damn." He suddenly remembered something else. "I think she has to have treats of some sort for Daisy Scouts tomorrow. I'm going to have to stop and pick something up."

Derek shook his head pityingly. "My friend, you need a wife."

The desk chair gave an ominous squeak as Michael leaned

back in it. "That's not exactly a subject you've ever had much interest in." He eyed his vice president with sudden suspicion. "Have you been talking to Bernie?"

"As rarely as possible," Derek assured him with unfeigned sincerity. "And I wasn't talking about me. I'm not in the market for marriage." He made the word sound like a disease. But you…" He gestured toward Michael. "You've got Chloe to consider. You have to make a home for her, and let's face it, you're as domesticated as a lapdog." His face was bland when he noted, "With that haircut, you resemble one, as well."

Michael raked his hand through his shaggy brown hair. "I cut it myself last week," he said, just to watch Derek cringe.

"That's another thing a wife could do for you. Take over your grooming. And—" he gave Michael's attire a considering look "—maybe lay your clothes out in the morning."

"I've been dressing myself for years."

"I've never doubted it."

Michael's eyes narrowed. "Besides, that's not a wife you're describing, it's my mother. And I like her exactly where she is. A hundred miles from here." Derek and Bernie would be no one's idea of experts on the topic of marriage. At least he'd had some experience with it, if only the experience of failing. He didn't have the time or the inclination for dating these days, much less marriage. But there were times when he'd struggle with an aspect of parenting and wish he had another person to talk things over with. It would be a relief to have someone with whom he could discuss the unsettling visit he'd just had with Chloe's teacher. Although his relationship with Deanna was carefully cordial, he hated to bring up anything that might have her changing her mind once again about custody.

Derek shrugged. Unaware of Michael's flagging attention, he inquired, "Have you had any news from the lawyer on the acquisition of the microchip company yet?"

Michael shook his head. Right now, everything dimmed in importance compared to his concern for Chloe. The NASA contract, the computer bug and the takeover bid had just become secondary.

Michael Friday didn't tolerate complications in his life, he eliminated them. Chloe's teacher had just become a major complication.

Before he could get back to business, he had to eliminate Katherine Rose.

Chapter 2

Kate stood in the doorway of her classroom, monitoring her students' return from recess. Smiling, she stooped down and helped one youngster unknot a shoelace. She motioned for the last straggler to finish putting his shoes on in the room and closed the door behind him. The phone on her desk was ringing, so she flicked the lights once as a warning to the noisy first-graders before crossing the room to answer it.

"Kate." The voice of her principal, Carol Bleakney, sounded in her ears. "Are you free after school today?"

Kate looked at her daily planner. "No, I have a level meeting at three-fifteen."

"You'll have to postpone it," Carol said. "Mr. Friday has called and requested a meeting at three o'clock. I told him I thought it would be a good idea for the two of us to speak and then for the counselor, the nurse and you to join us to continue the discussion on Chloe."

Kate sighed. The slight throbbing in her temples signaled a return of the full-blown headache she'd had when she'd left Mr. Friday's office yesterday. After the way things had ended in that conference, the upcoming meeting wasn't entirely unexpected. "Well, I did warn you," she said half-jokingly.

"I'm sure now that Mr. Friday's had a chance to think about it, he'll be in a much calmer frame of mind," Carol said optimistically. "See you at three-fifteen."

Kate replaced the receiver, her gaze sweeping her first-grade class. Most of the youngsters had returned to their seats when she'd blinked the lights and were talking quietly. Two boys glanced at her, noted her gaze on them and slipped quickly into their chairs. That left one blond-haired pixie still on her feet, skipping across the back of the classroom.

"I appreciate the way most of you went to your seats while I was on the phone," she said in a quiet voice. "When you do that, you are a big help to me, and it shows that you know how to follow the classroom rules we set at the beginning of the year."

Twenty-four first-grade faces beamed up at her words. "I know how to follow classroom rules, Miss Rose." Chloe quickly took her seat, smiling winningly.

An unwilling smile tugged at Kate's lips. It was absolutely impossible not to respond to Chloe. She was amazingly engaging; amazing, because in light of the meeting Kate had had with Michael Friday yesterday, she definitely didn't take after her father.

The uncharitable thought was satisfying, even if not strictly true. Although there was nothing about Chloe's father to suggest where she got her tiny build and long blond hair, she did have his hazel eyes and that grin that could charm a snake out of its skin. It was just that show of charm yesterday that had had Kate's mouth drying out and prickles of awareness scampering down her spine. He radiated high-voltage magnetism, a simmering vault of energy waiting to erupt.

The force of his personality had been almost as daunting as his show of temper. Regardless of his mood, the man had presence. It reached out and commanded respect, forcing people to respond to him. He'd seemed to take up more than his share of space. His legs, propped up on the desk the way they had been at her arrival, had resembled sturdy oaks. His shoulders were massive, shown to perfection in the casual shirt he'd worn. He could never be described as handsome; his features had too many angles, his hazel regard beneath the sun-streaked brown hair was too piercing. But there was definitely something compelling about him. He'd been near irresistible when he'd been teasing. But the abundant charm had disappeared abruptly once he'd started listening to what Kate had to say. When his mood had altered, he'd become downright formidable.

The Beltway Raider. She'd heard the title his secretary had tossed at him, and it had struck a chord of recognition. Although she didn't follow the financial news, it was all too easy to understand how Michael Friday had acquired the nickname. He exuded power and control. It was equally obvious that he was a man used to wielding that power to bend others to his will.

The knowledge had her spine stiffening. Unfortunately for him, she had a lifetime of experience dealing with his personality type. She was used to holding her own, and no man would ever again be allowed to intimidate her. But there had been no denying that quick burst of wariness that had tempered her earlier, equally involuntary reaction. It was immensely gratifying to blame him for both responses.

"Everyone needs to take their science notebook out of their desks," she said, reining in her thoughts with effort. "Today we're going to the science table, and each of you will draw a picture to record how much your bean plants have grown since last week."

Chloe catapulted out of her desk toward the science table, eliciting a tumble of several other bodies wanting to be first. Kate waited until all the children were at the table and then said firmly, "Now each of you who didn't walk to the table will need to go to your desk and walk properly to the back of the room." Her gaze swept the group, lingering on the guilty parties. Five children did as she requested and rejoined the group at a much more sedate pace.

Chloe grinned up at her teacher, her mood not dimmed in the slightest by needing reminders twice in the last five minutes. She danced impatiently from one foot to the next as she listened to Kate's instructions, but managed to stay in one spot until her teacher had finished.

As the first-graders worked on the assignment she'd given, Kate walked around giving help where needed and encouraging others. As she did so, her mind wandered again to the upcoming meeting. Mr. Friday had lost no time carrying through on his threat to go to her principal. But Carol was a fair-minded administrator who favored a problem-solving model that included all parties. If he'd thought that he would have a free arena to complain about his child's teacher, he would be disappointed. Not, she grimaced to herself, that she relished having to undergo yet again his disapproving glare and biting tone, this time in front of her peers.

She looked around the table with a practiced eye, mentally tallying small bodies and coming up one short.

"Chloe?" She turned her head even as she heard the water in the classroom sink being turned on. Hurrying across the room, she was met with splatters of mud.

Stepping back, Kate let out a long breath. "Chloe," she said calmly but firmly, "turn the water off *now.*"

Obediently the little girl reached over, turned off the faucet and faced her teacher.

Kate struggled to keep a serious expression on her face, clamping down on her quivering bottom lip. Chloe looked up at her innocently. Dots of mud speckled her face, hair, neck and arms and hadn't spared her pink top. A drop balanced on the tip of her turned-up nose, threatening to slide down at her first movement.

"My bean plant was dry so I gave it a drink."

Glancing at the plant, which was currently swimming in a sea of muddy water, Kate nodded. "I see that. But what did I ask you to do?"

Chloe chewed on a muddy lip, then, grimacing at the taste, scrubbed the back of her hand across her mouth. Her gaze dropped. "Measure my plant," she mumbled.

"That's right. Did you follow my direction?"

The little girl shook her head, her voice woeful. "No, Miss Rose."

Kate reached for some paper towels, expertly wet them and started cleaning the little girl up. "So now we have a mess in the sink and a mess on you."

Chloe's eyes began to sparkle mirthfully. "You have a mess on you, too, Miss Rose. Right here." She pointed a grubby finger at her teacher's face.

Kate looked at the mirror hanging over the sink. Chloe was right. Two splatters of dirt marred one cheek. She wiped them off and then brushed at the matching spots on the front of her jumper before returning to her student. Casting a glance at the surrounding countertops and walls, she stifled a sigh. She was going to have a major cleanup job, one that would have to wait until after her meeting with Mr. Friday.

Once Chloe had been returned to a semblance of her formerly tidy self, Kate disposed of the paper towels and reached for the little girl's plant. Pouring out the excess water, she handed the pot to Chloe. "Get your measuring stick and join the others at the table," she instructed.

Chloe looked at the plant, which was bent over dispiritedly. "I don't think it's gonna stand up to be measured."

Kate surveyed the plant and then her student. Chloe was looking at her hopefully. "Bring me a new pencil and the thread from the supply drawer." With Chloe and a few interested students looking on, Kate stuck the pencil in the dirt next to the plant, then tied thread around the two. When she finished, she set the plant in front of Chloe, who enthusiastically began measuring it.

Her gaze sneaked to the clock. Less than an hour to finish the activities she had planned for the afternoon. Her stomach tightened as she remembered. Less than an hour before she faced Michael Friday again. She hoped the upcoming meeting wouldn't give rise to another lecture from Carol. She'd spoken with Kate twice before to caution her against getting too involved in her students' lives. It was fine to preach objectivity and distance, Kate mused as she bent down to soothe a little boy growing frustrated with his slippery plant, but much harder to practice it. At least for her. She knew from bitter experience what it was like to grow up in a home where love and acceptance weren't given freely. She'd never believe that it was wrong for her to fight for them on behalf of her students.

Michael rose courteously to greet each of the newcomers as they entered the conference room near the office. After fifteen minutes of talking to the principal, it was easy to tell that Chloe's teacher had the woman's respect. He sank back into his seat after being introduced to the school nurse.

He was surrounded by women at the table, a situation he would ordinarily enjoy. He'd grown up in a household headed by a single mother and was totally at ease around women. He enjoyed everything about them—their smell, their softness, their fascinating female rituals. It was odd that the one thing he missed most from his marriage to Deanna was watching her get ready to go out for the evening. He stifled a sigh. Derek was right. He *was* as domesticated as a lapdog.

The door opened inwardly again, and this time Kate filled it. His stomach muscles tightened reflexively. Rising, he held out his hand, conscious of the softness of hers as he met it briefly. He waited for her to sit before he followed suit. Today her curly hair was caught in a low ponytail, allowing her hair to drape around her ears without letting any tendrils free. It was long, hanging to the middle of her back, and too close to the fantasy he'd had about her yesterday for comfort. She was wearing another jumper, plaid this time, with large pockets, and dark tights. The outfit made her look like a schoolgirl herself, especially with the smear of dirt across her chest.

"Sorry I'm late." Her voice was just as he remembered it, its cadence soft with the rounded vowels of a native Virginian, slightly husky. "I had bus duty right after school."

"Well, let's get started then," Carol said briskly. "I've had an opportunity to discuss Mr. Friday's concerns with him for a few minutes before the rest of you were free."

Michael removed his attention from Kate's chest with effort. "I don't have *concerns.*" He stressed the last word ironically. "I'm damn mad." He paused, but his words didn't elicit any reaction from the group except polite interest. "It seems to me, Mrs. Bleakney, that your teachers are more concerned with trying to force conformity on the students than with encouraging originality."

"The concerns I shared with you yesterday, Mr. Friday, were not about Chloe's lack of conformity," Kate responded, "although I do expect some level of uniform behavior from the students. There are certain behaviors that are necessary in order for our school to be a safe environment where children can learn. But my main concern about Chloe is that she cannot adequately monitor her own behavior to the extent needed for her to learn at the same pace as others.

"Mr. Friday—" Kate leaned forward, her expression sincere "—Chloe is a sweet-natured, creative little girl. She has many friends and is truly a joy to teach. But I worry about her. Her activity level is a problem, but with careful manipulation of the environment, her needs can be met in the classroom. Her distractibility is more troublesome. She simply isn't capable of maintaining her attention long enough to complete a task."

His brows lowered. "She's excitable, I know that. But that doesn't mean something's wrong with her, for Pete's sake. I can't believe she's all that different from the other kids you teach."

"I believe what Kate is saying is that it's the degree and frequency of Chloe's behaviors that make her stand out from the others." An older lady was speaking. The counselor? The nurse? Michael couldn't remember. "We are not doctors here, Mr. Friday. But hyperactivity, distractibility and a short attention span are symptoms of Attention Deficit Disorder. We could clear up our questions about Chloe if you would agree to take her to her pediatrician for an evaluation."

Michael stared hard at the woman who was speaking. He focused on the last word of the ominous-sounding name. *Disorder.* They were asking him to believe that something was wrong with Chloe. That she was abnormal in some respect. He shook his head disbelievingly, swinging his gaze from one somber expression to another. They had to be kidding. Chloe was the light of his life, the most precious thing in it, and so sweet and good he frequently wondered how he'd ever gotten so lucky.

"I can see it was useless to come here." He addressed the principal in a tight voice. "It's obvious that I made a poor choice when I selected your school for Chloe. If your employees can't accept their students as individuals—"

"I can assure you that you didn't make a mistake in choosing the Children's Academy for your daughter. At the risk of sounding biased, we're the finest private elementary school in the state. I'm sorry that Chloe's attention problems have taken you by surprise, but surely the kindergarten teacher at her school last year shared similar concerns."

"She was living with her mother last year. I never actually spoke to her teacher. Deanna gave me regular reports on her progress."

Carol exchanged a look with Kate and then pushed a white folder toward Michael. "This is Chloe's cumulative folder, containing all her school records. As her parent, you have a right to examine it at any time and to receive copies of anything you wish."

Frowning, Michael picked it up and flipped through it. The contents were scanty. A copy of her birth certificate, a card documenting childhood vaccinations and copies of her report cards. He skipped the ones she'd received this year and looked at her kindergarten reports. His stomach did a slow roll as he read the comments from last year's teacher.

Overly active...hard to keep her attention...very distractible. He closed the folder, but not before the words had branded themselves onto his brain. Long moments ticked by in which no one spoke. For a short time, Michael forgot about the others in the room, immersed as he was in the realization that Chloe's reports last year highlighted the same concerns that Kate had come to him with yesterday.

Kate. His eyes lifted and met hers.

"Your ex-wife hadn't shared those reports with you?" she asked, sympathy tinging her voice.

He cleared his throat. "Not copies of them, no," he said. He was searching his brain, trying to remember exactly what Deanna *had* told him about Chloe's schooling last year. Certainly nothing that would have prepared him for what he'd just read. Or for what the people around the table were trying to tell him.

"It's a lot to take in all at once," Kate said gently. "Only a qualified physician can diagnose Attention Deficit Disorder. I'm just asking that you consider seeking such a medical opinion. It's no more than you'd do if we suspected a hearing loss or allergies, is it?"

"As Kate said, this is a lot to think about," Carol put in. She handed him some brochures. "Here's some information about ADD. Maybe you'd like to take some time to look these over and then get back to us about your plans. If you have more questions at that time, we could meet again."

Michael took the information she was holding out, because he couldn't think of anything else to do. All his protective instincts, seldom dormant, rose to the surface. "This is a waste of time. I may not know anything about this...attention thing, but I know my little girl. She's a perfectly normal, energetic six-year-old."

"Perhaps that information will help clear up some questions for you, though," Kate suggested. "Read it and see if the descriptions match what you observe of Chloe's behavior at home."

The women rose, and Michael stood slowly. Clearly the meeting was at an end. Clutching the information in his hand, he followed them out into the hallway. Kate was speaking to one of the women, the counselor, he thought. His gaze lingered on the hand she'd placed on the woman's arm. The sight of that smooth skin and those long, tapered fingers stirred something inside him, something he didn't want to feel.

"Miss Rose." The flicker in her eyes told him his tone had been harsher than he'd intended. The counselor walked away and left the two of them together. Kate waited patiently for him to speak. Something about that calm, waiting air rankled him. His world was being kicked out from under him, and she was entirely too serene about the part she'd played in it.

Deliberately he came nearer, close enough to invade her space, and felt a savage surge of satisfaction when her eyes flickered. "This—" he indicated the papers he clenched tightly in his hand "—isn't going to change anything. There's something you should know about me, Kate." He rolled his tongue around her name, enjoying the uncertainty that flitted across her expression at its sound. "I protect what's mine. I can make things extremely difficult for you if I choose to. I suggest you drop this whole ridiculous idea."

But he must have overestimated his effect on her. That softly rounded chin came up in the air, and she matched him look for look. "My students are very important to me, and I'll do whatever it takes to help them succeed. And there's something you should know about me, Mr. Friday." Her voice held a hint of a dare. "I don't give up easily."

Chapter 3

The three-hour trip to her parents' home in Longstron, West Virginia, seemed to go even more slowly than usual. Kate passed the scenery unseeingly, not noticing the bright green that had spread across the countryside. Spring was beautiful on the East Coast, and it had always been her favorite season. A season of renewal. Of hope: When she was a child, she'd always thought that with each spring's rebirth there was a chance, just a chance, for things to be different. They never had been.

Her attention was diverted by a new rattle her car had acquired since she left her condo. An addition to the usual symphony of squeaks and coughs, it was an ominous heralding that her fifteen-year-old car's demise was approaching, probably more rapidly than she could afford.

She just needed to baby it along for another year or so, she thought. Since she'd finished financing her master's degree program, she'd been able to start a new-car account, but its contents were still woefully inadequate. She crossed her fingers on the steering wheel. With a little luck and a lot of help from a mechanic, the car's life might be spared another year.

Longstron was a tired little town with twins across the na-
tion. Rural and poor, it had nothing on its side but a small
citizenry who obviously had nowhere else to go. It had the
same dispirited appearance as the five other towns she'd lived
in while growing up, as if people had long ago given up trying
to better it or themselves. The streets were as tired and
washed-out as the rest of it. Kate turned onto a road that still
bore the ruts worn by winter.

Pulling up in front of the small house on the outskirts of
town, Kate shut off the ignition and got out of the car. Within
moments, a young girl raced down the sagging steps of the
frame house toward her. Smiling, Kate caught her in a quick
embrace before her sister broke away and said, "You're almost late. Dinner's just about ready and Papa said they'd go
on and eat without you if you didn't have the good sense to
wear a watch."

Kate pulled one of her sister's braids teasingly. "If dinner
is so soon, Miss Rebecca, how is that you're out here with
me and not in helping?"

Rebecca gave her a mischievous grin. "I *was* helping. I
was looking for you. Did you bring me anything?"

"I just may have."

The girl peeked into Kate's bag, and her eyes lit up.

"There's one for each of you. Go ahead and take them,
but put them away until after dinner."

Rebecca nodded eagerly and snatched the candy bars, slipping her free hand into Kate's.

"Charlotte's pouting again," the girl announced impor-
tantly as they climbed the tired wooden steps. "Papa says it
ain't gonna do her no good."

"Isn't going to do her any good," Kate corrected amusedly.

"'Cuz she still ain't goin' to the dance with that Wilson
boy in his souped-up truck," Rebecca finished hurriedly. Her
ringing voice preceded them into the kitchen, earning her a
scowl from sixteen-year-old Charlotte, who was setting the
table.

"Seems like there's plenty to do around here, Rebecca, so

why don't you quit your blabbing about my business and get to work?''

"I can help," Kate offered, slipping out of her coat and hanging it on the hall tree. "What needs to be done? Hello, Mama."

Kate's mother straightened from where she was bent over the oven and carried the ham to the table. "Katherine. Why don't you put those hot pads on the table, right there." She set the platter on the table and bustled over to the refrigerator. "You might go tell your father it's time to carve the meat."

She didn't need to ask where to find her father. It was Sunday afternoon, and that day had always had an unvaried routine. She went to the tiny living room right off the kitchen, where her father sat in his tattered recliner, watching the portable color television she'd bought the family last Christmas. "Hello, Papa. Mama says it's time to carve the meat."

Calvin Rose grunted. "I heard her." He slanted a look upward at his oldest child. "I ain't got no check from you this month, young lady. You ain't startin' to forget where you come from, are ya?"

Kate stared at her father silently. Someday it should stop surprising her how he seemed to shrink in the time since her last visit. Her memory of him from childhood was of a man of stature, of power. Yet with the onset of adulthood came a more mature vision. A lifetime of manual labor had stooped shoulders that had surely once been wider, straighter. Inches had miraculously disappeared from his height, pounds added to his girth. Now he was just a man whose only power in life stemmed from the iron control he wielded over his family. She'd long ceased feeling guilty about the tangled feelings of blame and dislike she had for him. It was a measure of her loyalty to her mother and the younger children that these monthly contacts continued.

"I brought the check with me," she said tightly, reaching into her purse. "I had a bit left over at the end of the month, so it's for a little more than usual." He didn't spare it a glance before folding it and slipping it into his shirt pocket.

"Go on out there, then, and help your mother get that meal on. I swear, the woman gets slower every passing day."

The meal was like countless ones before. There were fewer members around the table now. The older boys, Lucas, Steven and Paul, were married, living in towns much like this one, not far away. William was twenty, still living at home but working in the coal mine ten miles north. A good job, her father bragged as the family silently went through the routine of Sunday dinner. He never forgot to bring part of his check home, too.

"Something you could learn from, missy."

For one irrational moment, Kate was transported back in time, complete with mingled feelings of panic and remorse. But then she realized that his gaze was leveled at Charlotte, who was regarding her plate with sullen defiance.

"The few hours I work at the Laundromat don't make me much," the girl muttered.

"Just enough for some fancy lipstick and nail polish, I reckon," the man said. Shaking his fork at her, he continued sternly, "Time you learned to pull your weight around here. Why, at your age, Katherine was taking care of all you kids and helping your mama with the sewing, too. I reckon you could do a bigger share."

Charlotte flicked a look at her older sister then, and it was like looking at a reflection of herself ten years past. Kate recognized the trapped hopelessness and despair, the yearning for something more. She looked away, shaken. She'd like to speak to her sister about it privately but knew from experience it would be futile. Charlotte was too locked in her teenage angst to believe that any before her had experienced the same. Books had been Kate's way out, earning her scholarships and a chance for higher education. Charlotte lacked the interest in schooling. Her ticket out was likely to be Charlie Wilson, or someone like him, with whom she would start a new life, a carbon copy of the one she was living now.

"Boy!" Her father's disapproval thundered across the table as Emmett's milk glass tipped over.

Emmett froze, his shy, gentle eyes behind the thick glasses alarmed, but Kate rose smoothly and returned with a rag.

"I'm sorry, Emmett, I bumped your elbow, didn't I?" She ignored his confusion at her words and her father's lowered brows as she mopped up the mess. "I must be getting so used to eating alone that I'm taking up more than my share of space at the table."

She patted his shoulder in recognition of the grateful look he sent her. Her father's displeasure still radiated.

"I swear, if you ain't bumpin' into things, boy, you're bolting across the room and knockin' things over. Ain't never seen a clumsier kid, less'n it was Katherine at your age."

"Well, that's true enough," agreed Dorothy Rose. "Remember, Katherine? You was forever jumping around like your skirts was on fire. Thought you'd never learn to sit through church service."

Ben and Rebecca grinned at her, and Kate made herself smile back. "That's what gave me the experience to deal with twenty-four first-graders," she told them.

"You was always real good help," Dorothy went on. "The neighbors were forever carrying on about how good you were with the younger children. Course, you spoiled them all, forever picking them up and carrying them around, fetching for them. I like to never get William to bed without you rockin' him first."

The smile was harder to force this time. "You don't spoil children by letting them know you care about them."

"Hope you're firmer with them kids at school," her father grunted. "That's one of the problems at schools nowadays. The teachers don't make the kids mind. Ain't nuthin' wrong with rapping a few heads to get their attention."

With a deliberate shift of topic, Kate said, "I was hoping we could set up a time for Charlotte, Emmett, Ben and Rebecca to visit me." Aware that four pairs of eyes fixed hopefully on her, she continued, "There's so much to see in D.C. It would be a wonderful educational opportunity for them. And I'd love the chance to spend more time with them."

Dorothy sent an uncertain glance at her husband and said,

"Well, you can't have enough room for these four, Katherine. Best to just let them be."

"But, Mama," Rebecca burst out, "I want to go."

"Me, too," Ben put in. Emmett and Charlotte nodded in agreement.

"I can make room. The kids won't mind sleeping bags on the floor. It will be like camping indoors."

"They ain't going." Calvin Rose spoke with finality.

Kate's throat tightened, but her voice remained steady as she looked at her father. "It wouldn't be for very long. I can come get them and bring them home. It wouldn't be any problem for you at all."

He glowered at her. "You forgettin' who's in charge 'round here? I said they ain't going, and that's that." His gaze swept the rest of the group seated around the table. "Ya'll got your chores to do every day. Don't be thinkin' you're gonna run off to the city and forget your work."

Despite the anger his attitude sparked in her, Kate tamped down the emotion to smile encouragingly at her siblings. She'd lost this argument with her father before, but determination would have her raising the issue again. She didn't want her family to take the brunt of his ill temper once she'd left, so she let the subject drop. But his small-minded tyranny merely stiffened her resolve to win this particular battle in the future.

The rest of the afternoon dragged by. Charlotte disappeared, as was her wont, to the room she shared with her sister. Kate spent some time outside with Rebecca, Ben and Emmett before she reentered the house to say her goodbyes to her parents.

Her father never took his gaze off the ball game on the television. "Make sure next month's check is on time. You know we count on it."

Kate stared at him silently for a moment, biting back the words that threatened to tumble from her lips. Whatever he might think, the checks didn't come because he demanded them. She knew the extra money went a long way in providing for the younger children and eased her mother's load of worry. Life with Calvin Rose wasn't simple under the best of circumstances. Money problems only worsened the situation.

Dorothy got up from her sewing. "We'll expect you next month, same as always." She stood stiffly in Kate's embrace, accepting the kiss on her cheek stoically. Breaking away, she returned to her mending. "Go on with you, girl, no more of your fussing. Next time you're home, William may be here. Might be we'll have us a nice pot roast for dinner."

"We ain't havin' no pot roast," Calvin declared, his brows lowering. "You know it gives me gas."

Dorothy sent her husband a weak smile. "Well, of course it does, dear. Don't know what I was thinking. We'll have us a ham, just like you like."

Her mother's docile tone echoed in Kate's head as she made her escape out the door. The air outside seemed fresher and tasted like freedom. The run-down house seemed to grow as she walked away from it, becoming a vacuum that threatened to suck her back inside. With trembling hands she opened the car door and snapped her seat belt. It wasn't until she was driving away that the pent-up breath lodged in her lungs escaped.

You ain't startin' to forget where you come from, are ya?

Her fingers clutched the steering wheel in white-knuckled tension. No, Papa, she answered silently. I doubt that will ever be possible.

The hammering on her door would have splintered a less sturdy structure. Kate wiped her hands on a dish towel and looked at the kitchen clock. Barely nine o'clock. After arriving home from her parents, the silence and solitude of her home had been a soothing balm for her jangled nerves. She felt only curiosity as she hurried to answer the impatient knocking. Although she didn't know many people in her condo unit, she had several friends from school who would often drop by unexpectedly. Swinging the door open, she was confounded simultaneously by the appearance and proximity of Michael Friday.

He had one arm braced against the door frame. They were separated by only inches, and once again Kate found herself reacting to his nearness. His eyes tracked her movement, halting her automatic, almost imperceptible retreat.

"Mr. Friday." She made no effort to mask the wariness in her voice. She looked past him, saw he was alone. With the help of the lighting out front, she could make out the outline of an expensive sports car parked in front of her condo.

"Hello, Kate."

Her voice was cool when she looked back at him and asked, "How did you know where I lived?"

That grin was back in place, no less charming, no less lethal than she remembered. "The school directory. Actually, I tried calling you all afternoon. You were out."

She felt no compunction to explain where she'd been. It was no business of his what she'd done with her Sunday, and given his attitude the last time they'd spoken, she was more than a little suspicious at his sudden appearance.

Kate studied him. His only concession to the unseasonably cool breeze was a leather jacket. He wore no gloves or hat, and the jacket was unzipped, revealing a denim shirt. When her eyes trailed back to his, she caught a gleam in his gaze as it wandered over her figure, and she was made self-consciously aware of her casual attire. Pushing her hair back over one shoulder, she wished that she'd restrained it that morning.

"I rang the bell a few times, but when no one answered, I wasn't sure it was working."

"Oh." She looked from him to the bell and back again. "It isn't."

His lips twitched. "So I assumed."

"The landlord has been promising to repair it."

His smile faded slowly. "I have something I need to discuss with you. Do you have a few minutes?"

Muscles knotted as tension returned. "I think anything we have to discuss could be done at school tomorrow."

He nodded. "I thought about that. But I was afraid you wouldn't have anything in your classroom to put these in."

He picked up a long white box he'd had lying on her wooden banister and offered it to her.

Kate eyed it guardedly. "What's that?"

His eyes crinkled at her distrustful tone. "A peace offering." He stepped forward and thrust the box into her hands. Fingers closing over it, she took an unconscious step back, which he took as an invitation to enter. He shut the door behind him. With the panels of the white steel door as a backdrop, he seemed bigger than she remembered, with a barely restrained masculine strength. He filled the small foyer in which they stood as much by the force of his personality as by his physical presence.

"Something smells good," he said, sniffing the air appreciatively.

"It's cookies. Every student in my class had a perfect paper in spelling this week, and I promised them a celebration."

A slow smile crossed his face. "I heard from Chloe. She can't wait."

Kate didn't return his smile. This wasn't the same man she'd met with at school last week. He'd reverted to the charmingly casual manner of their first encounter, and alarm bells were going off inside her head. Michael Friday engaging and teasing was no less dangerous than Michael Friday in a temper. She hadn't forgotten his parting threat. He might use different methods than her father, but they shared a similar need to control others. She'd do well to remember that.

He nodded to the box she was holding. "Go ahead and open it."

His gaze held hers for a long moment before she did as he requested. Slipping the ribbon off the box, Kate lifted the lid and pushed aside the tissue paper. An involuntary sound of delight escaped her when the twelve long-stemmed yellow roses were revealed. "They're beautiful."

When her gaze met his again, he was watching her with an arrested expression, his face intent, no longer amused. Suddenly breathless, she parted her lips to speak, but no words came out.

Then he looked past her, a slight frown between his brows. "Is something burning?"

Kate's eyes grew wide. "Ohmigosh," she muttered, before turning and dashing back to the kitchen.

The view from the rear was at least as tantalizing as the one from the front. Her tightly curved bottom moved enticingly in rhythm with her quick steps. Michael watched appreciatively as she hurried into the kitchen and bent over the oven door. Those shapeless jumpers he'd seen her in had done little to enhance what nature had blessed her with, and nature had, in fact, been more than generous. He'd been dumbfounded by the transformation a pair of snug-fitting jeans and V-necked T-shirt could have on her appearance. But it wasn't really the clothes that had his hormones kicking into overdrive. It was seeing those riotous curls that had been left free to cascade over her shoulders.

All in all, his ability to breathe had been impaired at roughly the same moment she'd opened the door. Which shouldn't have surprised him, given his reaction to her both times they'd met previously. But he couldn't deny that he liked the sight of Kate Rose in jeans, liked it very much.

He followed in her steps, unabashedly ignoring the fact that he hadn't been invited in. She looked at him warily before sliding a spatula under the next fresh cookie and placing it on the brown paper where she had the others cooling.

"Can I do anything?"

She shook her head but didn't pause in her task. "No. I'm just going to get this next batch in the oven."

"How about if I put the flowers in water?" he offered. He didn't wait for an answer before he started pulling cupboard doors open. "Where do you keep your vases?"

"I don't think I have any."

"Never mind," he said, his voice muffled. When she turned back to him, he had two large jars in his hands. "These should do." She was visibly uncomfortable at having him in her kitchen, browsing through her cupboards, he noted. He matter-of-factly went about filling the jars with water and arranging half the roses in each one.

When the last pan had gone into the oven, she said, "The roses are gorgeous, but they really weren't necessary."

"I thought they were," he returned easily. "But if you're feeling indebted, those cookies look pretty tempting."

Being pushy had its advantages, he thought a few minutes later as he munched on warm chocolate-chip cookies. Without that quality it was a sure bet that he'd never have gotten in her door and inside her kitchen, and it was certain that he wouldn't be sitting at her table watching her pour him a glass of milk. He was feeling pretty expansive. The day was turning out much better than he deserved.

"I'm a sucker for milk and cookies."

"You're easily impressed."

"Not easily." His gaze was direct. "But I am impressed. Very." With fascination, he noted the delicate color that bloomed in her cheeks. "You're being much more gracious than I deserve. I wouldn't blame you for throwing me out after the way I acted at our other meetings."

"You didn't need to bring the flowers. I certainly understood your being upset."

"I wanted to apologize," he said soberly. If he hadn't been so engrossed in his own feelings of self-recrimination, he might have wondered at the shock widening her eyes. "When I left you at the school, I had every intention of contacting the superintendent and having you removed from your teaching position." He had no doubt he could have done so, had he not come to his senses. The academy was a private institution, and like most private schools, it relied heavily on donations to maintain its outstanding educational reputation. "I know what kind of bastard that makes me, and I'm not proud of it. I hope you'll accept my apology." He watched her carefully, but her expression had blanked. No doubt she was agreeing with his self-assessment.

Shame had a bitter flavor. He'd sworn long ago that he wasn't going to be the kind of man who would use his power to hurt others. It still shook him to realize just how close he had come to doing so.

She released a long breath. "Well. That's...honest, at least."

Her reaction encouraged him. "So we've declared a truce?"

A small smile crossed her lips. "I don't think our disagreement could qualify as war. Maybe a minor skirmish." Her gaze direct, she asked, "Have you had time to read through the information we gave you?"

He drew in a breath, then expelled it slowly. "You're tenacious, aren't you?"

"I can be."

"Well, to answer your question, yes, I've read it. And I understand your concern. There are some common points that I can see in Chloe," he said reluctantly. "But I still think you'd find commonalities with almost any kids. I'm not convinced that Chloe has Attention Deficit Disorder." He pronounced the name precisely. After a pause, he added grudgingly, "But I'm willing to learn more about it."

Her sudden smile sent thought momentarily careening away. Foolishly, he wondered for a brief second what it would take to get Kate to smile that way again, the pleasure reserved for *him* this time, rather than for his words.

"We have some excellent sources at the school," she responded. "I have copies of a few books myself. You're welcome to use them."

"Thanks. Trask is gathering up all the resources he can for me. He's read the material I brought home, as well. He's pretty attached to Chloe."

"Have you discussed this with Chloe's mother?"

Michael's hand halted halfway to his mouth with another cookie. "God, no," he muttered feelingly. Though she didn't say anything, he could feel her disapproval. "First I want to learn more about it myself. If I ever do decide to take Chloe to a doctor about it, I'll talk to Deanna then." He wouldn't look forward to that discussion, but he wasn't going to worry overmuch about it yet. He still believed that the possibility of Chloe having the disorder was remote. He wasn't going to put himself through a tangle with Deanna unless he was certain there was a need for it.

He dismissed his ex-wife from his mind with casual ease and returned all his attention to Kate. She reached for a cookie from the plate between them, and his gaze lingered on the delicate wrist, the long, slender fingers. She was fairly tall for a woman but still came only up to his shoulder. He'd dated a few models and had always enjoyed not having to fold himself in half to kiss them. But this woman would make a little effort worthwhile. He hadn't liked the bony angles and lack of feminine curves on the models, preferring instead a woman with defined female attributes. Kate's breasts were shown off to perfection in the thin cotton shirt she was wearing. High and round, each would be a luscious handful.

Suddenly aware of where his gaze had lingered, Michael looked quickly at her face to see if she'd noticed. Judging by the color that had returned to her cheeks, she had. Deliberately changing the subject, he said, "Actually, I had another reason for coming to see you today." He leaned back in the chair and stretched his legs out, crossing them at the ankle. "Chloe has a birthday coming up next week."

Kate nodded. "Yes, I know. We celebrate birthdays in the classroom, too."

"Deanna has arranged a party for her and a few friends the weekend after her birthday, but I'll be spending the day with her, and I wanted to do something special. She's made the plans, and they include you."

"Me?"

Michael's eyes glinted with humor. "Yes. You, Miss Rose, are her idol. You can do no wrong, and there's nothing she'd like more than to have you join us for a trip to—" he barely restrained the grimace "—Freddie's Funhouse."

Kate appeared to choose her words carefully. "That's sweet, but I don't belong at a family celebration."

One eyebrow cocked, he inquired, "You wouldn't by any chance be turning us down because you have an aversion to Freddie's, would you?"

She shook her head. "Actually, I've never even been there."

"Ah. Well then, you should know that at Freddie's, they use only real cheese on their pizzas, the tokens for the games are four for a dollar, and the fun never ends."

Her lips twitched. "It's a very attractive offer, but I still would feel out of place."

Michael leaned forward, suddenly serious. "I hope you're not turning down the invitation because of the way I acted at our previous meetings. I'd hate for Chloe to be disappointed because of my behavior."

He'd succeeded in flustering her. Her gaze bounced to his, and then away. "No. We've reached a truce, remember?"

His shoulders relaxed against the back of his chair. "Good. I don't want you to feel uncomfortable, but I really do hope you'll consider joining us, Kate. I wasn't exaggerating when I mentioned how much Chloe likes you. You've been a major topic of discussion over the dinner table since the first of September. We've heard about what you wear, what you say, and I must tell you, Chloe is quite impressed with your prowess with a jump rope."

She bit her lip. "Oh, Lord."

"Seriously," he continued, "I was relieved to find that she took to you so quickly. She was pretty young at the time of the divorce, but when the living arrangements changed, I was really worried about the transition."

"She seems very well adjusted."

He nodded. "I think so. She gets a lot of attention, but I don't want her to become spoiled. She really seems to be okay with the reversed custody." He gave a rueful shrug. "I can't tell if it's wishful thinking on my part, but she appears happy. She loves our place, loves having the dogs and horses around. Doesn't even seem to mind roughing it with two old bachelors who aren't always sure of what they're doing."

Kate leaned forward impulsively and touched his hand. "Chloe speaks of you often, and of Mr. Trask. And from the frequency with which you both appear in her pictures, you're at least as popular with her as the dogs and horses."

Her slightly teasing tone wasn't lost on him, but his attention was arrested by the feel of her fingers on his skin. The easy warmth that was so much a part of her was transferred by her touch, and a corresponding heat spread through him. She did that often, he realized. By the end of their last meeting he'd been a little dazed, but not so much that he couldn't remember the way she'd walked out of the office ahead of him, her hand on the nurse's arm as they spoke.

When she would have withdrawn her touch, he neatly reversed their positions, capturing her fingers in his. "Thanks for the vote of confidence," he said, his wry tone meant to distract her from the thumb he sent skating across her knuckles. "I'll take your word for it, since you're the expert here. There are actually times when I think Chloe has me at least as well trained as our golden retriever."

Her gaze dropped to their hands then, and after a moment Michael let go of hers, saying easily, "If I don't miss my guess, that last batch of cookies should be just about finished."

He watched her take the pans out of the oven and turn off the controls. Reaching for another cookie, he chewed slowly, thoroughly enjoying the situation. He couldn't remember the last time he'd sat in someone's kitchen enjoying freshly baked treats and conversation, but undoubtedly it had been when he was a child. Not his own kitchen then, of course. His mother hadn't been the type for baking before his father had walked out, and afterward had been too tired from her jobs to do much cooking. But he'd been to friends' houses, had occasionally stayed with his grandmother, before her health had failed.

While Kate started putting cookies in plastic storage containers, he studied his surroundings with interest. Her condo was small, but unlike most of the new buildings springing up around the D.C. area, it didn't lack character. Bright curtains hung at the kitchen window, and the narrow woodwork gleamed with a fresh coat of white paint. He was sitting at a wicker table, obviously an antique that had been carefully restored. There wasn't a lot of furniture in the rooms he'd passed through, but all of it looked as though it had been chosen carefully. Framed prints dotted the walls, green plants brightened corners, and photographs in antique frames were carefully arranged on top of the TV.

The total effect was of a home, a reflection of the woman who lived here. He frowned a little, wondering just how she'd managed to convey the feeling of warmth that emanated from the place when he, for all his money, couldn't find a decorator he didn't feel like strangling after two minutes.

"I should hire you to decorate my house," he muttered.

She looked at him askance. "You have a taste for Early American Poverty?"

"It's not what you have in it," he tried to explain. "Or it is, sort of."

"You scientific types are very succinct, aren't you?"

He grinned. "What I mean is, the place looks like a real person lives here. It has personality."

"And what's your house like?"

"Empty, mostly. It literally echoes. I just bought it a year ago, and I haven't had time to do a lot of furniture shopping. Plus, I have no idea about colors or styles. I just know—"

"What you like," she finished for him.

"Exactly."

"There are all kinds of interior design businesses who specialize in such things. I wouldn't think it would be too difficult to find one who could come up with something to your taste."

"I don't want a place that looks like it's been 'done,'" he explained. "I want a real home, one that looks like real people live there. I've never met a decorator who could coordinate homey with classy. I got so desperate I almost asked my mother for advice." He shuddered. "Luckily I remembered what her place looks like in time to save mine from being turned into a museum."

"How about Chloe?" Kate asked, her interest clearly piqued. "Sometimes kids come up with creative ideas. Have you asked her opinion?"

"Oh, yes. And it was very creative." He rolled his eyes

expressively. "She thinks we should put a trampoline in the living room."

That smile showed up again. It transformed her features in a totally unexpected way, turning her lovely, slightly serious expression into an intoxicating vision that had his loins tightening, his pulse ping-ponging with physical chemistry. This woman had the potential to wreak serious havoc with his cardiovascular system, not to mention his libido, which seemed to simmer in a semistate of arousal just in her presence.

All in all, he was pleased with the events of the evening. It had gone well, better than he'd expected, much better than he'd deserved. She'd been guarded but gracious when he'd barged into her home, showing a sense of humor and genuine warmth that he found too enticing to be physically comfortable.

He tore his eyes away from her with effort and made a show of looking at his watch. "I've taken up too much of your time," he said, attempting to sound regretful. He rose and lifted his coat off the back of the chair where he'd hung it. He shrugged into it carelessly, not bothering to zip it, and headed toward her front door. She followed him.

At the door he turned and looked down into her face. "Thank you again."

Her head tilted upward to meet his gaze. "For the cookies?"

"For not throwing me out."

"I told you, it's all right." Her smile was wry. "Believe it or not, you're not the first parent to disagree with me."

"You're too generous," he said soberly. Without conscious volition, he reached out one blunt-tipped index finger and brushed a curly tendril of her hair over her shoulder. It sprang back into place beside her delicate jawline as soon as he removed his finger. He smiled bemusedly. It felt alive, as if it had a will of its own. The rest of his fingers itched to bury themselves into that thick mass of hair, to feel it tumbling over the back of his hands and wrists.

His pulse slowed to a heavy thud at the evocative image. For a moment, before rational thought kicked in again, his face moved closer to hers. Her eyes widened, but she didn't move away from him. Her lips parted a bit, and he imagined he could feel her breath on his chin. All it would take was a couple more inches. If he lowered his head just that small amount, he would be close enough to…

Violently he jammed his hands into his jeans pockets, then stepped back. "I appreciate your hospitality. We plan to go out on Wednesday, fairly early so that we don't keep Chloe out past her bedtime. How about if we pick you up at four-thirty?"

Kate blinked a couple of times and then shook her head. "That won't be necessary. I can just meet you there in my car."

"It's no problem. Besides, you don't know where we live, and we'll have to go back to the house after Freddie's." He winked at her, turning to open the door. "What's a birthday without ice cream and cake?"

Before she could summon a protest, she was faced with his retreating back.

Only after Michael's taillights had disappeared did Kate become aware of the brisk air. Stepping back into her condo, she closed the door, shaking her head wryly. She felt as if a steamroller had entered her life, then just as quickly left it. She would have preferred arriving at the party in her own car. The thought of going to Chloe and Michael's home afterward filled her with a sense of unease. She couldn't shake the feeling that this whole episode today had been part of a well-orchestrated plan, with her being herded, ever so good-naturedly, directly down the path that Michael wished her to go.

She headed back for the kitchen, then paused for a moment in the small living room. She looked at it, trying to see it as a stranger would, as Michael had. The carved oak rocker had reminded her of the one in her grandmother's house, so she'd had to have it. The afghan draped over the back of it had actually been her grandmother's, given to Kate for her sixteenth birthday. The telephone sat on a whimsically carved table next to the television, and the couch, although bought new, was reminiscent of styles a century ago. She'd skimped on the curtains, choosing filmy fabric that let in the light. She was satisfied with the effect she was slowly building. It was comfortable, it was home for her. But she saw nothing here that would impress a man of Michael's wealth. Perplexed, she finally shrugged and went back to the kitchen.

Running water in the sink, she concentrated on washing the dishes she'd used baking. Even though she was aware that she had been finessed by an expert, she truly didn't mind being part of Chloe's birthday celebration. She enjoyed all of her students but privately had to admit that Chloe had become a favorite from the first day, when Kate had had to persuade her, gently but firmly, that she'd have to sit at her desk and not in the windowsill. The little girl had willingly complied, shooting Kate a grin that could melt steel. Even though Chloe had spent only five minutes at her desk before getting up again, her teacher's heart had been stolen.

When the child was a teenager, that appeal was going to give the boys some very uncomfortable nights. She'd gotten it from her father, of course. His crooked smile did unbelievable things to his rough-hewn features, softening all those blunt angles and making him much more attractive than mere handsomeness could. All in all, Michael Friday was an explosive waiting to detonate, and she was glad that she would never see the full extent of his overwhelming charm. A man like that could haunt a woman, ruining her for safer, more ordinary men.

Her actions stopped as she remembered the long moment before he'd left. When he'd touched her hair, all hints of teasing had abruptly fled from his face. He'd seemed closer somehow, but instead of stepping away, she'd remained rooted to the floor, tempted by his proximity.

She felt a flush crawl up her cheekbones, and she scrubbed harder at the cookie sheet in the sink. For just a split second, for one desire-laden instant, she'd been tempted to go up on tiptoe and press her lips against Michael Friday's. The memory was humiliating but true. Her gaze had focused on his mouth, entranced by the sensual curve of his full lower lip. And then he'd turned away, thankfully unaware of her uncustomary lapse of logic.

He was unlike anyone she'd ever considered dating, anyway. A man didn't get to be that wealthy and powerful without gaining quite a bit of experience along the way. She'd almost found out firsthand how ruthless he could be when he wanted something.

No, he wasn't the sort of man she'd ever get involved with. She'd escaped from a father who'd brandished control over his family like a weapon. From the distance of adulthood she could see that he'd clung to it as his only way of exerting some sort of power in his life, but she found that quality of his, and the misery it caused, difficult to forgive. Michael wasn't a man who would need such a contrivance. He radiated power and control. That made him a dangerous man to her, regardless of his charm.

Her gaze landed on the yellow roses, and an involuntary smile played across her lips. A simple apology wouldn't be enough for him. The lavish gesture hadn't been completely wasted on her, though she'd striven not to show it. Drying her hands, she crossed over to the elegant flowers and finally gave in to the urge to bury her nose in their delicate petals. She loved flowers; as a child she'd filled their home with wildflowers she'd picked from nearby meadows. Buying fresh-cut flowers seemed an extravagance to her, one she could ill afford. Which meant she would savor these lovely roses.

Picking up both jars, she carried them to the living room and sat them on the coffee table. Such generosity was probably of little consequence to Michael, and he couldn't have predicted her reaction to the gesture. He didn't need to know that he was the first man to ever utter an apology to her.

She inhaled deeply of the roses' delicate scent. And under no circumstances would she let him guess that he was the first man ever to bring her flowers.

Chapter 4

Chloe whispered her idea to Kate and then sat back with her hands clasped over her mouth, her eyes wide and waiting.

Kate blinked. "You want a big clown's mouth to hang on your bedroom wall?"

Clapping her hands, Chloe nodded gleefully. "Just like the one my daddy has to talk into when he orders my hamburgers."

Kate finally understood. "You mean at the fast-food place." The chain of restaurants the child was referring to had a garish three-foot clown with an enormous mouth one had to speak into when placing an order. In her one visit to the restaurant, Kate had found the process unappetizing enough to prevent her from returning.

"I can talk into the mouth and it will talk back to me," Chloe said. "Just like it talks back to my daddy."

Kate slid a glance at Michael, who was taking care of the bill at Freddie's Funhouse. "What does your father think of this idea?"

Chloe dimpled. "It's gonna be a sa-prise," she whispered loudly.

Michael rejoined them in time to overhear Chloe's last words. "If you're talking about that clown mouth for your bedroom again, shortstuff, then you're going to be the one 'sa-prised.'" Swooping down, he caught her up and raised her until they were face-to-face. "It ain't gonna happen."

Chloe wrapped her arms around her father's neck. "Yes, it is," she said confidently.

Michael sent Kate a harried look. "You see what I'm up against? If she had her way, our home would be turned into a circus tent."

"Surely there's a decorating firm you can hire."

"No dekraters," Chloe said wisely from her perch in her father's arms. "They're brainless bozos who have as much taste as a dog in—"

The rest of the sentence was mercifully cut off by Michael's hand over Chloe's mouth. A dull red flush crawled up his cheeks. Glaring at his daughter, he muttered, "You know what I say about big ears on little pitchers?"

She peeled his fingers away from her mouth "You say I'm pretty as a pitcher."

Michael looked hunted. "Not quite the same thing," he muttered.

Kate burst into laughter. Chloe joined in mirthfully.

"I'll go get the car," Trask said. Kate looked at him from the corner of her eye. His deep voice matched his daunting physical appearance. He was several inches taller than his employer and was solid enough to qualify as half a defensive line. His hair was black, without a trace of gray, although his face bore signs of at least five decades of hard living. With his deep-set eyes and prominent forehead, he made an imposing figure. Even at the conferences, he'd never looked directly at her, instead examining the ceiling or a spot past her left shoulder with great concentration while she'd spoken. But he seemed more comfortable in the company of Michael and Chloe and, indeed, had been as patient with the child tonight as her father had. Kate was beginning to suspect that beneath the man's rather alarming appearance existed a good-size soft spot for his small charge.

"Me, too," Chloe declared. She wiggled down from Michael's arms and danced over to Trask, slipping her hand into his. "I'll drive, Trask. You can rest."

As they walked toward the door, Kate heard Chloe tell Trask earnestly, "Maybe we can get you a clown mouth for your room, too, Trask."

The man's tone was dry. "You're too generous."

Michael shook his head as they walked out of sight and glanced at Kate. "You wouldn't happen to still be laughing at me, would you?"

Kate feigned astonishment. "Me? Take amusement from another's embarrassment?" Then she ruined it by giggling again. "You should have seen your face."

A corner of his mouth kicked up engagingly. "I've found the refreshing honesty of children to be vastly overrated. I swear, the kid can't remember that I asked her to hang up her coat, but she's as good as a tape recorder when it comes to repeating things she shouldn't have heard anyway."

"That's children," Kate agreed. "Sometimes my students will play school, and I have to wince when I hear the one playing teacher. I know they're mimicking me, and I have to tell you, the experience keeps me humble."

He moved closer to her to allow a family more room to enter the restaurant, and when he looked down at her again, the smile had faded from his lips. One long, curly tendril had escaped from the low ponytail she'd secured her hair in, and he reached up and smoothed it away from her face. She started a little at the intimate gesture.

"You're a good sport, you know that? Not many women would want to give up an evening to help a little girl celebrate her birthday at 'Freddy's House of Horrors.'"

"Oh, come on," she chided. "It wasn't that bad."

He cocked an eyebrow at her. "Which part? The part where you got the Skee-Ball dropped on your toe, or when you wound up wearing half a pizza?"

"My toe is fine," she assured him. "I'm sure your clumsiness was only due to the fact that I was beating you. And it was one slice of pizza. The blouse will wash."

He eyed the still-visible stain on the front of her silky white blouse doubtfully. When Chloe had made that sudden grab for another piece of pizza, he and Trask had reacted like old pros. He'd reached for the pitcher of pop, while Trask had steadied the table. He'd made a move as if to stop the pizza from reaching its inevitable destination but had checked himself. Kate had been grateful. She'd much rather deal with the stain than his hand's proximity to her breast.

"Like I said," he repeated, "you're a good sport. Send me the bill for the blouse."

She shook her head. "I think I'll be able to get the stain out. And Chloe really seemed to enjoy herself tonight."

"With three adults lavishing her with their undivided attention, what's not to enjoy? But judging from the number of times she said so, yeah, I'd say you're right. And we haven't even got to the best part of the evening yet." At her uncomprehending look, he explained, "The presents."

"I really should be getting home."

"What? And miss all the 'sa-prises?'" Michael asked, his tone shocked. His voice lowered as he leaned toward her and murmured, "Stick around, Miss Rose. The best is yet to come."

"You hid the sa-prises real good, Daddy," Chloe said as the car moved up a long driveway. "I never did find them."

Michael snagged one of his daughter's pigtails. "Are you admitting that you were snooping, munchkin?"

She shook her head vehemently. "Uh-uh! Honest! I was just helping Mrs. Martin clean. I cleaned in all the closets and under all the beds."

"And anywhere else a present might be found," Michael added amusedly. "I'm sure Mrs. Martin appreciates your yearly acts of assistance."

"Do you still need to stop in the stables to speak to Hank, Michael?" Trask's deep voice rumbled.

Michael snapped his fingers. "Gosh, thanks for reminding me, Trask. I do have to talk to Hank tonight. You don't mind, do you, munchkin?" he asked Chloe. "It won't take long."

He explained in an aside to Kate, "Hank's our stable manager. I need to stop in and talk to him about my stallion's training."

"Can I come in and pet Diablo?" Chloe wheedled.

"No!" Michael and Trask answered as one. Michael went on, "I mean, you can come in, but you mustn't try to pet Diablo. I've told you that. But you can look at him."

"Okay," Chloe said cheerfully, and Kate knew that the little imp had gotten what she'd wanted all along. Meeting Michael's gaze, she smiled inwardly. The poor man really did have his hands full.

Dusk was beginning to blanket the ground in long shadows, but outside lighting had been strategically placed along the winding drive. Kate gasped in spite of herself when they got closer to the house. *Gone with the Wind*'s Tara had nothing on this home. It had Southern antebellum architecture, with porches on each of its two stories. Graceful white columns lined the front of the house.

The stables stood near the back of the property. At Michael's urging, Kate got out of the car and joined them. She didn't understand his grin or the long look he exchanged with Trask when Chloe ran into the stables ahead of them. Then came an earsplitting shriek, and both men burst out laughing.

"Daddy! Daddy!" Chloe exited the stable the same way she'd entered it, at maximum speed. "Daddy, come look! There's a new horse in our stable."

"A new horse?" Michael said, sounding puzzled. "Now, how do you suppose a new horse got in our stable, Trask?"

The man's mouth twitched. "Couldn't say. Maybe Chloe's just seeing things."

"Am not, am not! Come look!" she demanded, tugging at her father's hand. Michael caught Kate's hand in his free one, and she was pulled in with them. The stable was spotlessly clean, and the smell of leather and straw mingled in the air. Stalls lined the corridor. From the first one a brown-and-white pony watched them curiously.

"He's beautiful! And he's mine, isn't he, Daddy? You got him for my sa-prise, didn't you, Daddy? For my birthday."

"Slow down, honey." Michael laughed, reaching down to ruffle her hair. He still hadn't relinquished Kate's hand, and if he noticed her subtle attempts to free herself, he was pretending not to. "It's a she, not a he. And yes, she's your birthday present."

"All right! Just what I wanted! I'll bet she goes really, really fast, doesn't she, Daddy? As fast as Diablo, right?"

"She goes plenty fast, kiddo. Just fast enough for a big seven-year-old girl like you."

"Have you seen her, Trask?" When the big man nodded, Chloe turned her attention to her teacher. "Come pet her, Miss Rose. She won't hurt you."

Kate's hand was released, and she moved toward the stall with Chloe. The animal pushed its soft muzzle into her hand and looked at them with soft, good-natured eyes.

"Well, I'll be darned, Trask. I think I see a couple of saprises in here that the Clo-worm hasn't even discovered yet."

"Where?" Attention momentarily diverted, Chloe darted back to her father. "Oh, I see it. Oh, Daddy, it's awesome!" She ran over to the child-size saddle and ran her hand over it reverently.

"Thought you might be needing this, as well." Trask held up a shiny leather bridle that matched the saddle.

"Thank you, Trask, thank you." Chloe threw her arms around his legs and hugged him.

Kate found herself being drawn away and looked at Michael quizzically. He gave her a crooked grin. "Now I get to show you *my* horse," he said. They went to the end of the stable. This stall was bigger than any of the others, and there were bars on the stanchions too narrow for the horse to get his head between.

"Good Lord," she said faintly. "He's huge."

The stallion was jet-black with white markings on his face. He was powerfully muscled and so high-strung she imagined she could see him quiver at their scent.

"He's a beauty, there's no doubt about it. Just got him this year, and we still don't have him completely broken. Hank works with him every day, and I exercise him every chance I get. He loves to run, don't you, boy?''

The horse fidgeted suddenly, and Kate backed away, coming up abruptly against Michael's chest. His hands grasped her shoulders, and he held her in place. "Do you like horses?''

They were close enough for him to speak the words in her ear, a low, husky rumble. She shivered, a totally involuntary response to his nearness. She could feel the solid width of his chest pressed against her, and his fingers kneaded her shoulders lightly. It didn't take much imagination to envision being wrapped in those arms, pressed tightly against his solid strength, his heat enveloping her. Deliberately, she stepped away and turned to face him. "I haven't been around horses much. I'm fascinated by their power, though. I've often thought it must be a wonderfully liberating feeling to race along on top of a horse.''

"It is. We'll have to get you on one someday so you can see for yourself. But first,'' he said, looking at his watch, "I have a daughter who's going to miss her bedtime if we can't drag her away from her sa-prises.''

It was the temptation of ice cream and cake that finally proved strong enough to entice Chloe back to the house. She kept up a steady stream of chatter throughout dessert. "Someday my horse will be as big as Diablo, right, Daddy?''

"'Fraid not, shortstuff. She's a Shetland pony. She won't get any bigger than she is right now.''

"I'll feed her really good,'' Chloe said earnestly over her ice cream. "She'll grow, you'll see. She'll get lots bigger.''

Michael caught Kate's eye and shrugged. "What are you going to name her, honey? Have you thought of that yet?''

Chloe nodded vigorously. "I'm going to name her Rosy. 'Cuz she's the beautifullest horse in the world, and Miss Rose is the beautifullest teacher.''

Kate choked on the piece of cake she was swallowing. Michael roared with laughter. Even Trask's normally gloomy expression lightened a fraction.

Michael said, "Miss Rose might not want to be the namesake to a horse, sweetheart. Maybe you should think of another name.''

Chloe's brow wrinkled. "What's a namesake?"

"It means when you name something after someone else. And Miss Rose doesn't mind a bit," said Kate. She smiled and added, "I think you should name your pony anything you want."

The matter settled, Kate rose and went to the counter, reaching for the package she had set there. Offering it to Chloe, she said, "Maybe you can use this to decorate your bedroom."

Chloe ripped the paper with little fanfare and let out a scream of delight. "It's one of mine, Daddy, look."

Michael looked at the drawing that Kate had had professionally matted and framed. "It's wonderful. Now you have something to hang in your bedroom. It's lots better than a clown head, isn't it?"

Chloe went over and hugged Kate. "Thank you, Miss Rose. Do you want to see where I'm going to hang it?" She led Kate through the house and up the stairs to her room. Michael followed them.

"What do you think, Miss Rose?" asked Chloe as she surveyed her bedroom from her teacher's side. The bed and dresser were the only furniture in it. Toys, Rollerblades, a skateboard, various articles of clothing and scraps of paper littered the floor.

"Well…" Kate tried to come up with a tactful response. "You have lots of space."

"I need to do something," Chloe said woefully. "But I hafta have help, and Daddy's *hopeless.*"

"Hey!"

Ignoring her father's objection at her description, she turned her face guilelessly up to her teacher's. "Could you help me, Miss Rose?"

Kate looked down into Chloe's hopeful eyes and swallowed hard. "Oh, honey, I don't think so."

"Why not?" Chloe wanted to know. "Don't you have a bedroom?"

Kate slid a glance to Michael, who seemed to be enjoying the exchange hugely.

"Well…yes, of course."

"Is it pretty?"

Damning her fair skin for the blush she knew was staining her cheeks, she tried to focus her concentration on Chloe and ignore her father. She smiled weakly. "Yes, it's…pretty."

"Daddy doesn't know how to make a bedroom pretty," Chloe confided in a loud whisper. "His bedroom is worse than mine. It only has a bed in it. Do you want to see it?"

"No!" Kate said quickly. She tried for a smile. "No, that's okay."

"It's a really, really big bed," Chloe told her earnestly. "Lots bigger than mine. But you're not supposed to jump on it, not ever."

Having heard more than enough about Michael's bedroom, Kate bent down and took the little girl's hands in hers. "You know what, Chloe? If your dad doesn't mind, maybe I can give you a little help. How would you like it if I took you to pick out some new curtains and a bedspread?"

"Yay!" Chloe catapulted into Kate's arms and squeezed tightly. "Thank you, Miss Rose." She leaned back to peer up at her teacher. "Can we pick out paint for the walls, too?"

Kate felt her heart contract at the little girl's excitement. Memories of the cheerless cramped space she'd shared with two siblings sneaked into her mind and lingered. Smoothing Chloe's hair back with a gentle hand, she said, "That's up to your dad."

"If Miss Rose doesn't mind, it's fine with me, Chloe," Michael said.

"And carpet? And furniture?" she queried, wiggling away and dancing from one foot to another.

Feeling as though she were getting in far deeper than she'd planned, Kate stood and sent an uncertain glance toward Michael. "You'll have to discuss that with your father."

Chloe launched herself across the room, and Michael scooped her up. "If Miss Rose and I work together, you'll have to stay out of our way, Daddy. And we're going to need *lots* of money."

"You sound like a decorator already," Michael replied with amusement. He lifted his daughter high. "You and Miss Rose will have to start on your room another day. Right now, it's bedtime."

"But, Daddy…"

"No buts," he said firmly. "You have to go to bed on time, and your teacher is going to know for sure why you're sleepy in the morning if you're not in bed by eight-thirty."

"Good night, Chloe," Kate said. "I'll see you in the morning."

"G'night, Miss Rose. Thank you for my picture."

"Give me a few minutes, Kate, would you?" Michael asked. "I'll help Chloe get ready for bed and then give you a ride home."

It was actually closer to an hour before Michael came down the stairs again and found Kate sipping coffee in the kitchen.

"Sorry it took so long," he said. "Bedtime every night is an adventure, and on her birthday…well, I'm still not sure she's down for the count."

"That's all right. Trask made me some coffee before he disappeared." Her lips tilted up. "I think I make him uncomfortable."

"All women make Trask uncomfortable," Michael responded with amusement. "For a man who can look so fierce, he turns absolutely green at the thought of having to make conversation with a female over the age of ten. He's probably hiding out in his room right now, the big wuss." He circled the table and came to stand near her. "Did you look around the house while you were waiting?"

She shook her head.

"Well, you've already heard about my bedroom," he said wickedly. "Let me show you around the downstairs."

They walked through room after room, each one larger and emptier than the next. "I told you I was desperate," he reminded her.

"Chloe was right. There's room for several trampolines."

He grimaced. "Don't even joke about it." He opened the next door and showed her the family room. It was fully furnished with comfortable-looking couches, chairs, bookcases and a large entertainment center.

Kate raised her eyebrows. "Furniture. Michael, I must say, I'm impressed."

His mouth went dry at her half laugh and the teasing cut of her eyes. His response to her was becoming all too predictable. He was coming to anticipate it, enjoy it. "It wasn't too difficult. When Deanna and I separated, I moved into a town house for a while. I just moved most of my stuff from my last place into here when I bought the house last summer."

"It's gorgeous," Kate said sincerely. "And so is the property, what I could see of it." They moved down the hallway to another doorway, this one closed. He punched a quick succession of numbers into the elaborate switchboard mounted in the wall. The door slid open.

"Two furnished rooms?" Kate put her hand to her heart. "You should have prepared me for the shock."

"I sometimes work from my home, so I needed to get this room ready. Actually, as soon as I get a few more things cleared up at the office, I'm going to be spending quite a bit of time in here. My company was just awarded a big contract, and I'll be doing most of the work from my den."

"Why would you do that?" she asked. "I mean, don't you need...I don't know, special equipment or something?"

"All I need is a high-powered computer, and the rest is all up here." He tapped his temple with his finger. "Actually, this computer will be a lot safer than the ones at my office. No one will have access to it but me."

"Sounds secretive."

"It's a security system to keep NASA's computer files safe. There's lot of competition out there. That's why I'll be working alone."

Michael closed and locked the door and caught Kate looking at her watch. "I've kept you out too late?"

She smiled regretfully. "I keep pretty early hours on school nights."

"Then I better get you home, hadn't I?"

He had her accompany him to the attached four-car garage and seated her in his sports car. As the car moved down the long drive with a powerful purr, Kate said, "I should have driven myself and saved you a long trip taking me home."

"I don't mind. I'll be going on in to work for a while anyway."

"At this hour?"

"I don't need much sleep. And I have a lot to take care of in the next few days before I can afford to leave the office for a while."

"Sounds like you're going to be busy."

Michael took a few moments to reflect on her words. "I haven't been too busy to have done some of that reading you recommended." At Kate's quick glance, he said, "Wasn't that what you were going to bring up?"

"Eventually," she admitted sheepishly. "But I would have given it a few more miles before broaching the subject."

"Tactful to the end, huh? Well, to save you from asking, I've looked over the material on Attention Deficit Disorder that Trask put together for me."

"And?"

"I'll admit that some of the stuff sounds like Chloe. She's certainly active, and she can be unpredictable. But a short attention span? The kid can spend an incredible amount of time drawing and painting. That just doesn't seem to fit."

"That in itself is not so unusual for ADD kids," Kate said. "They are often able to attend much better in one particular area that's of great interest to them."

Michael guided the car around the curves on the narrow roads with ease. "I'm a long way from considering consulting a doctor. Even if I did believe she has ADD, I don't think I could ever go along with medicating my daughter. The things I've been reading about some of the drugs they prescribe to control the behaviors is enough to turn any parent's blood to ice."

Kate touched his hand, which was clenched on the gearshift on the console between them. "I can appreciate how difficult a decision that would be. But you're getting ahead of yourself. She hasn't been diagnosed yet, and even if a physician recommended medication, the choice would remain yours. If you decide you don't want Chloe on medication, at least you have a heightened understanding of her behavior. That can be very helpful in learning to deal with situations that arise at home."

He was silent for a long time. When he finally responded, his voice was low. "I'm not ready to make a decision yet."

"I'm not trying to push, Michael. I just wanted to make you aware of the issue."

"Believe me," he said grimly, his eyes on the winding road ahead of them, "some days it's all I can think about."

When they reached her condo, he insisted on walking up to her door with her. "Go ahead and open the door," he instructed.

Indulging him, she did as he asked, and then had to stand aside as he did a walk-through of her home. When he met her back at her front door, her eyebrows were raised.

"Satisfied, Detective Friday?"

"You can't be too careful, Kate." All hints of humor were absent from his voice. He was dead serious. "A woman living alone has to be damn cautious. You could use a good security system for this place."

"Are you trying to scare me, Michael?"

"No. I'm trying to get you to agree to let me do a little work on this place, to make it more secure for you."

She seemed speechless at his offer. He pressed his case. "It's the least I can do after you were so kind to Chloe tonight. And it wouldn't take long."

"No, thank you," she said dismissively, once she'd found her voice again. "I can call a security company if I think I need further protection."

He regarded her with amusement. "Kath-er-ine," he said, drawling the syllables of her name out. "What do you think I operate?"

She blinked at him. "Well, you're computer security, aren't you? I mean, passwords and codes and whatnot for computer files."

"We're into all sorts of security. I designed the high-tech security system for my property," he informed her. "As well as the one protecting my den. It would be no trouble—"

"Thank you, but no," she said with finality. "I'll take care of it myself."

He regarded her from beneath lowered brows, but she returned his gaze steadily. "Stubborn, aren't you?"

"You, Mr. Friday, could have invented the word."

There was no reasoning with the woman, he saw that at once. Quiet, reserved Kate Rose was as implacable as steel when she had her mind made up. There was pride hidden beneath that lovely exterior, and a will that would rival his own for sheer stubbornness.

His lips curved. He never had learned to resist a challenge. "Well, would you at least allow me to—"

"No, Michael, no. There's nothing—"

"Allow me to thank you," he concluded. He'd succeeded in stopping her flow of words. "It was very generous of you to join Chloe's birthday celebration this evening. You made her day for her."

"I enjoyed the evening, too."

He savored her words and the light of sincerity in her eyes. He moved closer to her and cupped her face in both of his hands. Her skin was soft beneath his fingers, tempting them to linger, to stroke. There was a brief moment when logic could have fled, to be replaced only by instinct. But then he recognized the flicker of panic in her eyes and contented himself instead by brushing a kiss across her forehead.

"Thank you again, Miss Rose," he murmured huskily. Then he turned and went through her door before logic vanished completely.

The night was still fairly early, at least by Michael's standards, so he headed back to the office. But even as he sat behind his desk, faced with the mountain of file folders he had piled on it, his mind insisted on wandering to the woman he'd just left. He stared blankly at Derek's analysis report of the computer program he'd completed, the words jumbling together meaninglessly. He didn't want to rush his fences with Kate. She was a wary little thing, and she was nowhere near trusting him yet. She'd bolt at the first sudden move he made. Still, it was hard not thinking about the moves he'd *like* to make. He hadn't met a woman who interested him in a very long time, and he didn't think he'd ever met a woman like her.

His office door pushed open then, interrupting his thoughts. "Michael, I didn't know you were coming back tonight." Derek ambled into the room and dropped into a chair in front of Michael's desk.

"You're working late."

"Carla's been after me to get her a date for the completion of that new security system I'm working on so she can start planning the marketing blitz."

"Carla's still here?"

"Just left. Say, how was Chloe's birthday? Did you get together with Deanna?"

Michael shook his head. "She's got something planned for this weekend. Trask and I took Chloe out for pizza. Along with her teacher."

"Her teacher?" Derek shot him a surprised look. "Why was she there?"

"Because it was Chloe's party and she wanted her invited. She's very attached to Miss Rose."

"I had a teacher named Rose once," Derek reminisced. "Actually, it was Sister Mary Rose. She wore long black-and-white habits and shoes just like the ones Bernie always wears." After a moment of reflection, he added, "Looked a lot like Bernie, as a matter of fact."

"I can guarantee you that Kate Rose looks nothing like Bernie," Michael said wryly. "She's actually quite... intriguing." Yeah, that would explain the amount of time he'd spent thinking about Kate since they met. He was intrigued by her. She was gorgeous, sexy and strong-willed.

There was a sensitivity about her that lent her an air of vulnerability, but the lady had made it clear that she called her own shots.

And she had his hormones kicking into overdrive every time he got within ten feet of her.

Derek let out a chuckle. "Oh, my friend, if you're finding yourself intrigued by a schoolteacher, you have definitely been alone too long. Why don't you come with me some night and we'll find you some real reasons to be intrigued?"

"No thanks. That scene wore thin quickly."

Derek shook his head in bemusement. "There's no accounting for taste. How long are you going to be here? Do you need help with anything?"

Michael shook his head. "I got that bug worked out of the system we were stumped on. It's ready for you to take over. I'm just going to finish up a few more things here, and then starting tomorrow, I'm going to be working at home on FORAY. Anything you need, you can reach me there."

Derek nodded. "I'll do that. And I'm going to be working on something else for you, too, Michael. I've given this a lot of thought, and I've decided that you need to get out more. I'm going to find someone perfect for you. A real nice, old-fashioned girl."

Sending his vice president a jaundiced look, Michael noted, "I've seen your dates, Latham. You don't know any nice, old-fashioned girls."

"Well, no, not personally," Derek agreed cheerfully. "But I do know lots of women. Who know lots of other women..." He waved a hand carelessly.

"Don't bother," Michael advised him. "I don't need any help."

Derek's parting chuckle still rankled long after he'd left the office. Michael jammed papers into file folders and then placed them in some sort of order in the file cabinet located next to his desk. He didn't know why he was being treated like some pathetic date dork lately, but his recent absence from the frenetic social scene was by choice. Since Chloe had come to live with him, he'd been busier than ever. Settling into their life together had taken up all his time, and now that they had some sort of routine worked out, casual dating didn't seem worth the effort. Besides, he hadn't met a woman in the last few years who could hold his interest for more than a few minutes.

Except for one. His hands stilled and he leaned against the file cabinet reflectively. Kate Rose had definitely sparked his interest, among other things, from the first second he'd laid eyes on her. Even at the school, when he'd been angry, even when he'd been focused on having her removed from her job, he'd been aware of her in a way that hadn't been totally comfortable.

He slammed the file drawer shut. One arm was still draped over the edge of the cabinet, and his fingers drummed against the front of the drawer restlessly. She was a mouthwateringly attractive woman. Not beautiful like the coolly remote faces that graced magazine covers. But much more real. More approachable. More touchable.

His fingers tingled at the thought. Because he did want to touch Kate. Very much. She had everything he'd ever thought he wanted in a woman. Looks, brains and a good sense of humor. And the icing on the cake was that she already cared about Chloe. Really cared about her. She knew how to talk to children like they were people, not the way some adults talked down to kids as if they were alien life-forms.

He dropped down in his chair. As he'd told Derek earlier, he found Kate intriguing. Had from the start. He'd already half planned to pursue her, but he could see now that wouldn't be a good idea.

No, he mused, tipping back in his chair and perusing the ceiling, pursuing Kate Rose wasn't the answer. Dating her was out. He'd been crazy to even consider it. He didn't want another casual relationship in his life. He didn't want anything casual with Kate at all.

Bernie and Derek had been right all along. What he needed was a wife.

He examined the idea. Instead of the amusement he'd felt when Bernie had first mentioned it, and his irritation with

Derek's harping on it, the idea now seemed…right. Now that he was considering Kate for the position.

It was perfect. The chair came upright with a loud squeak, and he slammed his hand on his desktop. No, it was better than perfect, it was ingenius. He'd marry Kate Rose. She was exactly what he needed in his life, exactly what Chloe needed. And the fact that she torched his hormones by merely entering the room was a sweet little side benefit.

He considered the matter from every angle, with the fierce concentration he usually reserved for the minuscule details of preparation for a hostile takeover war. He'd have to approach her very cautiously, of course. He'd have to take it slow, win her trust. And then, of course, her love.

The thought filled him with a surge of heat. The idea of being loved by Kate Rose fired currents beneath his skin like warm rivers of electricity. He was more convinced than ever that he'd just come up with the most brilliant idea he'd ever had.

Fingers drumming on his desk, he plotted and polished his strategy, much as he did when he was readying for corporate warfare.

The thought of failure never even entered his mind.

Chapter 5

"Well, of course I agree that you need to work on FORAY from a secure computer," Derek allowed. "I'm just saying it's damn inconvenient. Especially now with the takeover deal heating up."

"Jake has things under control," Michael said calmly. Jake Winslow, the firm's lawyer, could be counted on to handle all the details as they came up.

"How often will you be in the office?"

Michael shrugged. "Whenever I need to be. You can keep things running there, can't you?"

Derek grinned. "You know it. Bernie is in seventh heaven at your absence."

"I think it's been the best two weeks of her life. She's got my number for the times when she feels the need to reach out and nag someone. Which she does," he added wryly, "on a regular basis. She thinks I'm playing hooky."

"Which you're not, of course."

"What do you think?"

"I think," Derek announced, rising from his chair and strolling around the room, "that the deadline for FORAY is a killer, and you don't have a minute to waste." Contrary to his words, he slouched against one of Michael's bookcases, clearly in no hurry to leave. With his hands in the pant pockets of his Italian suit, he resembled a *GQ* advertisement for CEO wanna-bes.

"Which makes it difficult to justify prolonging this conversation with you." Nodding at the sheaf of papers on the table beside him, Michael said, "Take those files back to Carla and tell her things are a go. She can start a marketing strategy for promoting the new home computer security system. You did a good job on it, Derek."

"Thanks. If you need any help on FORAY..."

"I'll let you know."

Derek gathered up the papers he'd brought for Michael's signature and placed them back in his briefcase. "Shouldn't Chloe be home by now?"

"She's upstairs," Michael said. "Every day for the past week and a half she's been holed up in her bedroom after school. She's redecorating."

Derek's eyebrows rose. "Alone?"

"She has help," Michael said cryptically. Glancing at his watch, he added, "Shouldn't you be getting back to the office? Maybe you can catch Carla before she leaves for the day."

"I'll just go up and say hi to Chloe on my way—" Derek's sentence was interrupted by the sound of small feet running down the hallway.

"Daddy, Daddy!" Chloe burst into the room. "We finished painting. And now my wallpaper can go up, and then the carpeting will come, and my room's gonna be awesome!" She stopped for a breath before adding, "Hi, Mr. Latham."

"Hi, squirt. What's this I hear about you redecorating your room?"

Chloe nodded enthusiastically. "I had to get help, because Daddy's hopeless."

Derek chuckled. "So I've often said." In an aside to Michael, he asked, "Which of those interior design businesses that I recommended did you decide to go with?"

Before he could answer, another voice asked, "Michael, do you have some place I can rinse out these brushes?" Kate peeked into the room. Her hands were full of brushes and a paint can. She was clad in jeans and an oversize man's shirt. It was one of his, and the sight of her had satisfaction curling through him. She hadn't wanted to wear it, but he'd insisted, citing a worry about her with Chloe in an enclosed area with fresh paint. The solution he'd suggested had been too practical for her to refuse. But practicality didn't explain his reaction. He liked the sight of her wearing his clothes, liked it very much.

As a matter of fact, he liked the sight of her, period. Wayward strands had escaped the hasty knot she'd confined her hair in and now curled around her ears, across her forehead. A smudge of paint decorated one cheekbone. She looked capable, efficient and faintly mussed. She was adorable.

"Well, well, no wonder Michael's so content to work at home," Derek murmured, his eyes gleaming. Stepping forward, he said, "Hello, I'm Derek Latham, Michael's vice president."

The hair on the back of Michael's neck rose as he watched Derek spring into action. The man was polished, there was no denying it, and he'd seen the effect that adroit charm could have on women. Derek wasn't discriminating; he felt the need to impress every woman he came across. And Kate made a definite impression herself, even dressed as she was. He watched her carefully for her reaction, but Derek's introduction elicited nothing but polite interest. His muscles unbunched slowly.

"Derek, this is Kate Rose. She's been kind enough to take pity on Chloe and help her fix up her bedroom."

"It's nice to meet you," Kate said politely.

Derek stared at her. "Kate Rose."

She exchanged a look with Michael. "Yes."

"You're…Chloe's teacher?"

She nodded, but Derek's gaze swung to Michael, as if to validate her answer. When Michael inclined his head, Derek looked back at her. "Well, I have to tell you, Kate, that if

I'd had a teacher who looked like you when I was in the first grade, I would have been heartbroken to be promoted to the second.''

His voice carefully bland, Michael said, ''Chloe, why don't you help Miss Rose find Trask. He'll show you where to wash the brushes out in the basement.''

''Okay.'' Chloe was plainly delighted to have a reason to escape the adult conversation. ''C'mon, Miss Rose.'' She dashed from the room, and Kate followed her.

Derek watched them exit, then turned to his boss with a wide smile on his face.

Michael waited with resignation for his reaction. It wasn't slow coming.

''Well, you've been even busier than I thought. What have you been up to, working during the day and getting tutored at night?'' His chuckle was loaded with meaning.

''You've got a predictable mind, Latham. You know how hard it is to say no to Chloe. Kate was kind enough to agree to help her out with her bedroom.''

''When she finishes in Chloe's bedroom, will she be starting in yours?'' Derek inquired.

With effort, Michael kept his temper in check. The fact that it took effort didn't escape him. He was used to the innuendos and the one-track mind Derek could have when it came to women. But he never recalled wanting to bury his fist into the man's perfect capped teeth for making a suggestive remark before. ''You're way off base, Derek. She's a nice woman, going out of her way for a student. It would be a stretch, even for you, to make something dirty out of it.''

Derek held his hands up in mock surrender. ''Okay, okay, just kidding. She's a damn good-looking woman, though. I know that hasn't escaped your attention. I take back everything I said before about schoolteachers. I could easily become—what was your word?—intrigued by her myself.''

''I don't think you're her type.''

Derek gave him a knowing grin. ''Staking a claim, boss?''

Irritation, tightly banked only a moment ago, seeped into his voice. ''If you don't get out of my den in five seconds, you're going to be free to stake a claim yourself—in the un-employment line.''

Unperturbed, Derek reached for his briefcase. "On my way." At the doorway, he paused. "If you learn anything new, you'll teach me, right?" He ducked out of the room, chortling at his own wit.

Michael dropped back into his chair, staring at the wall broodingly. He didn't spend a lot of time in self-analysis, but even he could recognize the emotion that had threatened to choke him as soon as Derek had laid eyes on Kate. Although unfamiliar, it was easily identifiable. Pure, unadulterated jealousy.

Serious, gorgeous, sexy Kate Rose had something that set his pulse pounding.

And Derek had been right about one thing. He was definitely staking a claim.

"Pay me?" Kate could feel her blood pressure rise threateningly. Her eyes narrowed and shot daggers at Michael. "You will not pay me for helping Chloe. I wanted to do it, and I enjoyed myself. I was happy to…"

The rest of her words were muffled by the placement of Michael's fingers against her lips. Amusement curled his mouth and tinged his words. "You didn't let me finish, Kate. May I finish?"

Shock held her immobile for a few seconds at the feel of those warm fingers, large, yet curiously gentle, pressed against her mouth. Even after she gave a stiff, self-conscious nod, he seemed slow to remove his touch. When he did, his fingers left a lingering warmth in their wake.

"I wasn't offering to write you a check. Not that your help hasn't been worth it," he added. "But I would like to do something to repay you for all the time you've given to Chloe. So how about it? Will you have dinner with me? If you like seafood, Masterson's Wharf is great."

Kate blinked at him, trying to still the foolish leap of her heart that his words had elicited. Michael Friday moved in a world that was totally outside of her experience. The man had the wealth and power to be a player in corporate takeovers and multimillion-dollar contracts. He emanated energy and confidence. He was also, undoubtedly, the most mind-numbingly, knee-shakingly sexy man she'd ever had occasion to meet. Have dinner with him?

"No," she heard herself say, as if from a distance, "I can't have dinner with you, Mr. Friday."

"*Mr.* Friday," he repeated, his voice husky. "Have I been demoted? A few minutes ago I was Michael."

Feeling a blush heat her cheeks, Kate persisted. "I don't need any repayment. I helped because I wanted to."

"I don't want you to think of the dinner as repayment, Kate," he chided. "It would hardly do justice for all you've done for us, at any rate. But you're right, I would like to at least thank you."

She shook her head again with finality, fighting off an absurd sense of disappointment. It had been surprisingly difficult to work here almost daily for the last couple of weeks with him around. He'd had a habit of showing up to check on her and Chloe's progress unexpectedly, sending her pulse scampering. Now that she was finished with the help she'd promised the little girl, there should be very little reason for the two of them to see each other.

Just then an earsplitting shriek sounded and the front door slammed. Michael winced and sent her a crooked smile. "Speak of the sweet little devil..." He began to talk rapidly as Chloe's footsteps came closer. "I promised to take Chloe to the movie tonight, and tomorrow I have to work all day. She'll be at her mother's after school. I could pick you up at six-thirty, I'll get reservations for seven. We'll be two adults having a quiet, uninterrupted meal. C'mon, Kate, how about it?" He finished the sentences in a rush, just as Chloe slid to a halt beside them, her voice still raised with excitement.

"Dad, Dad, Miss Rose, guess what? I taught Rosy to eat sugar cubes *right* out of my hand, and it doesn't hurt at all, it kinda tickles, and know what I'm going to teach her next? Guess! Guess what?"

Michael fixed her with a look of polite interest. "To roll over?"

Chloe rolled her eyes. "Da-a-d! I'm going to teach her to come when I whistle, that's what. Hank is teaching me to whistle, and listen to this." She screwed up her face, stuck a finger in both sides of her mouth and blew. The sound that emerged was reminiscent of a screech from a set of bagpipes. Michael winced again, and Kate recoiled a little.

After a moment, Chloe took her fingers from her mouth and looked from one to the other of them eagerly. "Well, what do you think?"

"You're a very...enthusiastic whistler," Kate said gravely. "I can tell you've been practicing."

The little girl nodded. "Uh-huh, and Hank says if I keep on practicing *day and night,* I'll be so good Rosy will know my whistle and come to me."

"Not in the house, okay, small fry?" her dad said. "Do your practicing outside, all right?"

"But, Dad!" Chloe wailed. "Hank says day and night. And Miss Rose always says if we want to be good at something we have to practice, right, Miss Rose?"

Kate smiled gently and said, "I think it's time for me to go." She headed toward the door, pausing to retrieve her coat from the front closet.

"Are you in a hurry, Kate?" Michael inquired, trailing after her with his hands shoved in his jeans pocket. Chloe chose that moment to try another whistle, and a pained look settled on his face.

"Lots to do," she replied, slipping into her jacket. As Chloe whistled again, her pace quickened.

Michael's hand beat hers to the doorknob, halting her escape. "Coward," he murmured, his lips close to her ear.

Kate turned her head and looked at him uncertainly. What was he referring to? Her hasty departure or her refusal of his dinner invitation? His body seemed to surround her, even though they weren't touching, and he felt like a furnace. The warmth lured her; all she would have to do was lean back a fraction of an inch and she'd be pressed against him, would feel that heat firsthand. She held herself rigid.

"Am I going to have to send the whistler home to serenade you, or are you going to have dinner with me?" he asked.

She slid a glance at Chloe, who looked ready to launch into another high-pitched noise. The idea occurred to her that her opportunities to speak to Michael were diminishing as Chloe's room neared completion. And she very much wanted to find out if he was any closer to taking her advice about making a doctor's appointment for his daughter.

Her gaze met his. His eyes were alight with purpose, and she knew that he had never accepted her refusal; giving up wasn't something this man would do easily.

"What do you say, Kate?" he asked again.

His gaze tracked her lips as they formed the words.

"I say…yes."

Kate had ample time to regret her decision as she got dressed that evening. Michael's nearness must have overpowered her usually logical thinking processes, she decided. She should have set up a conference at school to discuss Chloe with him, although with his propensity for missed appointments, it was just as likely that he would forget it. She and Chloe were almost done with her bedroom, and there was only one more week of school left. After that, she would never have occasion to see Michael again. She owed it to the little girl to push aside her uneasiness at being alone with Michael and use the opportunity to discuss his decision with him.

She'd never been to the restaurant Michael had mentioned, but she'd heard about it. It had a reputation for outstanding food, outrageous prices and snooty waiters. The narrow black dress she'd selected was the dressiest thing she owned. It had long sleeves and a scooped neckline and was made from a fabric that skimmed but didn't cling. She picked up two jet combs and fastened her hair back on both sides. Casting one last doubtful eye at her reflection, Kate left the bedroom before she could change her mind, and her clothes, again.

The pounding on her front door heralded Michael's arrival. She opened the door, and conscious thought deserted her.

She'd gotten used to seeing him in jeans and sneakers. She thought the casual wear must accentuate his strength, make him appear bigger, tougher, more dangerous. She'd been wrong.

The double-breasted gray suit he was wearing had to have been tailor-made for his muscled form. It fit his wide chest and shoulders to perfection. The white shirt and muted tie should have lent him an air of tamed civility. It failed to do so. Though his unruly tawny hair had been forced to a semblance of order, and he'd apparently recently shaved, he looked no less lethal. More so, really. All that power and presence forced into a polished package gave him a barely leashed energy that fairly crackled in the air between them.

Swallowing convulsively, Kate took an involuntary step backward. Michael followed, stepping into her hallway and immediately shrinking the area with his size.

His hazel eyes reflected the admiration in his voice. "You look fantastic."

So do you, she thought a little wildly. Murmuring her thanks, she turned blindly to the closet, staring at the contents without seeing them. This was a mistake, a huge one. What had she been thinking? It would have been infinitely safer to confer about Chloe at school or on the phone, anyplace where she wouldn't have to face that megawatt energy focused totally on *her*. Used to having the force of his personality defused by Chloe's or Trask's presence, she'd allowed herself to forget the sheer power of his regard. It was like being caught in an electrically charged field.

His arm reached past her then, and she started a little. He pulled her long black leather coat from its hanger and held it out for her. When she didn't move immediately, his eyebrow climbed.

"Is this coat all right?"

Her gaze met his for an instant. "Yes," she said, allowing him to help her with the coat. "Thank you." She stepped away from him as soon as she was able, using the opportunity to button up her coat. Michael wasn't wearing one, she noticed. Apparently that furnacelike heat he radiated was a sort of personal insulation.

"Kate?" His voice was quizzical.

Her gaze flew to meet his.

"Do you need anything else before we leave?"

She shook her head and then remembered her purse. Flushing, she backtracked to pick it up from the hallway table. He was holding the door open, waiting for her to precede him.

"We'll leave right away, if that's okay with you. I left the Jag running, and I'm double-parked. It will probably take us the full half hour to get to Masterson's. Do you have your house key?"

"Yes, of course, but there's no reason to worry. I keep a spare in back of the mailbox."

A genuinely pained expression crossed his face. "You must know how risky that is."

She walked by, leaving him to pull the door closed behind him. "Not as risky as finding myself locked out some night."

Seated in the powerful car, Kate discreetly ran her hand over the smooth leather seat. The luxury was hard not to appreciate. Then Michael was folding his long length into the vehicle, and nerves began to cluster again. He put the car into gear and it moved forward smoothly.

"Would you mind putting a CD in?" he asked. "The case is on the seat next to you." He flipped on a courtesy light, and she quickly made a selection and slipped it in the player. He pressed a button and they were shrouded in darkness again as the strains of the saxophone music filled the car.

"So, what did you do all day, since you didn't have to spend the afternoon engaged in slave labor for Chloe?"

Amusement laced her voice. "As taskmasters go, she's not quite up there with Simon Legree yet. But I had some free time, so I spent the day studying for my comps."

"Your what?"

"Comprehensive exams," she explained. "They'll complete my master's degree. I've already completed the coursework requirements. The exams will take place in another six weeks.''

''That's quite an accomplishment.'' There was no mistaking the admiration in his voice. ''You took courses while you were teaching?''

''One night a week during the school year, and two classes each summer.''

''Well, congratulations. Sounds like a lot of hard work. You'll really have something to celebrate when you finish up.'' He launched into a hilarious recounting of his exploits during his college years, and it would have been impossible for her to remain on edge when she was helpless with laughter.

''I don't believe you,'' she exclaimed after one particularly outlandish tale. ''You could have been thrown out for pulling a stunt like that.''

''The dean was really never able to pin it on me,'' he explained. ''But I have to admit that particular prank had a profound effect on me. Scared me enough to keep me out of trouble for a while, anyway. I couldn't afford to lose my football scholarship over a goat.''

''Well, I'm glad you came to your senses about the value of your education,'' she teased. ''Even if it did take livestock to convince you.''

By the time they were ushered to a table in the restaurant and she was seated across from Michael, the fluttering in her stomach had calmed. Until she opened the menu and saw the prices. She swiftly calculated that the combined price of their meals would be a close equivalent to the amount she spent on groceries for two weeks.

''What will you have, Kate?'' Michael inquired.

A coronary, she answered silently. Nothing could have pointed out so vividly the differences between them. He was a man used to money and the luxuries it could buy. Her idea of a meal out was pizza or fast food.

''If you're having trouble deciding, the seafood platter has a little of everything. I've had it here—it's very good.''

At her nod he gave their orders to the tux-clad waiter and

then turned back to her and grinned. "You know, when I was a grubby kid I used to dream about coming to places like this to eat. Now that I can afford it, I always have to fight an overwhelming urge to do something to shock the staff out of those professional masks of superiority."

He surprised a smile from her. "I know what you mean. Where's a goat when you need one?"

He reached over and clasped her hand. "What could we do to force a human emotion from these tuxedoed wax stiffs, hmm? A run through the fountain, maybe? A tap dance on the buffet table?"

"Either should do the trick." Growing serious, she asked, "Why do you come here if you don't like the atmosphere?"

"The food is great, but they don't do takeout," he said simply. Spreading his hands, he added, "Believe me, I asked. And I'm not easily intimidated."

That she could believe. If there was intimidation to be done, this man would do it. Although he wore his most charming persona this evening, she'd had an up close encounter with his temper and sensed the determination he was capable of. He would make a dangerous enemy.

He would make a dangerous lover.

The thought jolted her, suffusing her with heat. She wasn't in the habit of picturing men she barely knew in such a role. She wasn't, in fact, used to picturing *any* man in such a role. But the uncustomary thought brought her back to reality. It would be all too easy to let herself be lulled by her surroundings, to bask in his attention. But her purpose for coming here tonight was for Chloe.

As the meals arrived, she reached for her purse and withdrew two pamphlets and handed them to him. "I almost forgot. I picked these up for you."

He read the title from one aloud. *"Preventing Bedtime Bedlam."* His eyebrows rose. "You must have been spying on us. *Bedlam* is a good word to describe our house at eight-thirty every night." His gaze shifted to the other pamphlet. *"Homework Habits."* He looked at her. "Homework? She's a little young for that, isn't she?"

"Good habits take time to learn," Kate replied. "Both of those brochures have tips helpful for all children, not just those diagnosed with ADD. I think you'll find them..."

Her voice tapered off as she realized his attention had shifted. The change in him was startling. His expression went set and still, and his entire body seemed to tense, although he didn't move a muscle.

"Well, Michael, I shouldn't be surprised to see you here."

At the interruption, Kate turned to look at the man who stopped at their table. A well-preserved sixty-five, she estimated, with chiseled features and iron gray hair. In his dark blue suit he managed to look at once elegant and remote. It was his eyes, she decided. The pale blue gaze held all the warmth of the North Atlantic.

The man smiled, a cold, humorless stretching of his lips. "After all, sharks like their fish, don't they?"

Michael clenched his hand where it lay on the table. "An interesting analogy coming from you, Jonathan. You've always been the most ruthless predator I know."

"Congratulations on that NASA contract, by the way," Jonathan said. "I won't inquire as to how you won it. Heard it comes with a tight deadline. It would be a shame if you didn't make it, wouldn't it? I doubt those folks would be too understanding."

"Your concern, as always, is touching," Michael drawled. "But you might want to spend a little more of it on yourself. From the looks of you, your fourth—or was it fifth—marriage was a rough one."

"Not so rough, actually. I'm accomplished at extricating myself while holding on to what's mine."

"Don't I know it." Michael's voice was hard and bleak, and Kate looked at him, mystified. She didn't understand what was going on here, but the undercurrents of animosity were unmistakable.

Suddenly, the penetrating beam of the man's chilly blue eyes were turned on her. "As usual, Michael has forgotten his manners. Although we haven't been graced with an introduction, I'll do you a favor and give you a little advice." He leaned toward her, and Kate had to restrain herself from recoiling. "Don't trust him, not even for a second. He's the most ungrateful, ruthless bastard you'll ever meet, and the instant you take your eyes off him, he'll have the shirt off your back." Straightening, he added, "Or in your case, that pretty black dress."

Michael's chair clattered as he rose abruptly. His voice was low, icily controlled. "Your time just ran out, old man. I'd advise you to leave. Now."

Jonathan gave her a wintry smile. "Remember what I said." Then he turned and strolled away.

Michael remained standing, his gaze burning a hole in the man's ramrod-straight back. Time stretched, and still he didn't move. Kate grew concerned and touched the back of his hand. His gaze dropped to where her hand lay on his, and slowly, imperceptibly, he relaxed. She watched him reach for the rage that had enveloped him so briefly and tuck it back out of sight.

He sat down again and said grimly, "I'm sorry you had to witness that."

When it became apparent he was going to say nothing more, Kate burst out, "Michael, what just happened? Who was that awful person?"

He gave her a terrible parody of a smile and reached for his wineglass. Toasting in the direction of the man who'd just left their table, he replied, "That 'awful' person is Jonathan Garrett Friday." He took a sip from his glass before adding, "My father."

Chapter 6

Michael reached across the table and tipped more wine in her glass. He took a few moments before he spoke again. When he did, neither his face nor his voice revealed his earlier anger. "As you could probably tell, the Fridays aren't a particularly close-knit bunch." He picked up his fork and cocked an eyebrow at her. "What about you? What's your family like?"

Kate picked up her glass, considered the wine bubbling inside. Witnessing the earlier scene had left her shaken. And despite Michael's sternly controlled features, she was aware of the emotion still swirling beneath the surface.

"I'm the oldest of nine children."

He paused, his fork half-raised to his mouth. "What was it like?"

"It was...poor." Invariably people romanticized her childhood, imagining something out of an Alcott novel, with a house full of a noisy brood stringing popcorn together. She'd always been thankful that people couldn't know how wrong they were.

"Your parents?" Michael reached for a roll, breaking it apart to butter it, his gaze never leaving her face.

"Live in West Virginia, where I was raised. We moved several times when I was a child, always small towns, though, always in the state. Right now my father is a custodian for a rural church. My mother has never worked outside the home. She takes in sewing."

"How many of your brothers and sisters are still at home?"

"Five. My youngest sister is ten."

"Do you get to see them often?"

She almost flinched, as if he had touched a particularly painful bruise. "Not as often as I'd like."

"I can't even pretend to imagine it. I was an only child and on my own a lot. I wished for brothers and sisters...well, mostly brothers." He took another bite of lobster, chewed reflectively. "I imagine our childhoods had more in common than you think, though."

Kate looked at him askance. "I can't imagine what that would be."

He continued to eat, his face expressionless. "You said you grew up poor. When I was eight, my father walked out and took his money with him. My mother worked two jobs most of the time to pay the rent on our apartment." He shrugged, as if his next words were of little consequence. "I spent the better part of the next twenty years hating him."

Michael turned off the ignition and went around the car to open the door for Kate. When they reached her porch, he silently held his hand out for her key. She opened her mouth to protest, but one look from him silenced her. She handed it to him, and he followed the same routine that he had the last time he'd seen her home, entering the door ahead of her and doing a quick, thorough search of each room.

"You missed your calling," she drawled when he finally joined her again. She slipped out of her coat and turned to hang it up. "You should be with the DCPD." Even as she spoke, he went into the living room and pulled her curtains aside, examining the latches and frames on her windows.

"Hazards of the job. No matter what kind of security we're in, we tend to be paranoid." He moved to the kitchen, leaving her to trail after him.

"Don't tell me. You're looking for a burglar in my pots and pans."

He turned back to her with a quick grin. "No, I'm looking for a cup of coffee. What are my chances of having you offer me one?"

His tone was undeniably wheedling and had its desired effect. "All right. I'll make us some."

Minutes later they were facing each other across the small kitchen table, sipping coffee.

"Déjà vu," he said. "When I came here before you fed me cookies and milk."

"I remember."

"There are no cookies this time, of course," he went on, shamelessly hinting.

"No," Kate said firmly, her eyes meeting his. "No cookies."

He smiled and shrugged, unembarrassed to be caught begging. "I have an acquired appreciation for baked goods," he said. "Trask, despite his many fine qualities, doesn't claim to be a cook."

"Just what is it that Mr. Trask does for you?" Kate asked curiously.

"Not 'Mr.,'" Michael corrected. "He's just Trask. He started out as my security adviser. He became much more." He stopped, considered for a moment. "Since Chloe's come to live with me, he more or less runs the house, keeps track of appointments." He gave her a sidelong glance. "Had you made the conference appointments with him rather than me, he'd have made sure I got to them."

"You don't have a secretary to do that for you at work?"

He grimaced. "My secretary and I don't always communicate effectively. But speaking of Chloe, we never did. Finish, I mean."

Kate wrapped both her hands around her mug. "No, we never did," she said steadily.

"I've made an appointment for her to be seen by a pediatrician," he said bluntly. He waited for her startled gaze to meet his. "I still have a lot of doubts, but I remembered what you said. I figured too much information is rarely a problem."

He paused for a moment to enjoy the sudden transformation as her smile lit up her face. A corresponding heat bloomed low in his belly. That smile of hers should be outlawed. It had the impact of a thousand volts of electricity and, aimed at him, was damn near lethal. He basked in its glow for a moment.

"I'm so glad, Michael," she said, impulsively leaning forward to touch his arm. "I know you won't regret it."

He stared at the slim, elegant hand lying on his broad forearm. His gaze followed the slender line of her arm up to her shoulder and across the delicate hollows of her throat and settled, finally, on her mouth. It was getting more and more difficult to remember his plan, his strategy to go slow. Especially when she looked at him like that. Touched him like that. As the moments stretched, her smile wavered and faded away. But when she would have withdrawn her touch, he covered her hand with his.

"I'm not promising anything else," he warned. "Just that I'll get a medical opinion and listen to my options. Even if Chloe is diagnosed with ADD, I'm nowhere close to agreeing to medication for her. Right now, I can't promise any more than that."

"For right now, that's enough."

He looked down to where his large hand completely covered her much slimmer, more delicate one. "I made the appointment with Dr. Sachar. Do you know her?"

Kate thought for a moment and then shook her head.

"She's supposed to be very good. Her office is downtown D.C., and we're on a standby list. She was booked two months ahead, but if I agree to very little notice, I can get in when she has a canceled appointment." And it had taken fifteen minutes of his most persuasive coaxing to convince the receptionist of that idea. But once he'd reached the decision that he would proceed with a medical evaluation, he hadn't wanted to wait two months. "I'm going to have to talk to Deanna about it soon."

"How will she react?"

He lifted a shoulder. "I'm not sure." He hadn't ever really known what to expect from Deanna. He'd been wrong when he'd thought they shared the same interests, the same dreams. He'd been wrong about a lot of things.

"Does...your father...ever see Chloe?"

"No." He released her hand and pulled away from her touch. Her eyes were wide, somber, and he knew she was judging him, weighing him. As he'd so often weighed himself. "To tell you the truth, I'm not sure he's aware of her existence. I know damn well he wouldn't care."

"How do you know that?"

He simply looked at her, wondering if she could begin to understand. She'd come from a large family. Though she'd said they hadn't had money, there must have been plenty of love to make up for the lack. His own experience was just the opposite.

When he spoke again, it was without passion, the resentment safely buried again. "He didn't care about his own son when he left. Hell, I'll say this for him—he didn't make me a bunch of empty promises that he never delivered on. The only vow he left us with was when he told my mother she'd never see another nickel of his. That was true enough."

"He didn't keep in touch with you?"

"I didn't hear from him again until I was sixteen. I was making a name for myself in high school football, being mentioned in the papers." He lifted a shoulder. "I don't know what was going through his head. Maybe in some weird way he thought I'd proven myself worthy of his attention. Because all of a sudden, that's what I got. He started sending me things, issuing invitations." He fell silent then, the taste of remembered bitterness filling his mouth. If the old man had shown him even a fraction of that attention after he'd left, maybe it would have had some effect. A boy of eight or ten would have been dazzled by the authentic athletic jerseys, the autographed game balls. But at sixteen, Michael hadn't been a boy.

"I went with him once. My mother made me. Said he owed me, owed both of us. I think I was supposed to be impressed when he took me sailing. Instead, I kept thinking that for the cost of that damn boat, my mother and I could be living in a real house, in a decent neighborhood. Maybe even have a car that actually ran." Maybe she could have quit one of her jobs. Perhaps the lines would have faded from her face, the weariness lifted from her shoulders.

"So you refused to go with him again," Kate guessed.

Michael reached for the coffeepot and refilled his mug. "Yes. But people don't say no to Jonathan Friday. Six weeks later my mother was slapped with a summons. He took her to court to sue for custody." It had been an ugly, vicious battle. The old man had had a set of witnesses bought and paid for to testify to his former wife's supposed lack of morals, her unfitness as a mother. It had made a lasting impression on Michael. Money, when used callously, could buy almost anything.

Kate's gaze was sober and steady. "Did you have to live with him?"

He shook his head. "I was plenty old to have a say in the proceedings, and I told the judge in no uncertain terms where I wanted to live. He must have believed my mother and me, because he allowed me to stay where I was."

"That's it, then? That's the reason he seemed so hateful to you this evening?"

"Oh, I have no doubt he hates me, all right." His voice was carefully blank. "I started my own business right out of college. I worked hard to get ahead, acquired some contacts who helped me." He held her gaze deliberately, wanting to watch her reaction to his next words. "And the first company I ever took over was my father's." He'd dismantled it piece by piece, raided the solvent funds and sold it off in parcels. And he'd enjoyed every second of it.

"I had my mother quit her jobs. I took some of the money from the old man's business and I bought her a house on a golf course. One of those country club places, you know. A couple of cars..." His voice trailed off. He'd gone about setting his mother up in the life the old man had robbed her of when he'd dumped them both. His mouth twisted. "Very Freudian, huh?"

He didn't see the horrified fascination in her eyes that he'd learned to expect. Didn't see the pity that he'd learned to despise. The absence of either nearly undid him. Her voice was soft when she replied, "Human, at any rate."

It would be all too easy to lose himself in her clear blue gaze, which reflected the easy warmth that was so much a part of her. There was compassion there, the kind that had a man blurting out his life story, that made a man feel he was better than he was. He wondered how much understanding he'd see there if she realized how close he'd come to the abyss. How close he'd come to turning into a heartless SOB, just like his father.

She looked past him at the clock on the wall. "It's late."

He wondered—hoped—he heard a tinge of regret in her voice. Surely he had enough regrets for both of them. Regret for the way the evening had ended and for giving her a guided tour down his own personal path of grief. She could tempt a confession from a closemouthed priest.

Discomfit filled him. This hadn't been part of the plan. By baring his soul like that, he'd risked making her even warier of him. For the first time it occurred to him that his plan for luring cautious, sexy Kate Rose closer wasn't going to be as clear-cut as designing a dispassionate corporate takeover bid. When he was with Kate, emotion crept in. And emotion clouded logic, turned objectivity aside. When he had a goal in his sights, retaining his objectivity was imperative.

He got up and followed her to the front door. When she reached the hallway, she turned around, seeming unsure about what to do with him. He crooked a smile at the flicker of uncertainty on her face. It wasn't as strong as the full-blown trepidation she'd worn when she'd opened the door to him tonight. As the evening had worn on, that expression had eased. Now an echo of it was back, just enough to let him know that she wasn't all that comfortable with a man in her apartment after midnight. The knowledge was primitively satisfying, and rather than moving toward the door, he deliberately stepped toward her.

He recognized her reaction in the way her mouth trembled for a moment before she made a visible effort to firm it. His gaze lingered on the combs holding back her hair, and he let his imagination go for just a second as he wondered what she would do if he reached over and released them.

He remembered the last time he'd left her like this, and the frustration he'd carried with him that he hadn't given in and tasted her, just once. He didn't want to scare her, didn't want to give her a reason for the anxiety to bloom into real fear of him. His goal for the evening had already been accomplished. She'd agreed to spend a few hours with him, alone. They were closer than they had been before, even if things hadn't progressed exactly as he would have liked. Michael was a careful man, one who'd never been accused of rushing his fences. A retreat was in order now, a little space in which Kate might wonder, might crave more.

But his mind didn't seem to have any control over his body. Instead of moving toward the door, he closed the distance between them and allowed himself to breathe in deeply of the scent at her delicate jawline. The pulse that beat below it was an overwhelming temptation, and he wasn't doing too well avoiding temptations right now. The tip of his tongue touched that delicate pulse, and at her shudder, his lips pressed there, lingered.

Her breath came more rapidly, in short, staccato gasps. Her hands pushed against his chest. "Michael."

If that word was meant as a warning, her voice shouldn't have been so soft. So full of longing.

"Kate," he murmured. He waited for her gaze to meet his, waited for the last remnant of determination to fade from her expression, to be replaced by a fraction of the desire he knew was reflected in his own, before his mouth covered hers.

The first touch of his mouth against hers was whisper-light, a mere brushing of lips. He returned again and again, taking

slow, sipping tastes. Her lips were soft and full. He could feel
the bottom one tremble slightly against his mouth, and he
soothed it gently with his tongue. He changed the angle of
the kiss to draw that fuller bottom lip into his mouth, and his
teeth closed on it tenderly.

She shuddered against him and he held her closer, tighter.
His mouth left hers and went to the delicate place behind her
earlobe. Thoughts of carefully plotted strategy faded as he
drank in the scent of her, greedily filling his senses with the
pleasure of her smell. It was a fragrance that owed less to the
light perfume she wore and more to the uniquely feminine
essence that was Kate.

A necklace of kisses was strewn with deliberate care from
one end of her collarbone to the other. He paused in his ministrations to give equal attention to the exquisitely soft skin
at the base of her throat. He took immediate advantage of the
way her neck arched beneath his mouth and closed his teeth
gently on the sensitive cord exposed there.

The sound she made was one of mingled shock and acceptance. And then she was moving closer, her hands at his nape,
tangling in his hair as she coaxed his mouth back to hers. His
lips crushed hers and found them open, the trembling gone,
and just as hungry as his own. Where before she'd accepted
his kiss, now she was returning it, demanding in her own
right.

He could feel reality edging away. He'd thought of this
moment often enough, from the first second he'd laid eyes
on her. Fantasized about it. Planned for it. But he hadn't foreseen the intoxicating effect her taste would have on him.
Hadn't planned on this fire licking through his veins, fueled
by the liquid pool of heat in his groin. He was wallowing in
the sensation of her slim, taut body close to his, so close that
he could feel her breasts, high and firm, flattened against him.

Her pointed tongue made a timid foray into his mouth,
engaging in a shy duel with his own. A groan was torn from
him and his fingers delved into her hair, cupping her face as
their mouths twisted together with savage intensity.

He moved forward, trapping her between the wall and his

body. And still he couldn't get close enough. The beckoning warmth that was so much a part of her nature was liquid fire now, trailing over his skin everywhere they touched. He'd never dreamed she'd be this hot, this soft, this silky. And he wouldn't have let himself imagine the pleasure he would get being this close to her, feeling her use that sweet little tongue to incite his own.

His hand went to her shoulder, slipping inside her dress to caress the smooth skin there. His fingers lingered for a moment, then delved lower to cup her breast. Drinking her moan, he teased her nipple into a tight, hard knot. It wasn't until he bent his mouth to replace his hand that she stopped him.

"No, Michael, don't."

He stilled immediately, wishing he could deny her breathless whisper. His face was level with her breast, his breath against it keeping the nipple drawn. Taking a deep, torturous breath, he rose slowly, dragging her dress back into place with one long finger.

Kate's beautiful blue eyes were still smoked with passion, but that soft mouth was determined. "We have to stop," she whispered.

He wondered if he was only imagining the regret in her voice.

"This wouldn't work."

His hard, pulsing length was still pressed against her stomach. "At the risk of sounding crude," he corrected dryly, "everything appears to be working just fine."

Her eyes flickered, then followed the direction of his gaze to where it rested between their bodies. Her eyes widened in fascination. Her palms pressed against his shoulders firmly. "We need to talk, Michael."

His forehead dropped to lean against hers. "We were already communicating," he murmured. His lips pressed against her temple. "Very nicely, I thought." The shiver that skated down her body filled him with a sheerly masculine pleasure. But her voice was no less firm when she spoke again.

"Please let me go."

He sighed this time and moved carefully, painfully away from her. She took advantage of the space to smooth her dress, fingers fidgeting with the neckline, the shoulders, the sleeves. It took him all of two seconds to realize that she was focusing on anything except him.

She turned away and appeared appalled at her reflection in the mirror. He didn't know what she found so objectionable. He much preferred the wildness in her hair, hanging as it was around her shoulders, across her breasts. He watched as she snatched out the comb that had come loose and restored it. Bending down, he scooped up the other comb from the floor, the one that had been sent flying by his eager hand, and she took an inordinate amount of time replacing it.

He watched her reflection from over her shoulder. "It's no use, you know."

Their gazes met in the mirror.

"You can't wipe away what happened here as easily as smoothing the wrinkles from your dress. It still shows where I kissed you. Here." His finger touched the side of her jaw, where his rougher chin had left an abrasion. "And here." His touch whispered over her lips, still swollen from his.

She pulled away jerkily, making sure to keep a careful distance between them. "This was a mistake. Mine," she hastened to add when his eyes narrowed. "I'm sorry I let it go this far. I appreciate the news you shared with me about your decision for Chloe. And the meal," she added, almost as an afterthought. "But I'm your daughter's teacher. Surely you understand how unprofessional it would be for me to get involved with…"

"Get involved with…?" he asked helpfully when she hesitated.

She made a helpless gesture with her hand. "With…this. With you. With…anything."

"Am I to assume from that explanation that your only objection to what happened here stems from the fact that you're Chloe's teacher?"

A frown worried her brows. "No…not exactly."

Frustrated desire shortened his temper. "Well then, what...exactly?"

"It wouldn't be right to have this sort of relationship with a parent, that's true. But you and I...we're not compatible at all."

"No?" he asked softly, moving toward her.

Her eyes tracked his movements warily. "No. Our life-styles. Our values. We have nothing in common."

"Did you like the seafood at the restaurant tonight?"

She tried, and visibly failed, to make the connection. "Yes, but..."

"So did I. Do you like my car?"

"What?" He was very close now, and he could read the effort it took for her not to retreat. "Your car? I...yes, I guess."

"Me, too. And I like your condo. We both like kids. I'm kind to dogs. We've got more in common than you're letting on. How about this?" he dared her, pressing his lips against the rapid pulse in her throat. "Do you like this?"

She took a deep breath. "Michael."

He raised his head slowly.

"This can't happen again."

"Let's negotiate."

"No."

He clenched his jaw and threw her one last fierce look. She returned it steadily, her breathing a little rapid but her expression determined. He opened his mouth one more time to make one last attempt to get her to see reason. She gave a slight, imperceptible shake of her head, her answer devastatingly apparent. Turning jerkily, he yanked at the door to let himself out. The brisk night air held no previews of the coming summer weather, but its chill came much too late to cool unquenched fires.

"Lock the door after me," he commanded, his voice low and harsh. It gave him a reason to linger there on her steps, when common sense and raging hormones would have dictated otherwise. It was an excuse to wait to hear the unmistakable click of the dead bolt, the jangle of the chain.

His ears strained, and he could almost convince himself that he heard more, as well. That he might have heard a tiny sound against the door that could have been her body relaxing against it. An almost imperceptible sigh that might have been a released pent-up breath.

A tight smile twisted his lips, at odds with the ache in his loins. If he tried hard enough, he might just convince himself that he heard his name whispered.

On the other side of the door.

Chapter 7

Kate released the breath that was strangling her lungs. Shakily, she pushed away from the door and headed to her bedroom. *A close call.* She shivered. For a moment she hadn't thought he'd leave, had been afraid that he might reach for her again. And if he had, she was all too aware that the evening would have ended much differently. Another minute with his mouth on hers, hot and hungry, and she wouldn't have been able to formulate a coherent sentence, much less an argument for sending him away.

She pressed a hand to her jittery stomach and climbed the stairs, wondering why she'd ever considered that she could have a calm, uneventful evening with Michael Friday. She'd rationalized her decision by focusing on the dinner as an opportunity to further discuss her very real concerns about Chloe. Underlying her relief that he had decided to take Chloe to a doctor was dismayed shock at her own weakness. Her mistake had been in thinking that she and Michael could have such a discussion free of emotional entanglements. But the last several minutes had made a mockery of that belief.

She entered her bedroom and crossed to the mirror. Her

reflection was somber, face flushed, her breathing still uneven. She released the combs in her hair, replacing them in the carved wooden box on the dresser. Her hair tumbled forward, its disarray an uncomfortable reminder of the way it had looked after Michael's hands had been in it. Kate stared at herself wide-eyed, barely recognizing the woman in the mirror. This was the woman Michael had seen. Hair wild, lips swollen and the marks of passion still very much apparent. One finger went to the slightly reddened spot on her neck, and for an instant she could imagine the drag of his lips over her skin, the slight abrasion of his beard.

Turning jerkily away, she released the zipper on her dress and stepped out of it. She'd known that he packed a powerful, sexual charge, but she hadn't been prepared for its impact. Hadn't been prepared for the tidal wave of her answering need.

She puttered around the room, using time and the mundane tasks of hanging up clothes and getting ready for bed to calm herself. She slipped into bed suspecting that sleep would be a long time coming, and contemplated the shadows that danced across her ceiling. It wasn't as though she should be surprised. Michael burned with the sort of fierce masculinity that would be a magnet to most women. She'd been aware of the force of his appeal from the instant she'd met him.

But she hadn't been prepared for the intensity of her reaction to him. Kate rolled to her side, bunching her pillow beneath her head. She'd been aware of him from the first, but even in her inexperience she'd known better than to let him get a hint of her response to him. He was much too aggressive not to press his advantage. The high voltage of his sexual energy would have been difficult to withstand, but under other circumstances she thought she could have resisted easily enough...if only he wasn't so darn likable.

She squeezed her eyes shut and then, when an image of Michael Friday swam beneath her lids, popped them open again. She had always been cautious in her relationships. She would never willingly relinquish control to a man the way her mother had, bowing to her father's every wish and command. She savored her own independence.

But Kate could remember too well a childhood spent yearning for even a fraction of the unconditional love and acceptance that Michael showered on Chloe. A man who loved his daughter as fiercely and completely as Michael did had his own appeal.

She shifted restlessly, the sound of her skin against the sheets a whisper in the night. The darkness of the room was relieved only by the red glow from her clock radio. As she stared sightlessly into the shadows, she thought that the appeal of such a man would, by itself, represent a powerful tug to her emotions. Coupled as it was with Michael's megawatt sexuality, he was nearly irresistible.

The computer blinked with automatic staggered reminders, waiting patiently for Michael to attend to it. His attention was sadly lacking, however, and had been since he'd left Kate at her condo two days ago, her long hair tangled from his fingers, her lips swollen and wet from his.

That particular memory sparked an all-too-familiar physical response. He shifted uncomfortably. He'd moved too fast. He'd known it at the time, but his brain had had no direct influence over the rest of his body. Even now his lack of control was baffling. Damned if he knew just what it was about Chloe's straitlaced teacher that sent his libido into overdrive. He'd met women more beautiful, less inhibited and much less obstinate. But there was no denying it; there was something about Kate Rose that had drawn him from the first, something he found endlessly fascinating. Not to mention something that got him hotter than a randy sixteen-year-old under the bleachers with the head cheerleader.

Maybe it was that slim white neck, he mused. It had seemed to beg to be teased, tasted. Or maybe it was the feel of her hair tangled in his fingers and the mental image of it spread across his bare chest. Or it could be those steady blue eyes, which reflected every emotion she was experiencing. The memory of how they'd mirrored her passion before she'd stopped him didn't do anything for the rapidly tightening fit of his pants.

He stretched his long legs out in front of him and gazed at the screen unseeingly. He'd made a strategical error that night. He'd never been one to tip his hand, not when preparing a takeover bid or going after a new slice of the market. He'd known he needed to approach her cautiously, to give her time to get used to the idea of a relationship between them. And yet he'd risked all his careful planning when he'd given in to the temptation to taste her. Just once.

A grimace crossed his face, and his fingers drummed against the side of the keyboard. Although he was a born risk taker in his career, the risks were always calculated, the percentage for success carefully formulated. There had been no such logic governing his actions with Kate. One taste might have been forgiven. It might have made her think, gotten her used to the idea of his wanting her. But he hadn't been able to stop at one taste.

He crossed his arms and slouched down in his chair. If he hadn't felt the shudders that had racked her body, hadn't caught her little gasps in his mouth, he'd think the reaction was all on his part, the aching, the wanting. But it hadn't been. He was sure of it. So all wasn't lost. He just needed to fine-tune his strategy a little.

Of course, he admitted morosely, scowling at the keyboard, all the fine-tuning in the world would be for nothing if he didn't manage to keep his emotions under control. Passion, he mentally corrected himself. Emotion had never been a problem, had never been allowed to circumvent his objectives. Emotion clouded judgment and fit him as uncomfortably as an ill-fitting suit.

He'd probably scared her. He frowned consideringly. And maybe her own responses had alarmed her as much as his actions had. She'd lobbed excuses at him like grenades, hoping that one of them would convince him to back away. Sorting through them mentally, he decided the one that had the most validity was when she said they were nothing alike. She could have been talking about their life-styles, but he thought it was more complex than that. It didn't take a rocket scientist to figure out that Kate didn't have a great deal of experience. She had an innate caution that was a tantalizing contrast to the warmth that was just as much a part of her. And if the truth be known, he didn't have a lot of experience, either, not with women like her. She wasn't a woman to be taken casually.

A thoughtful look settled on his face. That was fine with him, since he wasn't feeling very casual himself. Perhaps it was time to show her that he could be serious.

A glow smile curved his mouth. He could be very serious, indeed.

"Am I bothering you?"

Always, he wanted to answer Kate's diffident question. *Completely. Achingly.*

"Not at all," he answered politely, turning away from his computer. As if his earlier thoughts had summoned her, she hesitated in the doorway of his den. His mouth quirked. She looked about as eager to enter as Daniel had been to join the lions.

He watched her approach. She was wearing her teacher face, serious, professional. It would have been too much to ask that she was here to make his life easier by admitting to an overwhelming urge to have him there, now, on the floor, naked and sweating. For the first time he noticed the manila envelope she carried in her hand and gave a mental sigh as his fantasy sprouted wings and flew away. Yes, that had definitely been too much to ask.

"Did you get the wallpapering done?"

"Chloe is finishing up."

His eyebrows shot up in mock panic.

"Trask is with her. They're really just cleaning."

"You two make a heck of a racket wallpapering."

She surveyed him patiently. "Chloe decided it would go faster if we whistled while we worked. Or rather, she whistled."

"And you worked," he guessed.

"She was a very willing helper."

"Oh, I can tell. You have wallpaper paste here." He rubbed a spot on his own jaw, not trusting himself to touch her. Her hand flew to her face, finding the substance dried there. "And I wouldn't be a bit surprised if you find some in your hair."

Kate shrugged. "I'll wash. The important thing is, Chloe's room is completely finished. There are no talking clown heads in the vicinity, and if you're very lucky, she may forget the idea."

He snorted. "From your lips to God's ears." Sobering, he added, "I want to thank you, Kate."

"You already have."

He let the silence stretch a few moments between them, long enough for awareness to flare into her eyes. "It wasn't enough," he murmured.

"Yes." She cleared her throat. "Yes, it was more than enough."

"It didn't feel like it to me."

She didn't look away from him, her gaze helplessly entrapped in his. He watched her soft pink mouth part, the lips trembling slightly. The sight tantalized, beckoned, reminding him of the way she had looked two nights ago before he'd kissed her. And then afterward, her mouth had been wet and swollen into a delicious pout.

Her chin came up, her mouth firmed, and another of his mental images took a flying leap.

"The dinner was all the thanks I need," she said clearly. "But I do have something to discuss with you." Coming forward, she took some papers out of the envelope and handed them to him.

"What are these?"

"We need your signed permission for the school to be able to share information about Chloe with Dr. Sachar. And the doctor will need written permission to share the results of the appointment with us. The bottom sheets are your copies."

Michael took the papers, each bound in triplicate, and scanned them quickly. Taking a pen out of his desk, he scrawled his name on each, then removed his copies before handing them back to her.

It seemed to take extraordinary concentration on her part to replace the papers in the envelope. "I'll take care of getting these copies to the doctor, as well as the behavioral scales I completed, her grade reports and a complete description of my concerns. When you go to the appointment, the doctor will want to see the behavioral scales you completed, as well."

"Yeah, that's what she said." He wondered how much longer she could avoid looking at him. "She also said that she likes to speak to someone from the school as well as the parents, once the examination is completed."

Kate nodded. "That's the way it's usually done."

Michael sat silent and patient, waiting for her nervous tension to peak. Finally, she slid a glance at him. "Well, that should be everything. You can let me know once you get a specific date and time for the appointment." As she was talking, she inched toward the open door. "I'm sure Chloe would love to have you look at her room. I have a meeting this evening, so I really need to go."

He let her get within a foot of the door before saying gently, "Oh…Kate?"

Her head jerked around. "Yes?"

He rose languidly and approached her. Her eyes widened as he drew closer, then passed her and pressed his hand flat against the door, closing it. Turning, he propped his shoulders against the door, folded his arms in front of his chest and deliberately crossed one sneaker-shod foot over the other.

"You said the other night that we couldn't see each other again."

"Not in a social sense, no."

"Because I'm Chloe's father."

"That was part of the reason," she said, watching him warily.

"You don't feel it would be…professional at this point."

"It wouldn't."

He nodded, as if in thoughtful agreement, and then said, "I can be a very patient man."

She blinked at him, puzzlement plain on her face. "I'm sure you can be."

"School will be out in a few days." Her silence told him that she had made the connection. "Chloe won't be your student after that." He pushed away from the door and closed the distance between them.

She wanted to back away. He could see it in her eyes. He was deliberately invading her space, forcing that awareness of him to spark.

"I never said your relationship to Chloe was my only concern," she reminded him shakily.

"It shouldn't be any secret that I'm attracted to you," he murmured, watching the delicate pink wash her cheeks at his words. "And you're too honest to deny that you're attracted to me."

"I don't feel the need to act on every passing attraction I feel."

"You don't know me very well, I realize that," he said, ignoring her words. He was a savvy enough strategist to smell fear, and what he needed to do now was calm hers. Partly. He circled her slowly, his head dipping to inhale deeply of the scent from her hair. His thigh grazed the back of hers and she shivered. "Deanna and I had our problems, but I never ran around on her. I was committed to my family. Things didn't work out."

"I never asked…" Kate started.

"I know. I wanted to tell you. Because I think you're afraid." He came to a stop in front of her, in time to meet her startled gaze. "I went through a period after my divorce when I…dated…a lot of women. Not anymore, though. I'm not interested in a casual relationship." He watched her carefully. "I don't think you are, either."

Panic and wariness flickered in her eyes. "We're too different."

"Trask once told me that it's not where people come from that matters, it's where they're going." His face moved closer to hers and his next words were whispered against her mouth. "Wherever you're going, I think I'd like to come along." He gave in to the temptation and pressed his lips, ever so lightly, against hers. His tongue traced their delicate inner lining.

It took several seconds for her to formulate a response once he'd lifted his mouth. "It wouldn't work."

"Why not? You like Chloe."

"Yes." The word was breathed against his lips, because he wasn't moving away. He dropped a little kiss at the corner of her mouth.

"And you like me."

"I...yes..."

She was rewarded with another tiny kiss for her answer. "You think I'm cute."

It took a moment for his outrageous statement to register, and then her head jerked back and her dark brows arched upward. "And how did you reach that conclusion?"

He gave her a slow, satisfied smile. "I figured it out the other night when you bit my bottom lip and ran your fingers through my hair."

This time when she stepped away, he let her go and watched, amused, as she paced the room.

"Apparently I wasn't clear enough then about what I want. Or don't want."

Because his hands itched to touch her again, he jammed them in his pockets to keep them out of trouble. "Oh, I thought you were pretty clear." He watched her movements, made swift and sharp from the nerves edging to the surface.

"Without going into the excruciating details, I'll just tell you that I have a long-standing aversion to men who are used to manipulating others. Men who use what power they have to bend others to their will."

"Is that what I'm doing?" he asked, his interest piqued.

Though the glance she sliced at him was laced with uncertainty, she didn't pause in her pacing. "I've always known what I want. Where I'm going. And I'm sorry, but the journey doesn't involve you."

"You're sure about that?" He really was curious. He knew

she was stubborn but hadn't realized she could be this single-minded.

"Yes." The word was firm, but her gaze wasn't meeting his. Because he needed to, he took that as a positive sign.

"Well, it sounds like you've thought this out." He strolled casually near her and watched her muscles jump with the instinct to move away. He knew her pride wouldn't let her.

"Yes." The word was hoarse, and she cleared her voice nervously. "I have."

He reached out one long finger and pushed a curly strand of hair back over her shoulder. "Okay."

Her gaze bounced to his, and for a moment she seemed speechless. "Okay?"

He gave a slow nod.

Her eyes searched his for a long moment. "Well…fine."

"Fine."

She seemed to be having trouble with her voice again. This time, it sounded strangled. "That's it, then." She looked to either side and took a deep breath. He watched, enjoying the moment. He had a feeling that Kate Rose didn't fluster easily.

"You'll let me know when Chloe's appointment is set?"

"I will do that," he said gravely.

"Well. Goodbye, then, Michael." Her hand shot out, a proper little gesture of dismissal.

He eyed it amusedly before taking it in his and caressing her soft palm with his thumb. "Goodbye, Kate."

She jerked her hand free and turned, almost fleeing from the room.

He watched her go, humor still twitching at his lips. If ever there had been a time to engage retreat strategy, this had been it. He knew from experience that showing too much interest in a rival company would tip his hand before he played it. Keeping a low profile went a long way toward soothing fears. He didn't see why the same wouldn't be true in a relationship.

He turned to go back to his computer, whistling softly between his teeth. But once seated there, he couldn't stop thinking of Kate. The range of emotions he'd seen from her today captivated him, enthralled him. Remembering the way she'd explained her lack of interest in him had a wide grin splitting his face. God, she was sweet.

And she was going to be his.

"I believe we could have a problem, Michael."

"Tell me about it," Michael muttered. Then it occurred to him that Trask probably wasn't referring to the problem Michael had had concentrating since he'd last seen Kate three days ago. He scrubbed his hands over his face and turned away from the computer to meet Trask's troubled gaze.

"What's up?"

"Word has it that none of your competitors were happy about losing the NASA contract, especially not to you."

Michael shrugged impatiently. "No one likes to lose."

The other man didn't change expression, just looked at him steadily. Michael stared back, then sighed. "All right, Trask, out with it."

"I've been hearing talk."

Michael didn't inquire into the man's sources. He had uncanny business instincts and he was always accurate. He was the one person in the world whose opinion Michael valued without reservation.

"What kind of talk?"

"Like what happens if you don't make the deadline on FORAY. Who'd be the forerunner in your place."

Michael shrugged again. "Sounds like the kind of talk that always accompanies a project this big, Trask. Rumors. You know how the business is."

"I do know it," the other man said, his gaze steady. "Might be a little more security around here wouldn't hurt."

Rubbing his jaw, Michael pondered Trask's suggestion. "The place is like Fort Knox already, thanks to the system you helped me install."

"Still," the older man persisted, "you can't be too careful." He cleared his throat and looked at the ceiling. "Especially with the little tyke around most of the time."

Shock held Michael still for a moment. He'd accepted the level of competition surrounding his field, actually relished it.

Success was always sweeter when it was hard-won. He'd never shied away from a calculated risk in his career, but there was no way in hell he'd take any kind of chance with Chloe's safety.

A tight, cold fist of dread squeezed his heart. He didn't question whether Trask was overreacting—or his own response. If there was even a fraction of a chance that his daughter could be affected, there really was no decision to be made at all.

"It wouldn't take much to figure that I would work on FORAY from the house," he said slowly. Trask waited patiently. Michael lifted his gaze to meet the other man's. "Hire some men," he ordered flatly. Trask nodded, relief flickering across his normally implacable exterior, and exited the room.

When Kate's phone rang at eleven-thirty that evening she woke, instantly alarmed. All her friends knew she retired early during the week, but her married brothers had phones. Bracing herself for bad news, she fumbled for the switch on the lamp beside the bed and picked up the receiver.

"Kate."

The voice was low and husky and filled with unmistakable weariness. But it was instantly identifiable. "Michael?"

"I must have wakened you. I'm sorry about that. How long have you been sleeping?"

"About an hour, I guess. " She stopped, mentally trying to arrange her thoughts. She hadn't heard from him since they'd decided to go their separate ways. At least she'd decided. And he'd given in with an alacrity that still rankled. It had been humbling to find that she was simultaneously capable of cool logic and wounded pride. She'd decided that reason and emotion didn't always coexist peacefully. "Is something wrong?"

"Nothing, really. I just wanted to ask you to do a favor for me."

Caution reared. "What kind of favor?"

"You said once that you led the children out at dismissal time."

She pushed her heavy hair off her shoulder, nonplussed. "Yes, at three o'clock I take them out and make sure they get on the bus or catch their ride home."

"Trask says things get a little hectic out there."

"When you have two hundred and fifty students anxious to get home, things do get exciting at times," Kate allowed. "But dismissal is well supervised by the teachers."

"I'd like to have Trask come into the building to pick Chloe up. He could come to your room at two fifty-five and get her before the rest of the students leave the building."

"I'm sure that would be okay," Kate said. "But I'd like to know why."

She could hear him release a breath, and a sudden picture of him leaning back in his chair, propping his long legs up on the desk, flashed into her mind.

"I'm just being overly careful," he finally replied. "The competition for this NASA contract was fierce. I'm probably paranoid, but I never take chances with someone I love."

In the pause that stretched between them, Kate came wide-awake. She pushed her pillow into position behind her and leaned against her headboard. "You think Chloe might be in danger?"

"I don't think anything," he soothed. "I'm paranoid, remember. I'm just being extra careful."

"My students always have the option to stay inside the classroom with me at recesses. Would you like me to keep Chloe in?"

"Yeah, if you can arrange it. I'll talk to the Clo-worm about it. Maybe if she could draw or something, she wouldn't mind it so much."

"I'll set up a paint station," Kate promised. "There's nothing Chloe would rather do at school."

"Thank you." His voice was lower. "I appreciate your help. And I'll talk to the principal tomorrow and arrange the dismissal procedure with her."

There was a long silence then, which seemed to get more intimate by the moment. Finally Michael spoke. "It's good to hear your voice, Kate."

She drew in a deep breath, released it slowly. "It's…thank you."

"How many days left of school? Two?"

"Yes."

"I'll be in touch."

She clutched the receiver several moments after he'd hung up, puzzling over his last words. He must have been referring to the appointment for Chloe. Irritated with the disappointment she felt at that conclusion, she replaced the receiver with a clatter. She should feel satisfied that he had respected her decision and dropped his pursuit of her. But she wouldn't be human if her pride wasn't deflated by how easily he'd managed to do just that. It was galling to realize she was capable of such diverse reactions to a man. Irritating to recognize that she could respond to him on two very different levels.

And it was incredibly annoying to admit, even to herself, that it had been good to hear his voice, too.

Chapter 8

"How come those men have to be here all the time, Daddy?"

Michael stifled a sigh at what was surely the tenth time Chloe had repeated that particular question. "I told you, bug, the men are here to help Trask."

Chloe crawled up to perch on the edge of her father's desk, secure in the knowledge that her presence in the den was completely welcome. "Trask doesn't need any help," she explained earnestly. "Alls he does is watch me and I'm not much work."

One corner of Michael's mouth kicked up. "You're more work than you could ever know, squirt." With one arm he swept her off the desk and into his lap, making her shriek with laughter.

When her giggles had subsided, she continued, "I'm not even here when I'm at school. Do the men go home then?"

"They do other work for Trask," he answered vaguely. "He has lots to keep them busy. This is a big place, you know."

Her brow wrinkled, Chloe surveyed him for a moment.

"But Hank takes care of the horses, and Mrs. Martin cleans the house, and Mr. Martin mows and does the flowers. Are the men gonna help Mr. Martin mow?"

"Maybe," he answered, feeling hunted in the face of his daughter's persistence. "But mostly they'll do other stuff."

"What kind of stuff?"

This time Michael did groan. "And I'm supposed to believe you have a short attention span?" he mumbled.

"What's a span?" she wanted to know.

"Never mind. Listen," he said, searching for an answer that wouldn't alarm her. "The men are here to be sure that...things don't get lost."

Chloe surveyed her father gravely. "We don't have lots of things, Daddy."

"Right. But we're fixing up the place, aren't we? Your room looks so great I decided it's time to start getting furniture and stuff in the rest of the house. So when you're out of school, we're going to start shaping this place up."

"Who's going to help?" she asked dubiously.

"What makes you think I need help? All right, all right," he hastened to add at the comical look she aimed at him, "maybe I could use a little."

"Ask Miss Rose!" shouted Chloe. She bounced up and down excitedly. "I bet she would help if you asked her."

"Think so?"

Her head bobbed enthusiastically. "And then I could see her this summer! And that would be good, 'cuz I'm gonna miss her when she's not my teacher anymore."

"Tell you what," he said confidingly, "I'll think of a plan so you can see Miss Rose this summer, but it's going to have to be a sa-prise, okay?"

Chloe's eyes widened in delight, and she nodded enthusiastically.

"And you know about sa-prises, right?" he continued. "They have to be a secret. So you let me be the one to talk to Miss Rose about this, okay? And you have to pipe down and keep it a sa-prise."

"Can't I even tell Rosy?" she wanted to know.

Michael pretended to consider her words. "Does she know how to keep a secret?"

His daughter rolled her eyes. "Da-a-d."

He rested his forehead against hers, staring into the hazel gaze that was so like his own. "I don't want to find out that your blabbermouth pony spread our secret all over the stables."

Chloe giggled. "She won't. Can I tell Trask?"

"Leave Trask to me," Michael said after a moment. "I'd like to tell him myself."

Chloe threw her arms around his neck exuberantly and squeezed. A second later she was wriggling off his lap and on her way to the stables, presumably to tell Rosy the news.

Michael leaned back in his chair, suddenly exhausted. He'd successfully managed to distract Chloe, but she'd ask about the men again. And by then he'd better have an answer prepared. He didn't want to alarm her with explanations of security and increased vigilance. He knew better than most how quickly a child grew up when faced with worries beyond his years. His daughter's childhood wasn't going to be like his, he vowed. He and Deanna might be divorced, but Chloe's life was going to remain just as safe and secure as he could manage. It was his habit to be carefully prepared. And it was his nature to protect those he loved.

Kate sighed and relaxed on the couch in uncustomary indolence. After saying emotional goodbyes to twenty-four first-graders and working late to finish closing her classroom for the summer, she was too exhausted to move. Her stomach was requesting food but she couldn't summon the energy to make anything to eat. She opened one eye lazily and looked at the phone. Pizza delivery was a definite possibility, but it would have to wait. Even the effort it would take to cross the room to the phone was beyond her at the moment.

She must have dozed for a while, because a sudden racket had her jerking upright so suddenly she nearly tumbled off the couch. It took her a moment to discern the source of the noise, and then she scowled at the direction of the door.

Crossing the room, she unlocked the door and threw it open, glaring at the offending visitor.

Michael grinned engagingly. "I would have called first…"

Her heart kicked a faster beat at the sight of him. He looked so good. The casual T-shirt emphasized his broad chest and shoulders, and what the man did for jeans should send stock skyrocketing all over Wall Street. "But…" she prompted him when he didn't go on.

He shrugged. "But I didn't. Figured you'd be hungry. Have you eaten yet?"

Suspicion at his unexpected arrival was tempered by greed. Kate eyed the sacks in his hands with interest. "You have food?"

"Chinese. Are you going to let me in? Please?"

Quickly she stepped aside and he walked in. "You said the magic word."

"Please?"

"Chinese."

They ended up eating in the tiny living room, cartons spread out on the coffee table in front of them. They were seated on the floor, backs propped against the couch. Despite the chummy atmosphere, or maybe because of it, Kate made sure to keep a careful distance between them.

"Is Chloe excited to be out of school for the summer?" she asked between bites of spicy cashew chicken.

"Excited doesn't even come close. Although judging from her tears when I came and picked her up, she's going to miss you a lot, too."

"Oh, she'll still see plenty of me."

"That's what I said to her."

Kate glanced at him uncertainly. "I mean, next year at school she'll still be in my unit. I'll see her frequently in the lunchroom and on the playground."

Michael nodded. "I told her that."

Kate went back to eating, feeling a little foolish. Of course he'd told her that. Why had she immediately assumed he was talking about seeing her on a more personal level? Because of a couple of phone calls they'd had? He must have been making time for a great deal of reading, because after the first phone call about Chloe's dismissal time, he'd phoned twice more to question her about articles he'd read on Attention Deficit Disorder.

The calls had always come at night, right before she was asleep. As innocent as they'd been, it had become entirely too comfortable for her to sit propped up in bed with only the lamp on the bedside table turned on, talking to him. Their conversations had lent warmth to the early summer nights, a warmth she didn't care to admit to.

Her family had never had a phone when she was growing up; her parents still didn't own one. She'd never had the opportunity to go through a giggling teenage phase when she'd hung on the telephone, talking to girlfriends about everything and nothing. She'd never experienced that kind of connection before, and it was a little frightening that the first time she had it was with this man.

"I have to ask you a favor," Michael said. He leaned back, his long legs stretched out under the table in front of him. His shoulders dented the couch cushions. Kate suddenly became more aware of their proximity when he turned to look at her. His face was close to hers. So near that it took physical effort not to inch away. Close enough that she had to concentrate in order to attend to what he was saying.

"I got a phone call from Dr. Sachar's office today. They had a cancellation for one forty-five tomorrow. I said I'd take it. Will you be able to come then?"

"Of course," she said immediately.

"Great." He seemed genuinely relieved. "Deanna has to try and change her schedule. She was supposed to hostess some kind of luncheon or something."

"How does she feel about the whole thing? I mean, I assume you've shared your concerns with her."

Michael's voice was noncommittal. "I've tried."

When he didn't go on, she prompted, "And..."

He lifted a shoulder. "She knows something about ADD, she says. I think she was involved in a fund-raiser dealing with it last year. Deanna is very big into fund-raisers."

"And…does she think Chloe has it?"

"She's 'open to the possibility.' That's what she said. 'Open to the possibility,'" he repeated softly, shaking his head. "She always did have a remarkable ability to remain dispassionate about any subject I could throw at her. Even her daughter."

Kate was unsure how to respond to that comment. He seemed to be brooding about something, staring into space. She didn't want to wonder what he was thinking, didn't want to care. But it was hard not to. He was a man used to being in charge of his own life. Now he was faced with a situation he had no control over, and given his love for his daughter, she knew that helplessness must terrify him.

Because she was too close to offering him comfort, a comfort she wasn't sure would be welcomed, she got up and began removing the cartons and wrappers from the table and carrying them to the trash.

She was surprised when he got to his feet and helped her. In short order the mess had been tidied and he had planted himself back on her sofa. She busied herself in the kitchen making coffee. The atmosphere in her living room seemed too cozy now without the activity of eating. Lounging with his back wedged in the corner of her couch, he was having difficulty arranging his long legs without tangling them in the coffee table. Finally, he pushed the table out of the way with one foot and then sprawled out comfortably.

He was having no problem relaxing, she thought. There wasn't a hint of nerves in him, if indeed the man even owned any. He picked up the remote and turned the television on, flicking through the channels in a seemingly aimless fashion. Her couch really hadn't been selected with someone his size in mind. His rugged strength made it seem almost delicate in comparison. He flexed his shoulders, as if working out a kink, and watching that wide expanse stretch and strain against the back of his shirt suddenly impaired her ability to breathe.

"Coffee?" She thrust a mug at him and hoped he didn't notice that her voice was huskier than normal.

"Thanks."

When he reached for the mug his hand brushed hers, his heat immediately transferring to her at the touch. She folded her hands together, trapping that heat, savoring the way it seemed to seep into her skin and shimmy through her veins.

"Aren't you having any?"

Her head jerked at his question. "No. Maybe later."

He lazily patted the couch cushion beside him. "Well then, why don't you sit down. We have something to discuss." He snapped off the TV and leaned forward to lay the remote on the coffee table.

She sat on the couch, taking great care to leave much more distance between them than he had indicated. "What might that be?"

"Our futures, of course. Yours and mine."

He'd caught her attention. "Our futures?" she repeated faintly.

He nodded solemnly. "You didn't think I'd let you ignore it, did you?"

"Ignore what exactly?" she said cautiously, anticipation humming up her spine.

He held out his hand and slowly uncupped it. There in his big palm were two wrapped fortune cookies. Kate's breath was released in a rush.

"I don't think so, thanks," she refused. "I've got my future pretty well planned out already."

One dark, thick eyebrow rose at her words. "Do you, now? No room in that future for a little advice from a Confucius wanna-be?" When she shook her head, he grinned slowly and taunted, "Afraid?"

"Don't be ridiculous. What would I be afraid of?"

"You tell me," he said softly. His gaze refused to release hers. There was teasing there, and more. He was a master at speaking on two different levels, keeping her off-kilter. But he was wrong if he thought she was afraid of him. Fear was one emotion he didn't stir in her. But afraid of herself? That possibility was too close to the truth to be entirely comfortable.

She snatched a fortune cookie out of his hand and opened

it. Retrieving the tiny slip of paper, she took an inordinate amount of time smoothing it before reading it out loud. "A patient man receives his just rewards." Her gaze slowly lifted to his.

"True beauty waits for those wise enough to find it." He recited his without releasing her gaze.

Seconds ticked by unnoticed as the silence between them grew taut with tension. "Kate." His voice was a low rumble. "I did come here today to tell you about the appointment."

She moistened her lips. "I…yes, I know that."

His gaze was intent. "But I would have been here regardless. School's out. I'm no longer the parent of one of your students."

Caught in the high-beam intensity of his gaze, she needed a moment to make the connection. Another to fashion a response to it. "Your relationship to Chloe wasn't my only concern."

He reached for her hand where it lay at her side and sent his thumb skimming across her knuckles. "I know," he murmured. His one-sided grin was meant to disarm. "I figured I'd handle them one at a time."

And suddenly she realized just how subtly she'd been finessed. He'd seemed to back off, and on one level she'd regretted it. He'd given her just enough space to miss him, to think about him. And more than enough time to wonder what a relationship with him would be like. To wonder what would happen if she gave in to those disturbing hormonal tugs that appeared in her system whenever she was near him.

She moistened her lips nervously. "I…"

"Needed time," he finished for her, raising her hand to his lips and pressing a kiss to her palm. "So I gave you time. The question is, was it enough time to change your mind about us?"

She couldn't form an answer. He moved closer, and she knew she should move away. The way he'd manipulated her should have filled her with anger. And anger would be easy to feel if the light in his eyes wasn't fueling the desire humming through her veins. If he didn't look so sinfully sexy and ruggedly male… If the fierce light of masculine desire wasn't so plain on his face…

And then his lips were on hers and reason swirled away. His mouth was hard, hungry and a little desperate. There was no patience, no gentle wooing. Perhaps that would have been easier to withstand. But his desperation fueled her own, his hunger fed hers. Her arms went to his shoulders and clung, and she was barely aware as he lay back on the couch, pulling her on top of him. His hands were on her face, keeping her lips above his. He pressed her mouth open and his tongue swept inside, and she welcomed it with her own.

His heart was hammering beneath her hand, and his heat was searing her everywhere they touched. Her hair draped around them, curtaining them from the rest of the world. Her hands came up to cup his jaw, slightly scratchy with the beginning of an evening beard, and she reveled in the friction beneath her palms. He released her mouth, spreading kisses across her eyelids, her cheeks, her throat. One large hand dropped to her hips and he pressed her close against his insistent hardness.

Her gasp mingled with his tortured groan. Her eyes flew open. His were slitted, the flush of desire stamped on his face, arousal apparent in the taut skin across his cheekbones.

Mouth trembling, Kate struggled to return to an upright position, her attempt bringing another groan to his lips. He followed her up, his lips catching hers again in another deep, openmouthed kiss, his hand tangling in her hair. They devoured each other for a long moment…two…three…before Michael tore his mouth from hers.

He caught her hands in his, stilling their unconscious caressing movements across his chest. He leaned his head back, taking big, gulping breaths.

"Kate," he rasped. His body shuddered against hers. She could feel every tremor that shook him, every breath he drew. "Believe it or not, I didn't come here to seduce you tonight."

"I know," she whispered. And she did. He'd come because he'd allowed her so much time and no more. She was to consider whether she wanted to see him again. Whether she wanted a relationship with him. Her breath hitched in her chest. "I still haven't answered your question."

His hand came up to rub her vertebrae, sending her arching into him. She sensed his smile before she saw it. "Yes, sweetheart, I think you have."

The waiting room of Dr. Sachar's office was pleasantly decorated in primary colors, with a wealth of toys designed to keep busy young hands occupied. Chloe wove a path around the room, trying all of them out, engaging the other children in conversation along the way.

Michael watched his daughter with a slight smile on his face, but his mind was occupied. Neither Kate nor Deanna had made an appearance yet, but he wasn't really worried. Kate had promised she would be there, although she had been resolute about driving herself. She was, he was discovering, an extremely determined woman.

An idiotic grin spread across his face as he considered the way last evening had ended. She hadn't liked his certainty about the result of her decision. But she hadn't made it difficult to guess. Her mouth had been just as demanding as his, her breathing just as ragged. The most difficult thing he'd ever done was to say good-night to her after allowing himself one more hard, quick kiss at her door.

She wasn't the kind of woman to leave alone too long; she thought too damn much. And she had a cautious streak running through her that he hadn't completely figured out yet. But he had time. Time was going to be his secret weapon with her; time to let her get to know him, to drop that cautious veneer and to allow him closer. He'd give her the time she needed, but not the space. He had a feeling that the more space between them, the more walls she'd throw up. And though she was worth scaling a few walls for he was alarmingly low on patience. Last night had proved that.

The office door opened then and Kate walked in. Chloe looked up and shrieked in delight, running over to give her an exuberant hug. As Michael watched, Kate bent gracefully and returned it. Watching them together had his throat clogging inexplicably. Kate's reserve was never present with Chloe. The warm smile was open, the caring in her eyes immediate.

"Come sit down," he invited, his gaze feasting on the sight of her in a sky blue suit. It was a color that matched her eyes perfectly and provided a stunning foil to her hair. All in all she looked good enough for him to start howling in another minute. He contented himself with draping his arm across the back of her chair when she sat next to him, his fingers cupping her shoulder.

"You look fantastic," he murmured close to her ear. He watched with fascination as the delicate hue of her cheeks deepened. "Is it too much to hope that you've sacrificed all your jumpers to an after-school bonfire?"

Her eyebrow arched. "*You're* going to get snotty about *my* wardrobe? Careful, Friday. If I start with yours, the possibilities are endless."

He chuckled. "You're welcome to change whatever you want of mine. I'm open to suggestion."

"Chloe Friday?"

Michael's head jerked up. He followed his daughter as she sped to the nurse standing in the open doorway. The woman smiled and stepped aside, indicating that they should precede her into the inner offices. He turned and held out a hand. "Come on, Kate."

He drew her after him even as she protested quietly, "Michael, I think I should wait outside until the doctor wants to speak to all of us together."

"Don't be ridiculous," he said. He didn't release her hand as he followed the nurse and Chloe down a long hallway. "Why shouldn't you be there the whole time?"

"Because usually the parents meet with the doctor, some tests are run, medical history is given, and then the school personnel is invited in. You and your—that is—Chloe's mother…"

"Deanna will be here soon," he said easily. "She would have called otherwise. But in the meantime you're going to be needed for emotional support and major hand-holding."

Kate looked immediately at Chloe, who was examining the thermometer the nurse was explaining to her. "Oh, I think Chloe will be fine."

"I was talking about me," he said in an undertone, and grinned when she suddenly tugged at the hand still clasped in his. He let her go but turned casually toward the nurse, making sure his position blocked any possible escape Kate might have made.

Chloe was weighed and her height measured. Michael didn't know how the nurse could get an accurate reading the way Chloe was fidgeting, but she seemed to be used to the challenge. In fact, he noted as he watched the woman carefully, she went to great lengths to put Chloe at ease. She explained the function of each utensil before she tried to use it with the little girl. Her patience with Chloe eased his own trepidation somewhat. At least until she took out a needle and some test tubes.

Michael interrupted the explanation the nurse was giving Chloe. "Wait a minute," he demanded. "Is that really necessary?"

"It is important that we have complete information about Chloe's medical condition. We have to be sure, first of all, that there isn't a preexisting physical ailment that we're unaware of."

"There isn't. She goes in for a routine checkup yearly, as well as any time she isn't feeling well. I don't see the need to put her through this."

"Is this like a shot?" Chloe wanted to know.

"Sort of." Both the nurse and Michael turned to look at Kate as she addressed Chloe. "The nurse will attach a little tube to the needle and she'll put the needle in your arm, right about here." She touched the inside of her arm. "You'll feel a little prick. That would be like a shot. The needle will stay in your arm a bit longer, though, because she'll be filling up some different little tubes with your blood. Then she'll take the needle out and mark all the little tubes with your name so they can run tests on them."

"What kind of tests?"

"They just want to see if your blood is healthy," Kate responded. She looked at Michael. She had obviously learned how to converse with Chloe. Answers with too many details only elicited more questions. However, he was the one who remained unconvinced.

The nurse continued quietly, "The tests are necessary before the doctor can make a diagnosis, Mr. Friday. Would you like to postpone this until you talk to Dr. Sachar?"

Michael looked at Kate. After sharing a long, steady gaze, he capitulated. "No, that's fine. We'll do it now."

"I don't like shots," Chloe informed them.

Michael sank to his knees in front of her. "I know you don't, honey. But sometimes you have to get one, just like you did before they could stitch up your hand last summer. Remember? And you know, Rosy has to get shots, too. The vet is coming out this week to give her some."

Chloe remained visibly uneasy. Kate bent down, next to Michael. "I'll tell you a trick we can do. You hold my hand and close your eyes. The nurse will tell you when she's going to prick you a little with the needle. That's when you'll squeeze my hand really, really tight."

"What's the trick?" Chloe wanted to know.

"Well, the trick is, as soon as you close your eyes, you have to start telling me every single thing you've taught Rosy to do since the last time I saw her. If you stop talking, even for a second, then you can't tell me any more about her."

"That's easy," Chloe boasted. "I can do that. And there's a whole bunch of stuff, too, because Rosy's been working real hard."

Kate took the little girl's hand. "That's good, but I don't think you're going to have time to tell me everything, because this isn't going to last very long. Can you talk really, really fast?"

"Yes!"

"Close your eyes, then."

Michael watched in bemusement as Chloe's eyes squeezed shut. The nurse quickly went to work. As she wrapped a piece of tubing around the small arm and swabbed it with alcohol, he swallowed hard and looked away. As if from a distance he could hear Kate say, "Ready. Set. Go."

Chloe's exuberant stream of words started as she tried to fill her teacher in on every single snippet of information about her beloved pony. Her voice faltered only once, when she interjected a loud "Ouch!" and then continued with her litany of praise for her pony's intelligence.

Michael's attention snapped to his child when he heard her cry. Her eyes were still closed, and her small hand was clenched tightly in Kate's. Her exclamation of pain had barely interrupted her monologue. His eyes remained glued in morbid fascination on the nurse. As he watched, she removed a small tube of blood, *his daughter's blood,* and smoothly put another in its place to be filled. All the while, the long, wicked-looking needle remained in Chloe's arm. Nausea twisted in his stomach, and he moved to lean against the wall weakly, closing his eyes.

Several moments later Chloe bounded out of the chair after the nurse had placed a dinosaur bandage on her arm. As the nurse led them to a conference room, Michael lagged behind. Kate shot him a concerned look.

"Are you all right?"

"I will be," he muttered. His throat felt parched, and he'd have given his Jag for a glass of water.

"Which was it?" she asked in an undertone as they walked into the room together. "The needle or the blood?"

"I don't mind *my* blood," he defended himself. "But the sight of Chloe's..." His voice trailed off and he swallowed again. "And I have to admit to an opinion similar to Chloe's when it comes to shots."

The smirk on her face was an open invitation, but he wasn't given any time to respond to it. As they walked into the conference room, a middle-aged woman in a brightly patterned dress approached them.

"Please come in," she invited them, shaking Kate's hand and then turning to Michael. "It's nice to meet you, Mr. and Mrs. Friday."

Chapter 9

Michael still couldn't decide whether to be amused or offended by the speed with which Kate had explained her identity. Confusion had reigned for a minute as Deanna had chosen that moment to enter the room, as well. After speaking to the three of them for several minutes, Kate had slipped back into the waiting room while the doctor examined Chloe.

He thought his daughter had held up pretty well, but sitting still had never been her favorite indoor sport. By the time the examination was over and Kate had rejoined them in the conference room, Chloe was showing noticeable signs of agitation. The third time she fell out of her chair, Deanna said, "For heaven's sake, Chloe, stop fidgeting."

"Would you like to put some puzzles together?" Dr. Sachar asked. "We have several of them in the next room."

"I want to go home," she said, swinging from the edge of the table. "I want to ride Rosy."

"Maybe if she had some paper and markers, she would be occupied for a while," Kate suggested hesitantly.

"You like to draw," Michael said with relief. "How about it, squirt?"

Dr. Sachar rummaged through some desk drawers. "Here we go," she said at last, finding a large white tablet and some pens. "You should be able to make some great pictures with these."

Once the child was settled, Deanna said, "That's exactly the sort of behavior I'm concerned about. She's a very bright little girl, interested in everything. But nothing seems to keep her attention for long. Just when I think I have her occupied with something, she's into something else. She makes me tired just keeping up with her."

Michael defended Chloe immediately. "She's active. She doesn't like being cooped up. At our place she's used to having the run of the house, the grounds and the stables."

"A high activity level isn't abnormal in and of itself at Chloe's age," said Dr. Sachar. "It's only when it's coupled with other symptoms that we start to look at a medical implication. Based on my observation of Chloe this afternoon, as well as the information provided by parents and school, I think it's likely that Chloe suffers from ADHD. That's the current term used to describe children with Attention Deficit Disorder, with hyperactivity as a component."

The words hit Michael with the force of a left jab. The room and its occupants faded as the doctor's opinion echoed and reechoed across his mind. He'd thought to cover his bases by setting up this appointment. He'd never knowingly ignore even the remotest possibility that Chloe needed any kind of help. But now he realized how unprepared he'd been for this moment. He hadn't believed the doctor would agree with Kate's concerns. He hadn't let himself consider it.

He hadn't felt this helpless since he was a kid, vainly loathing his father for abandoning his family. His childhood had helped shape him into the man he was today—one who would do anything to protect those he cared about. But how did he protect his little girl from a disorder whose name he'd never even heard of a month ago?

He didn't participate in the discussion Deanna and Dr. Sachar were having about the percentage of youngsters diagnosed with the disorder. What did that matter, anyway? The only child he was concerned about was the cute little blonde sitting beside him, kicking her legs in beat with the tune she was humming as she drew a darn good likeness of the room they were sitting in. He wanted to yell at the doctor, to demand that she look, really look, at his daughter. How dare she say there was something wrong with her? Anyone could see just how perfect she was. She was funny and sweet and terrifically talented. She was the single most precious thing in his life.

Chloe abandoned her markers and scrambled off her chair to sit under the table. The vise in his chest loosened a little. Regardless of the outcome of this appointment, regardless of whether or not Chloe was afflicted with this ADHD thing, she was still his same little girl; the one who ran recklessly to leap in his arms to welcome him home; the one who loved knock-knock jokes and animals; the one who brightened his life in a million different ways every day. He looked down to where she was crouched under the table, and she waved impishly at him, gesturing for him to join her. For a moment he was tempted to do so.

With effort he tuned in to the educational planning the doctor, Kate and Deanna were discussing. Kate. He fixed on her name gratefully, her form drawing his gaze. He trusted her to make the necessary recommendations to personnel at school. She cared about Chloe; she'd do everything in her power to see that his daughter was successful there.

"How do you recommend we handle this, Doctor?" Deanna asked. "I've heard that children can be put on medication to help with the symptoms of this disorder."

"Medication with side effects," Michael put in with a scowl. "Do we really want to chance insomnia, weight loss, headaches and stomachaches with our daughter, just for a quick fix?"

"There are several different medications that have proven effective," the doctor said. "All of them have good safety records. But the side effects you mention, Mr. Friday, are possibilities for some of them. That's why it's extremely important for Chloe to be monitored regularly by a medical doc-

Play "Lucky

when you pla
...then contin
with a sweeth

1. Play Lucky Hearts as instruc
2. Send back this card and you'll
   books have a cover price of
3. There's no catch. You're und
   ZERO — for your first shipr
   of purchases — not even o
4. The fact is thousands of read
   Reader Service™. They like th
   the best new novels BEFORE
   discount prices!
5. We hope that after receiving
   choice is yours — to contin
   invitation, with no risk of an

The Silhouette Reader Service™ — Here's how it works:

Accepting free books places you under no obligation to buy anything. You may keep the books and gift and return the shipping statement marked "cancel." If you do not cancel, about a month later we'll send you 6 additional novels and bill you just $3.57 each plus 25¢ delivery per book and applicable sales tax, if any.* That's the complete price — and compared to cover prices of $4.25 each — quite a bargain! You may cancel at any time, but if you choose to continue, every month we'll send you 6 more books, which you may either purchase at the discount price... or return to us and cancel your subscription.

*Terms and prices subject to change without notice. Sales tax applicable in N.Y.

tor. If side effects occur, we would of course adjust her dosage or change medications.'' She held up her hand when Michael opened his mouth again.

"We're getting ahead of ourselves here. Whether or not your daughter begins medication is a decision you'll have to make for yourselves. With or without it, there are many, many strategies and techniques you can try until you find workable ways to help Chloe manage her behavior, both at home and at school.''

After setting up another appointment for August, Michael rose. Deanna looked at him and said, "I really must talk to you, Michael. Do you have time now?''

"Sure.'' He turned to his daughter and caught her small hand in his.

Deanna hesitated. "This…needs to be just the two of us. Maybe I should come by later.''

"The Smithsonian is right around the corner,'' Kate put in quietly. "Would you like me to take Chloe there for a while?''

Michael's eyes cut to hers and he gave a slow nod. "I'll catch up with you there in about an hour.''

They found a cafeteria on the bottom floor of the office building, and Michael bought two coffees, which remained untouched between them. As his ex-wife smoothed her hair and adjusted her earrings, it occurred to him that she was nervous. Deanna didn't fidget. She was always calm, always collected and never at a loss for words. Her constant composure had irritated the hell out of him on more than one occasion.

"Look, if this is about the medication, I have to tell you, I'm not ready to make that kind of decision yet,'' he said bluntly. "I need time.''

"It's not that,'' she denied, folding both hands in front of her. "I wanted to ask to have Chloe tonight.''

He studied her. "Something special going on?''

"No, not really. Actually, we haven't spoken about her summer arrangements, and we need to get that ironed out, as well." Her voice tapered off in a very unusual way, and Michael's eyes narrowed. Something was bugging his ex-wife, and it was something big. He'd never known her to be shy about stating her needs. She'd even announced she was leaving him and taking Chloe in that same cool, well-bred voice he'd grown to detest.

"Why don't you spit it out, Deanna?" he said deliberately, knowing she'd hate his plain language and not caring. "There's something bothering you and you might as well just say it."

Her chin came up, the only visible sign of her displeasure. "Very well. I'd like to modify the custody agreement for Chloe."

Michael went absolutely still. Every nerve, every muscle were sheathed in ice. She wanted Chloe back. He'd known it could happen, actually should have been expecting it. She still had primary custody, with him supposed to be sharing a few days a week. A few days weren't enough, especially now that he'd had Chloe for so much more. He hadn't been able to change the judge's mind when his daughter was three, and he doubted he stood a much better chance now, despite Chloe's apparent happiness with the new arrangement. Old bitterness surged up inside him, and his hand on the table was clenched.

"Mind telling me why?" His voice managed to stay soft, revealing none of the rage and fear churning within him.

"Actually, I'm getting married."

Shock twisted through him, penetrating the haze of resentment. "Married? To whom? Chloe never mentioned anybody from her visits with you."

That nervousness was back, barely perceptible. "Chloe hasn't met Jeffrey yet. His schedule is unpredictable, and the timing was never right."

"You're expecting to take Chloe to live with you and a man she's never met?" The anger burst forth now, despite his efforts to control it. "What in God's name are you thinking, Deanna? Did you ever once consider how this would affect her?"

"Yes!" she snapped. "I've done nothing but consider Chloe. That's why I'm suggesting that we modify the arrangement so she can stay here with you, instead of my taking her out of the country."

Her words acted like a one-two punch on Michael's emotionally charged state, and it took several seconds to assimilate what she was saying. Then comprehension dawned, and his relief was so great it threatened to choke him.

"You...you want to give me primary custody?"

Deanna finally sipped at her coffee. "I don't think 'want to' is the correct phrase. Suffice it to say, I knew that you would be totally unreasonable about my taking her to Greece to live with me."

"You had that damned straight," he muttered. "Mind telling me why you decided to live in Greece?"

A familiar glint was in her eye, the one that told him she was extraordinarily pleased with herself. "My fiancé is Jeffrey Creighton, ambassador to Greece."

Michael leaned back in his chair and surveyed her amusedly. "Landed yourself a big one, Dee."

"Don't call me Dee," she snapped. "Jeffrey and I have a great deal in common. I'm looking forward to our new life together."

He smiled slowly. He just bet she was. She'd lived for the dinners and entertaining that had gone along with starting his business. She'd wanted money, prestige and power when she'd married him. He'd wanted her. They'd done fairly well until they started spending more time together and discovered they really didn't like each other very much. His only surprise was that it had taken her this long to find someone more suited to her taste.

"I'm going to ask that you be very flexible about scheduling visits. I'd like the freedom to see Chloe anytime we're in D.C., and of course I'll want her to spend part of her summers with us."

"We can work something out. She'll want to see you as often as possible, too." He was sincere about that. Chloe was going to miss her mother, and since he had just been given what he most wanted in the world, he could afford to be generous. "When's the date set for?"

"We'll be married quietly next month. I'll leave almost immediately for Greece afterward."

A long, awkward silence stretched between them, during which they both looked at each other and didn't say a thing. "About this appointment…" she finally began. "I want to be fully apprised of anything and everything that pertains to Chloe. I'd like her to try medication in the fall."

"We can discuss it," he said noncommittally.

She gathered her purse and prepared to leave. Before rising, she said in a low voice, "I really do love her, you know."

Michael looked at her. She was blinking rapidly to dispel the tears that had gathered. He reached out and took her hand. "I know you do, Dee. I've always known that."

A few moments later she was walking away. Michael surveyed the foam cup of coffee he didn't intend to drink. For some reason he was reminded of the last time Deanna had walked away from him, the time she'd taken his daughter, his whole world, with her. She'd cataloged his flaws crisply prior to her exit, with no hint of temper. The list of his shortcomings had long ago ceased to sting. There were plenty of women since who had seemed more than willing to overlook the defects in his upbringing. Money and power went a long way toward erasing the stigma of being raised in near poverty. But he didn't want any of those women. There was only one woman he wanted, and right now she was waiting with his daughter at the Smithsonian.

He rose and strode purposefully out the door, toward his future.

Kate sighed and stopped her pacing. She laid the textbook she'd been studying on the table. Her brain could only assimilate so much information, and right now it was saturated. There would be plenty more time to study in the remaining time she had before her comprehensive exams.

She glanced at the clock. It wasn't all that late, but the day had been long. She wondered what Michael was doing. He'd seemed preoccupied when he'd met her and Chloe, and they'd parted without him giving her much of an indication of just what was going on inside him.

To distract herself she tossed a bag of popcorn in the microwave and got a diet soda from the refrigerator. Though she usually wasn't much of a TV watcher, it would distract her from thinking of the events of the day. And of Michael.

The microwave dinged just as the pounding on her door began. She didn't wonder for a second who it was. Other people knocked, but not Michael. She was sure he tried, but those large fists probably weren't capable of anything so restrained. She crossed the room and threw the door open.

Her heart immediately kicked to a faster beat in her chest. He was lounging against her porch railing, his weight probably not doing much good for its sturdiness. His brows were lowered.

"You didn't even check the peephole before you opened the door."

She leaned against the door and surveyed him. "You didn't leave much doubt in my mind as to who my visitor was."

"You were expecting me?" He sounded surprised.

"No, but I don't know anyone else who sounds like a battering ram when they're announcing themselves."

"Your doorbell still isn't working."

"I point that out to my landlord on a regular basis." He looked tired. His hair, too long to begin with, showed the effects of fingers run through it. She wondered how much sleep he'd had in recent weeks. He always seemed to have an endless supply of energy but right now looked as if he'd just about depleted it. He smiled at her then, a slow, engaging smile, and her heart thumped at the difference it made to his harsh features.

"I smelled your popcorn and thought I'd take a chance on an invitation."

She teased, "So it was the hope of a handout that brought you here. Again."

The smile disappeared abruptly. "No," he said soberly. "I just didn't want to be alone tonight."

Kate stepped back wordlessly and he moved past her into the condo. His big body crowded her in the small area inside the door, but she didn't feel like moving away. She wanted to take a step closer, until she was in his arms. She wanted to hold him and touch those hard features, to make the weariness drain from his face. Flushing at her thoughts, she turned and walked to the kitchen, got the popcorn from the microwave and reached for a bowl to dump it in.

"You wouldn't by any chance have a beer in your refrigerator, would you?" he asked hopefully.

"I think so," she said. "Check in the back."

He did, and made a satisfied sound when he found one. She'd bought the six-pack for the occasional friend who stopped by. When she'd purchased it last month, it would never have occurred to her that the first beer out of the pack would be drunk by Michael Friday.

He trailed after her to the living room and disdained her couch for the floor. She watched him move her coffee table aside and take the pillows off the sofa to arrange behind him. Once comfortable, he looked at her and patted the floor next to him. "Come join me."

"Since you have the popcorn…"

She sat down next to him and he used the remote to flip through the channels. He finally settled on a popular late-night talk show.

"How was Chloe when you got her home?"

He took a long drink of beer. "I took her to her mother's after supper."

Kate looked at him, surprised. "She didn't mention that she had a visit planned when we were at the Smithsonian." Chloe had chattered about the exhibits, Rosy and her plans for the endless summer days but hadn't mentioned a word about the appointment or her mother.

"It just came up." He turned to look at her. "When I was talking to Deanna, she laid a few bombshells on me. She's getting married. Soon. And she won't be living in the country anymore. She's agreed to get the custody agreement changed to give me primary custody. She wanted Chloe for a few days to explain it all to her."

Kate was shocked into silence. She watched his face carefully. "How do you think Chloe will take this?"

He lifted one shoulder. "I'm not sure. I would have preferred being there when her mother talks to her, but that's not the way Deanna wanted to play it. Hell, she kept this whole relationship quiet, so it will be a shock, I'm sure. I really don't think Chloe will know the difference as far as the arrangement goes, because she's been living with Trask and me all year and seems happy. But visits with Deanna will be limited to the times she and her husband are in D.C. and in the summer. That's bound to be hard on her."

"How about you?" Kate dared to ask. "How does her decision affect you?"

"Deanna and I were over a long time ago," he said dismissively. "But we've always tried to make decisions jointly. On the one hand, I'm ecstatic that the custody arrangement will be made legal. I never questioned Deanna too closely about why she allowed me to have Chloe this year, but maybe she'd already met this guy and was dating him." He shrugged. "I could never have gone back to seeing Chloe a couple days a week. But the thought of having sole responsibility is scary as hell, too."

"You'll do fine," Kate reassured him softly.

He looked grim. "What if I screw up? What if she gets sick and I don't know what's wrong with her? What if she rebels as a teenager and does some god-awful thing to her hair and starts piercing her body parts? Or if she decides to skip college and go out to California and live in the back of some grunge rocker's van?"

It wasn't the panic edging his voice that made her chest tighten with emotion, it was the vulnerability layered beneath it. Some might think it odd that this self-made man who'd used cunning and a ruthless determination to overcome all obstacles could be leveled by such insecurities. But she found it incredibly endearing. Surely one of the most important measures of a man was the success he made of parenting. Michael's fierce, all-encompassing love for his daughter came as naturally to him as the corporate warfare he waged daily.

And that fact threatened her heart as nothing else could.

Chapter 10

It was a moment before she could speak. "Michael, whatever happens, Chloe knows she can depend on you. Just keep listening to her, supporting her. Loving her."

One side of his mouth curled. "You sound like the voice of experience. Is that what your father did for you?"

Her smile abruptly ceased. Her father's voice floated across her mind like a ghost that refused to stay banished. *You ain't startin' to forget where you come from, are ya?*

She turned away from the curiosity in his eyes. "No." Her voice was flat. "Not my father." Because it was more comfortable, she buried the memories that threatened and focused on evading the questions in his eyes. "You might want to consider signing Chloe up for dance, gymnastics or martial arts. Any of those would give her activity level a natural outlet and help teach her to channel it in a constructive way."

"I'm not sure I could stand going through a kung fu stage with her," he responded. "But gymnastics…that's a possibility. She loves doing cartwheels and stuff, although I'm constantly reminding her to do them outside." He pondered the idea for a minute. "I have been teaching her to swim, and she catches on really quick. I think she might have a natural affinity for gymnastics, as well." He smiled crookedly. "Speaking with the natural bias of a father, of course."

Her returning smile was strained. Rising, she muttered something about getting napkins and turned to flee to the kitchen. Her wrist was snagged with a suddenness that startled her.

He gently pulled her back down beside him and sent a thumb skimming across the sensitive inner skin of her wrist. His speed didn't frighten her, but his tenderness did. "Want to tell me about it?"

She sat very still, attempting to keep the emotion she was feeling from leaking into her face. It was amazing how old hurts and inadequacies never really went away. She could bury them for long periods of time, but then when she least expected it, the pain could slice through years and maturity with a sharpness that was unrelenting.

She was familiar with Michael's determination. There would be no dodging his questions, so she let him guide her head to the hollow beneath his shoulder. She had the distracted thought that they shouldn't seem to fit together so perfectly. He brushed a hand over her hair, smoothing it away from her face. And waited.

"I told you I grew up poor. " Her voice, when she finally spoke, didn't betray her. It was calm and matter-of-fact. "That never really bothered me. Few of the children I knew had a whole lot more than we did. But most of them had something that I envied, something that I knew was missing from our house, even before I was old enough to put it in words. And that was love."

He waited for her to go on, and when she didn't, he drew his own conclusions. His fingers cupping her shoulder tightened, but his voice was carefully blank when he asked, "Did your father abuse you?"

She glanced up at him, astonished. A muscle in his cheek tensed, and what she saw in his eyes shouldn't have warmed her but did. She reached up with one finger to soothe his tight jaw in a single light caress. "No, oh, no, Michael. Nothing like that. My parents aren't bad people. They're just... emotionally sterile.'' She'd wondered as a child if she was impossible to love. She'd been an adult before she'd realized that the failing belonged to her parents, not to her. She didn't know which was sadder.

He picked up her hand, measuring her palm against his, then laced their fingers. Skimming his mouth over her knuckles, he said nothing, but the caring in the gesture was as loud as a shout. With an effort she banished the tears that his concern threatened to recall. She'd long ago forgiven her parents for what they couldn't help, for the lack they'd never noticed. They weren't capable of giving love, at least not in a way she'd ever learned to recognize. What had passed for it, duty and obligation, hadn't been enough, but she was a woman now, and it shouldn't matter anymore.

For reasons she didn't want to identify, it did matter that Chloe had the understanding and support that Kate had lacked. Michael would always be there for his daughter. The knowledge was soothing and beckoned to the old yearning she was used to shoving into a pocket in her mind.

He seemed to read the regret that simmered inside her and didn't push. For long minutes they sat there, intimacy weaving between them. Michael's heart thudded hypnotically in Kate's ear. The sound was solid and comforting.

''Did Chloe say anything to you about the appointment today?'' he finally asked.

She shook her head. ''Did she mention it to you?''

''We talked a little. She told me she thought she had to go to the lady doctor because sometimes her feet take her places her head doesn't tell them to go.'' His voice grew rough. ''When she said that, it hit me right in the gut. Here I've been denying to myself that there was a problem and she's been aware of it all along. The doctor warned of the dangers of low self-esteem in these kids. What if I had never admitted it? Or worse yet, what if I—''

Kate's fingers pressed against his mouth, stemming his words. ''You didn't,'' she said simply. ''You're addressing it, and you'll be able to talk to Chloe about it. You'll learn together how best to deal with it."

He caught her fingers and pressed a warm kiss against her palm, then gave her a crooked grin that transposed his hard features. "You have a great deal of faith in me."

"Yes," she whispered, "I do." She watched his grin fade away and shivered inside when it was replaced with awareness and something else, a desire she'd seen on his face before. That powerful masculine intent was almost frightening in its intensity, but it was tempting, too.

"Do you know why I came here tonight?" he asked, his voice a low rumble.

"You said you didn't want to be alone."

"I wasn't alone. Trask was there. I needed to be here. I needed *you*."

A bittersweet blade of longing slipped into her heart. As his face moved closer, her eyes drifted shut in silent anticipation of his kiss. She could already imagine the feel of his hard mouth moving against her own, his rougher skin abrading her cheek.

The sensations didn't come. Instead she heard his voice in her ear urging, "Kate, kiss me."

Her eyes flew open. He was close, very close. She could see the heat in his hazel eyes, feel his warm breath on her face. For a moment she went blank. What was he asking? And why? The experience she had, depressingly limited, hadn't prepared her to be the aggressor. She had been the recipient of kisses many times, had responded to *his* kisses with an eagerness and an abandon that both terrified and exhilarated her. But there had been a comfortable familiarity in the passive role of acceptance. It seemed as if all her life she'd sought the human contact denied her by her parents. She'd lavished attention on her siblings; physical demonstrativeness hadn't been rejected by them. She sometimes thought that if she hadn't had that outlet, the emotional side of her nature would have withered away, much as her parents' had seemed to.

Other girls, starved for the kind of love and acceptance

she'd been denied, might have sought it in the arms of any boy who'd shown an interest in them. But Kate had been too fastidious, too cautious to fall into that trap. And so she'd somehow managed to reach the age of twenty-seven with some intimate experience, yet without ever having initiated a kiss with a man.

Her gaze fell to his mouth, to the chiseled lips, firm and waiting. Michael wasn't just any man. The attraction between them was there; she'd never been able to deny it. She already knew how he would taste, and the memory was exquisite. He was offering her the opportunity to venture into uncharted waters by taking a first with him, and the newness of the situation gave her pause.

He tipped the balance then by muttering *"Kate,"* his voice low and urgent. By moving only a fraction of an inch, she was able to catch the sound in her mouth.

His taste was familiar, yet the experience was foreign. The first kiss was a whisper, then her mouth hesitated for a moment, like a butterfly suspended in midair. Her lips parted over his, tentative at first. He held himself rigid, only his lips soft and pliant against hers, allowing her to mold them as she wished.

She forgot to be embarrassed, forgot to wonder about technique. Instead, she fell into the intoxicating pleasure of being the aggressor. Her mouth moved against his sweetly, tenderly. His lower lip was full and curved, equally capable of delivering a lopsided grin or a snarl. Her teeth scraped against it lightly, worrying it with delicate precision. She dared to use the tip of her tongue to trace the seam of his lips and was rewarded by his indrawn breath.

It was pleasant, but soon it wasn't enough. Unconsciously she moved closer, twisting her body to face him more fully. He reached out one long arm and helped her straddle his lap, and she accomplished the feat without releasing his lips.

Her arms went around his neck, her fingers curling in hair that had been neglected long enough to spill over his collar. She leaned against the solid breadth of his chest and pressed his lips open. As a demand, it probably was more tentative

than most. But Michael was helpfully responsive, and when
she dared to test her tongue on the ridge of his teeth, his
breathing grew choppy.

That evidence of his response tempted her to venture further. Her tongue slipped into his mouth to tangle with his,
savoring its rich, masculine flavor. She was lost in the experience; if he had taken over, if he had responded too quickly
or too eagerly, she might have awoken from the intoxicating
reverie and drawn back. But his hands remained motionless
on her waist. He was making no attempt to guide her movements or to change the pace.

The power of it was heady. Kate's senses reeled as she
allowed herself the pleasure of exploring his mouth with
quick little flicks of her tongue; along the sensitive roof of
his mouth, the inside of his lip, across the front of his teeth.
When a groan rumbled up from his chest, she almost echoed
it. She nibbled at his full lower lip, explored the corners of
his mouth, then pressed her cheek to his. Whisker stubble
prickled her skin; it had been many hours since his morning
shave. Her lips sought out the same experience, dragging back
and forth across his cheek. Her teeth caught his chin lightly,
and her tongue tested its rough surface.

She opened weighted eyes slowly. His remained closed, the
lashes thick brushes against his skin. His breathing was rapid
and the skin was pulled tautly across cheekbones that seemed
carved from granite. She'd seen him teasing, angry, laughing
and grim. But by far the most seductive sight was the image
of him now, muscles rigid with the enormous effort required
to hold himself in check.

Kate dropped kisses along the cord of his throat and lingered at the base. His top button was undone, and she lowered
her lips to the triangle of skin bared there. It was smooth and
heated, warming her lips. Her hands came down to clutch his
shoulders, kneading the tight muscles. An emotion was boil-
ing in the pit of her belly, one she had never quite understood
before.

Desire. Hot and naked, it was snaking through her veins,
leaving a conflagration in its wake. It singed her from her

toes to her fingertips, and suddenly kisses weren't enough. She wanted more. That vee of bare flesh was a taunting sample of the tightly muscled planes lying beneath his shirt. Her palms itched, and she fisted her hands as if to guard against the temptation.

Drawing her lip between her teeth, she stared hard at the next button. So easy, really. It would be so easy to slip that one small button open to expose another inch or two of flesh. Her fingers acted before her brain gave them conscious permission, and she couldn't help being pleased with her work. Brown chest hair covered the portion she'd revealed, and her lips went to explore the newest territory. It was surprisingly soft, not unlike the strands she'd recently had her fingers tangled in. No doubt it matched the rest of his chest, still hidden from her view.

Her fingers danced down his shirtfront, and her lips followed in their trail, welcoming each new inch of flesh revealed. When she finally finished, she pushed the shirt apart impatiently, her breath knotting in her throat. His chest was massive and solid with muscle. His heavy shoulders were almost as wide as the half of the couch he was propped against. His large form radiated power and strength, yet he remained still, only the muscles quivering beneath the smooth skin of his stomach giving mute testament to the effort it cost him.

She smoothed her hands up and down his torso, gasping as his heat transferred from his skin to her palms. Her fingers walked up his ribs and combed through the triangular mat of hair on his chest. Leaning forward, she sealed his mouth with hers again, reveling in the eager twisting of his lips beneath hers. She kneaded his chest, his shoulders before trailing her hands down to clutch at his massive biceps.

Michael shrugged out of his shirt and wrapped his arms around her waist, urging her closer. Kate complied, her mouth still moving on his, her hips intimately pressed against the thick ridge beneath his jeans. Hunger built as he pulled her T-shirt from her jeans and his hands swept inside, roaming over her back and waist restlessly. She squirmed against him, unable to get close enough.

Her hips rocked against him, and their moans mingled at the contact. That solid length of manhood assuaged the ache that had settled between her thighs, even as it fueled it. Her breasts were full and heavy, her nipples unbearably sensitive within their lacy confines. His hands flamed a path on her skin, leaving her wanting more. She waited, breath indrawn, for him to take the next step, to touch her as intimately as she touched him. Her movements became a little more frantic, a little more frustrated, and she nipped at his full lower lip before soothing it with the tip of her tongue.

"For God's sake, Kate," he rasped, his voice strangled. His fingers delved into her hair, cupping her head and holding her close for another deep, wet kiss that had them both shaking but still wasn't enough.

"Michael," she whispered, her tone rife with frustration, her kiss more so.

He tore his mouth away to murmur, "Take your shirt off, honey."

She dispensed with her T-shirt and undid the back clasp of her bra. The straps drooped on her shoulders, the lacy cups clung to her breasts. A measure of modesty filtered through her haze of desire, and her fingers faltered. She sucked at her lower lip, trying to garner flagging courage.

The harsh angles of his features were covered with a light sheen of perspiration. Desire had flushed his rock-hewn cheekbones. His hazel eyes were glittering slits, focused on the lacy garment. His fingers were clenched hard on her hips, his body otherwise still. She leaned forward and shrugged her shoulders. The fragile garment slipped down her arms.

His arm came hard around her and their bared torsos met, surprising a whimper from her. Her nipples were drawn in tight, sensitized knots, and the first contact sent twin arrows of pleasure shooting to her womb. His mouth caught hers, their hunger spiraling at the intimate contact.

"Michael," she whimpered into his mouth. "Please."

It was all the invitation he needed. His large hands swept

up to cup her breasts. The long-awaited contact was at first a relief and then quickly torched their desire. She arched her back and he leaned forward to take one tight nipple into his mouth.

A broken cry emanated from Kate's throat. Her fingers tangled in his hair, holding him to her breast, where his lips worked their incredible magic. When he grazed her nipple with his teeth her hands grew more frantic. All her senses were centered on the exquisite sensations that he was sending like rapid fire through her body.

She felt the carpet beneath her shoulders and blinked dazedly. Michael's hand went to the fastening of her jeans, and then he dragged them down her legs. One hand smoothed over her stomach, the large palm almost spanning the expanse. He kneaded the skin soothingly as he returned his attention to her breasts.

Brilliant colors fragmented behind her eyelids and she moved helplessly under his touch. Every muscle, every nerve in her body was drawn tight and poised on the brink of unfamiliar discovery. Her hands roamed over his shoulders restlessly, unable to concentrate on anything other than the pleasurable torment of his touch.

He stroked down her body, fingers dipping teasingly below the waistband of her panties. Kate writhed beneath him, barely conscious of anything other than the gnawing craving he created within her. When his hand slipped inside and tucked into the vee between her thighs, her body jerked and her eyes flew open. One of her hands went to his wrist as if to stop his ministrations, and for a moment their gazes melded, his heated, knowing and hungry.

"Do you want me to stop?" His husky question seemed to rumble up from the depths of him. Her mouth trembled, and she made an effort to still it. Both of them were aware of the slippery heat beneath his hand, the dampness that was even now dewing his fingers. Slowly, without taking her gaze from his, she shook her head.

"No," she whispered.

He relaxed imperceptibly, and she realized for the first time how rigidly he'd been holding himself. If her answer had been different, he would have withdrawn from her immediately, despite the cost to himself. She didn't question how she knew that or where the measure of her trust had come from.

"Then relax." His voice vibrated in her ear before he placed a warm kiss below the lobe. "Put your arms around me. I like your hands on me."

Slowly, she released his wrist and did as he requested, her hands sliding up his bulging muscles, stopping to squeeze them testingly. Her thighs quivered beneath his touch; she couldn't control the movement.

His mouth moved to her throat and trailed moist kisses across her collarbone. He gently stroked her with his fingers, using her body's dampness to ease his way. Involuntarily her thighs tightened around his hand and then slowly, gradually relaxed, giving him silent permission to continue.

One long finger eased inside her and she arched beneath him, a cry rising in her throat, her sensitized inner muscles tensing and contracting at his touch. Michael shuddered against her, his breathing ragged. Slowly, gently, he pushed another finger inside and Kate's whole body shook at the intimate invasion.

Her fingers dug into his shoulders as she struggled for control. The sensations he roused in her were wrenchingly intimate, and the slow thrust of his fingers stoked her inner fire until she was twisting helplessly beneath him. Then his rough thumb found the taut bundle of nerves hidden in her soft folds and pressed against it. Liquid flames licked through her veins, exploding her tenuous attempt at control. Her body was pure reaction, responding to every movement of his fingers with eager, helpless pleasure.

The sensations raced through her and the pleasure built to unbearable heights. His thumb circled and rubbed, his fingers moved in rhythm to her body's unconscious arching. Her nerves were coiling, her senses spiraling to the brink of some unfamiliar precipice. "Michael!" Her voice was anguished.

"Let go, sweetheart," he said hoarsely. "Just let it happen." His mouth covered hers then, his kiss hard, desperate.

His tongue swept into her mouth, repeating the invasive movements of his fingers, the pressure hard and urgent. Her body welcomed both, embraced his passion even as it fueled her own.

The tension built quickly. Her body drew tighter and tighter until it was too much. The explosion shook her body in uncontrollable spasms that went on and on while he held her close, sheltering her in the tempest.

Her body went limp, little aftershocks quaking through her, limbs still trembling. Gradually, her senses quieted, became attuned once again. She was aware of his hard arms around her, aware of his tensed muscles, his ragged breathing. Tenderly she cupped his hard jaw in her hand.

He quivered under her touch, then pulled away with an abruptness that almost had her crying out. Her eyelids opened, and her voice stilled the protest she would have made. He stood above her, the hands that had so recently brought her pleasure dispensing with the button of his jeans. He eased the zipper down more carefully, grimacing as he worked it over the bulge beneath his fly. Then in one violent stroke, he pushed jeans and briefs down his legs and kicked them away.

The breath was driven from her body. She'd recognized the power in his wide, padded shoulders and subtly layered torso. But she hadn't been prepared for the sight of his nude splendor. He was magnificent. Her gaze shyly skated over the lean, taut hips, muscled thighs and calves, and then up again. He was huge. All over. She swallowed. Her mental faculties began to function sluggishly, enough for trepidation to make a belated appearance. He knelt between her legs and reached for his jeans again. As he withdrew something from his pocket and moved to protect her, her inner muscles twitched. Despite her apprehension, her body responded to the sight of his. Moments ago she had been awash in sensations that he had caused, drowning in the pleasure that he had brought her. Still her body called for him. She was fulfilled in a way she'd never imagined, yet ached for him. Satisfied but empty.

He crawled over her, his weight heavy and comforting, the feel of his body against hers exciting. She could feel the urgency of his sex throbbing against the apex of her thighs. His muscled legs were an enticing contrast to her smooth ones, and she moved beneath him, everything feminine inside her reveling in his primally masculine form.

He braced himself on one elbow, and his other hand reached between them to guide his entrance as he pushed slowly into her. Kate abruptly stilled, senses scattering. His way was eased by the damp heat he'd caused within her, but he was bigger than his fingers had been, much bigger. Her delicate tissues were exquisitely sensitized after his attentions, and her breath became trapped in her throat. The sensations were flooding back, torrents that threatened to sweep her over the brink again. He eased farther in, stretching her, making a place for himself, then pausing as her muscles tightened convulsively.

Her hands went to his hips as if to still his movements, and he waited rigidly for a tense moment. Her fingers were sidetracked by the taut muscles beneath them, and she kneaded them reflexively. A shaky groan rumbled from Michael's chest, and with a smooth thrust of his hips, he drove himself deeply into her.

Kate gasped. She could feel his powerful body buried within her. The throbbing of his sex kept rhythm with the pulsing of her own inner nerve endings. He'd stretched her to the point of discomfort, but her body was given time to adjust, and she could feel the delicate convulsions as she accommodated him.

Then he started to move, and thought was no longer possible. She heard herself whimper, and he caught the sound in his mouth. Her knees came up and clenched his thighs. Her fingers dug into his hips, silently urging him on.

Her response must have sent his own flagging control up in smoke, for he lunged into her with heavy power, and his hands went below her hips to lift her closer. A rough sound burst from his throat and his movements became deeper, more powerful. She clung to him as his hips hammered against hers, his harsh breathing mingling with her helpless moans.

She'd wanted this, and she'd wanted him. Later she might

be embarrassed at the way she'd fallen to pieces in his hands. But now, faced with his need, she reveled in their passion. The physical aspect of being wanted by this man was satisfying; the emotional aspect impossible to resist. She clung to him, helpless to do more as his hunger grew more savage, his movements harsher. His frantic pace ignited the lingering embers within her.

He pushed her legs higher and she clasped them above his hips. Her body shook with the force of his desire, and he took a deep, gasping breath. She felt him tense and grow even bigger within her. And then with one last, heavy surge of his hips, he crested abruptly, groaning harshly against her mouth.

She stroked his back as he shuddered convulsively against her, tears pricking her eyes. She'd thought she understood everything there was to understand about need, at least emotionally. But physical need was something she'd known nothing about until Michael had shown her. She never would have believed that she could experience it, or that someone could feel it for her so urgently. The fierceness of their desire had shattered what little she had known about sex, and her senses were still reeling.

His weight was growing heavy as his limbs relaxed, but she didn't care. The aftermath of their mating was as shattering as the act itself had been, and if she had her way, they would stay like that forever.

Forever lasted only a few more moments. Michael stirred, then eased away, moving to lie beside her. His arm was a heavy anchor across her waist, and his fingers tangled in her hair, pushing the mass away from her forehead tenderly. Their lips brushed, hesitated, then lingered.

"You taste like roses," he whispered, smoothing one hand over her hair.

Her lips tilted a little. "What do roses taste like?"

"Soft. Sweet." His face was unsmiling, his gaze intent. "Like you could drown in the sweetness, and it still wouldn't be enough."

Her smile faded, and her gaze searched his. She'd never lain with a man like this, languorous after loving, bodies reluctant to move away. Moments after had been awkward, fumbling times, filled with hasty departures or snore-filled slumber. But Michael didn't look sleepy, and he didn't appear to be going anywhere.

He seemed mesmerized with her hair, the natural curls that had been the bane of her existence. He drew a lock over his shoulder, then another, repeating the process until her hair was cascading over both of them. "If you could know," he murmured distractedly, "how many fantasies I've had about your hair."

His compliment pleased her, even as it made her self-conscious. "I leave it long to drag some of the curl out of it. It's even more hopeless when it's short."

"Long is good. I like long," he assured her, stroking the thick curls.

Her fingers ran through the length of his. "I can tell," she teased. "A little more time and your hair will be the same length as mine."

He gave a quick smile. "I'm not real good about planning appointments with the barber. Or keeping them, actually. How are you at trims?"

"I used to do my brothers' hair when they were little."

He gave her a quick, hard kiss. "You're hired."

A few minutes later found them in her kitchen, with Michael seated patiently on a chair. He was bare-chested and hadn't bothered to fasten his jeans after dragging them on. He'd helped her into his shirt, doing up the buttons with great care. Despite her protests that she was rusty and the scissors were not appropriate, he insisted she try.

"It'll beat me doing it myself," he explained, and she gave his shaggy head a thoughtful glance. Her skills, limited though they were, had to be better than an impatient, inattentive man hacking away at his own locks.

No reputable barber would put up with him, she found several minutes later. He didn't stay still long enough for her to cut any of the strands the same length, because he insisted on looking at her while he kept up a steady stream of banter. All illusions of cooperation disappeared when she moved to the front. He drew her between his legs and then proceeded to undo buttons on the shirt as she worked.

"Stop it," she said in mock exasperation as he pressed a kiss to the skin he was baring.

"You did it to me," he reasoned logically.

"Not when you were holding scissors."

"Good point." He took the scissors from her hand and laid them on the table, then pulled her down on his lap. Her breasts pressed against him as he tasted her mouth lingeringly.

"You're a mess," she said breathlessly when he lifted his lips from hers. "You're covered with hair." She brushed the little clippings from his shoulders in vain.

"I know." He rubbed his chest against hers. "Now you are, too. I guess we'll have to take a shower." He got to his feet, still holding her in his arms, and headed for the stairs, inordinately pleased with himself.

"Most of my customers just leave a tip," Kate said with mock seriousness.

He set her on her feet in the small bathroom and turned on the water. "Honey, this is the tip."

They were still laughing when they stepped under the spray. Michael was solicitous about soaping her thoroughly, and she enjoyed the opportunity to touch him freely, as well. Hands slick with soap roamed over wet, slippery skin, heating as they cleansed. Minutes later the soap was forgotten and Michael crowded her against the wall of the shower. After preparing himself he lifted her, and she clasped her legs around his hips while he slid into her with a firm, deep stroke.

The water was growing cool by the time their breathing had calmed. He helped her from the shower and toweled her dry, handing her another towel for her hair. He dried off carelessly, then dropped the towel to the floor, modesty not an issue. As if he'd done it countless times before, he walked with her to her bedroom and crawled into the old brass bed with her.

Long after he had fallen asleep, his chest rising and falling evenly with his breathing, she lay awake, her mind refusing to rest. The events of the evening were totally unlike her, and she felt like a giddy stranger. All her life she'd been staid, sensible Kate, the envy of all her mother's friends. *You must be so proud of Kate. She's such a help with the little ones, isn't she?*

If her mother had ever shown that pride, Kate would have felt proud, too. But because she hadn't, Kate had felt used, trapped and resentful. No one would have suspected how many times as a child she'd longed to do something wild and impetuous, something to shock people into seeing her as a person. Something that wasn't sensible in the least.

Sleeping with Michael just might qualify. He called to every romantic instinct she'd buried so long ago. He'd become a part of her life almost before she'd realized it, and tonight he'd become something more.

All her life she'd wished for something more meaningful than being needed. Right now, lying in the arms of this man, she found herself wishing with all her heart that need would be enough.

Chapter 11

The hardest thing he'd ever done, reflected Michael as he went through the mail and memos that had piled up in his office during his absence, was to get up and leave Kate that morning. As big as he was, her double bed had felt cramped to him, but the close quarters had enabled him to keep her near all night. That had more than made up for the slight discomfort. He'd roused early, at first light, and just lay there watching her. She was even more beautiful in repose, with her long hair tangled around her bare shoulders. He'd wanted to touch her but had been unwilling to chance waking her. It hadn't been necessary. She'd opened those heart-stopping blue eyes sleepily and smiled at him, slow and welcoming. Their early morning kiss had started out sweet and quickly turned serious. So serious, in fact, that he'd had to rush to get home and changed before driving to the office.

Waking up in Kate's bed had been immensely satisfying. Sleeping next to her all night had been even more so. He could have slipped away and gone home earlier, avoiding the downtown traffic he detested, but he would never have left her like that. He hadn't wanted her to wake up and feel regret for what had happened between them. In his business, he was used to anticipating and planning for every possible outcome. He'd be willing to bet that her first response after making love with him would be to withdraw, to strive to rebuild her defenses. He wasn't going to allow her the opportunity to do so. He hadn't left until they'd finalized plans to see each other that evening.

He sorted the pieces of mail into haphazard piles, throwing a good portion of them into the trash without more than a cursory glance. It was a task that required no more than a fraction of his attention, leaving his mind free to linger over the woman who filled it. Every time he remembered the little she'd revealed about her childhood, a knot formed in his gut. All children needed to feel secure in their parents' love. His father had never provided that kind of support in his life, but he'd never had reason to doubt his mother's feelings for him. Kate had an instinctive warmth that demanded a corresponding emotion, but she hadn't received any such reassurance. She'd damned her parents with the little she'd said and with what she'd left unsaid.

He'd wondered about the cause of her wariness, and now he thought he understood. Because he did, he was more certain than ever that he could offer her exactly what she needed—the warmth of a real family, with the occasional craziness that went with it. They'd have the whole thing together. A family, pets, jobs—he figured she'd want to continue working after they got married—and more children. A surge of heat filled him at the thought. She would want children, and God knew he'd welcome them, as well. Chloe would be thrilled to have some brothers or sisters. It was almost uncanny how perfectly Kate suited him, when only a few weeks ago he'd have sworn he would never meet a woman who really interested him, much less one he'd want to marry.

Hands behind his head, he leaned back in his chair pensively. He wondered just how quickly he could convince her to marry him. He tempered his impatience with logic. It would be a mistake to push Kate too far, too fast. Maybe Christmastime. He examined the idea from all angles with fierce concentration and decided it was possible. It was far enough in the future to give her the time she'd need to get used to the idea. His contract with NASA dictated that he have FORAY ready to deliver by October, so the project would be out of the way. He rocked in the chair a little as he considered. The honeymoon would need to be somewhere tropical, but that shouldn't be a problem. The thought of spending a few weeks in the sun with Kate in a bikini had the blood pooling hotly in his loins.

It would work, he thought, satisfied. He always felt better when he had exact goals in mind, with timelines for their accomplishment. Their relationship was progressing smoothly, and as long as he remained patient, there was no reason to expect any obstacles. Restraint would be difficult when he wanted nothing more than to provide her with the kind of family life she'd missed out on as a child. The kind they'd both missed out on. But goals as important as this one were well worth the planning.

There was a knock on his door, but his secretary didn't wait for his invitation before she entered. Stomping over to his desk, she slammed his schedule book down in front of him and surveyed him with her hands on her hips.

Michael watched her blandly. "Is that a new dress, Bernie?"

She made a sound between a snort and a growl. "I don't know how long you're planning to be here, but your day is already filling up." She glared at him accusingly. "I thought you were supposed to be working at home."

"I was and I am. But I knew you'd miss me if I didn't show up occasionally." He gave her his most charming smile. It had no noticeable effect.

"That lawyer, Mr. Winslow, will be here at nine, but Miss Patrie from marketing needs to talk to you, as well. When should I tell her you'll see her?"

He considered for a moment. The meeting with his lawyer would be time-consuming. At the end of the day they'd make their move on that company he was intent on acquiring, and they needed to plot last-minute strategy. "Not until three," he finally responded. "And tell her she's only got an hour. I'm leaving early today." Ignoring Bernie's sniff of disdain, he continued, "Let Derek and Trask know what time Winslow will be here. And we'll need lunch sent in."

Without another word Bernie turned and marched silently for the door.

Ordinarily a day such as this one would fill him with anticipation. He enjoyed the adrenaline rush that resulted from matching wits with his competitors, the endless planning before making a move designed to take the market by surprise. But he was unable to drum up his usual enthusiasm. Glancing at his watch, he mentally calculated the hours until he'd see Kate. Too damn long. He wondered what she was doing right now, what she was thinking. He shifted restlessly in his chair before reaching for the telephone. His hand hovered above the receiver, then dropped. She needed some space, he lectured himself, though not too much. He forced down the impatience welling inside him. Business first. He'd savor the thought of his upcoming evening with Kate as the reward at the end of the day that stretched before him. She would be worth the wait.

Michael looked at home in the pizza and pool parlor, Kate thought, although his large frame dwarfed the ladder-back chair he was sitting in. That mouthwatering muscular build was tucked snugly into denim and cotton. Looking at him made her breath go short and her pulse ping-pong crazily. She knew from experience that he could wear an Armani suit with the same ease and look every bit as provocative.

He reached over and picked up her hand, measuring her palm against his. "What did you do today?"

Her thoughts splintered as heat transferred from his touch. "Studied for my exam. Did a little work on some lessons for next fall."

He looked surprised. "Getting kind of a head start, aren't you?"

"There are a couple of new units I'd like to prepare. Since I'm not taking classes this summer, I hope to get quite a bit of schoolwork done." She welcomed the simple conversation. She'd also spent a lot of the day thinking. But her attempt to balance the events of last night with a dose of realism had been frustrated by the intimate memories that had insisted on seeping into her consciousness.

"How was the office?"

The corner of his mouth pulled down. "Tedious. Things pile up when I'm gone, even when I stay in contact daily." He paused when the waitress came up to take their order.

Kate observed the way the girl lingered near Michael's chair. He had a sheerly masculine presence that any female couldn't help but react to. Certainly, she had done so last night. The memory washed her cheeks with color. The novelty of waking up with a man in her bed, with *Michael* in her bed, had filled her with giddy pleasure. And then he'd kissed her, and the pleasure had changed to the deep froths of passion he could evoke from her so easily.

He hadn't released her hand, and when the waitress left, the beam of his gaze was directed solely at her once again, bathing her with heat. He sent a thumb skimming over her knuckles. "You don't know how many times I reached for the phone today."

"You wanted to call?" The admission pleased her, made it easier to meet his intent hazel eyes.

He gave a slow nod. "Only about a hundred times. But I figured you needed the break, so I had to settle for counting the hours until I could see you again."

His words sent hot licks of pleasure flickering in her stomach. To distract him, and herself, she said, "You must have been busy today."

"Swamped," he agreed cheerfully. "We're moving on another company tomorrow and needed to get some final details ironed out."

Her fingers stiffened a little in his hand. "What does that mean? Moving on?"

"I'm hoping to acquire it."

Kate surveyed him carefully. *The Beltway Raider.* The term

whispered across her mind, leaving traces of uneasiness. "You mean a hostile takeover."

His fingers closed around hers, trapping them neatly. "We'll be offering a buyout, yes. Hummels, the owner, over-extended his company, put too much stock public. Since I now own a good portion of that stock, I'm in a position to make an offer."

Something inside her refused to leave the topic alone. "Will the owner be able to refuse your offer?"

"I doubt it. Not unless he has some reserve that can be easily liquidated for cash. And I don't think he has. Otherwise he never would have chanced putting that much stock on the market."

She dropped her gaze, strangely shaken. "You must have been planning this for a very long time."

"About a year." When her shocked gaze bounced back to his, he gave her a wry grin. "I told you once I could be patient, didn't I?"

"Yes," she murmured. "You did." That patience of his was a curious contradiction, since he struck her as a man who reached out and took what he wanted. She decided that corporate moves such as the one he was alluding to weren't about patience at all. They were all about planning and control.

A shiver trickled down her spine, stiffening her resolve. She liked knowing where she was going before starting out. Getting involved with Michael was more like jumping off the edge of a cliff than taking a journey, she acknowledged, but the analogy remained valid. If she was intent on taking the first step, she'd do so with a map in hand. *Her* map. *Her* route. *Her* destination.

Michael released her hand so the waitress could place the steaming pizza on the table between them. "When does Chloe come back?" she asked as she placed a slice of pizza on a plate and handed it to him.

"Not until tomorrow night. Mrs. Martin will go and fetch her. I've got a meeting that will last until late, and I want Trask there. He's also investigating teachers for dance and gymnastics. If Chloe is agreeable, he'll get her signed up at one of the centers.''

"She's going to love it.''

His mouth quirked. "Yeah, I think so, too.''

"You might also consider art lessons. She has natural ability, and it is the one area she can attend to for longer amounts of time.'' She eyed Michael thoughtfully. "But I suppose all these activities for Chloe could get to be a scheduling nightmare.''

"No, I think it would be great. I just can't believe I haven't thought of any of this on my own. I'm going to be spending most of the summer working at home, and either Trask or I would be available to take her wherever she needs to go.''

"Just how did you acquire Trask, anyway?'' She asked the question that she'd often wondered about. "He seems an unusual nanny.''

Michael almost choked on his second slice of pizza. "I wish he could hear you call him that.'' He shook his head. "Trask doesn't really have a job title. He just takes care of things for me. When I was trying to convince him to come and work for me, I told him he'd be head of security. He's become much more than that.''

She'd observed as much for herself. Both Chloe and Michael obviously cared for the huge, taciturn man, and she'd seen for herself how good he was with the little girl.

His eyes darkened, but his voice remained calm. "I met him about a month after I'd taken over my father's company, after I'd dismantled it piece by piece. I'd wanted to destroy my father for what he'd done to me and my mother, and I did it.

"Trask had worked for Jonathan, had been head of security for the old man's company. He just showed up at my office one day, demanded to see me. I was curious, so I met with him.'' Michael's gaze was still on her, but his sight had turned inward. "He said he just wanted to meet the son of a bitch who was a chip off the old man's block. I was furious when he implied I was anything like my father. I'd spent too many years hating Jonathan. I'm not proud to admit that until

Trask pointed it out to me, I'd never given a thought to the hundreds of employees I'd put out of work with my actions. I didn't think about the lives disrupted, the possible homes lost…'' His mouth tightened. ''Put in that light, I had to admit that I was more like my father than I'd ever dreamed possible. I wouldn't face it, of course. Not for a while. But eventually I found Trask again and convinced him to come and work for me.''

''How did you do that?''

Michael contemplated her question for a moment. ''I honestly don't know,'' he said finally. ''I'm determined when I want something, but Trask is an immovable wall. I guess I finally managed to convince him that he was the only one who could help me.'' .

''To head up security?''

He shook his head. ''No. To keep me from becoming my father.'' His voice was wry, but no less sincere, when he added, ''You could say it's become my life's work.''

His regret shimmered in the air between them and her heart cracked. In an unconscious effort to soothe, she touched his arm, stroked it slowly. ''You're nothing like your father. You would never walk out on Chloe.''

His thumb skated along the sensitive underside of her wrist. ''No, I wouldn't. And I decided the ultimate revenge wasn't putting that bastard out of business, it was making sure I didn't turn out just like him. The corporation is always expanding. But I never acquire another company now without making damn sure the employees can remain in their positions or offering them places in our other holdings.''

His gaze grew intent and he leaned closer. ''The similarities are there, Kate, like it or not. Jonathan and I are in the same line of business, and we've got the same knack for it. Within weeks of losing his company, the old man had lined up financing for another. But there's a difference between us, a huge one. I can't see the bottom line anymore without considering the people involved, and I know I have Trask to thank for that. Family is important to me.'' His voice lowered, a note of intimacy entering it. "When I care about someone, there's nothing I wouldn't do to keep them safe. Protected."

Her gaze was trapped by his, that soft, alluring voice rendered her defenseless. What he had told her should have shored up her store of caution, given her one more excuse for keeping a steady distance between them. Instead it threatened to flay at the very fabric of her reason. Old hurts and regrets shaped them all. He had, at least, used his to alter the course he'd been headed toward. And because he'd chosen a path filled with love for his daughter, she was, quite simply, captivated.

Shifting a glance to her empty plate, he asked hoarsely, "Are you finished?"

Without a second thought, she nodded. Her hunger wasn't for food, and her stomach was full anyway, churning with nerves and emotion. Gratefully she followed him to the front desk and put a look of amused tolerance on his face by insisting on paying the bill. Reminding him that she'd brought him here only made him smile wider.

Her hand trembled a bit as she was fitting the key into her car lock, then she was leaning across the seat to unlock the passenger door. She was glad she'd driven tonight, although she'd felt a tinge of remorse earlier, watching him trying to fold his large body into her car. She enjoyed driving; it symbolized freedom to her and it had seemed important to exert some measure of her independence. Last night had proven she was completely vulnerable to him. She wasn't going to become dependent on him, as well.

The car sped along the interstate, and Michael fiddled with the radio. His efforts were met with static. "The radio doesn't work?"

"Not for the last few months."

He turned it off and relaxed back in his seat as she expertly changed lanes. He cocked an eyebrow at her when she smoothly passed a semi. "Like speeding, do you?"

She smiled unabashedly. "I love it. I try to control my lead foot, though. Speeding tickets are such a wasted expense. And truthfully, this car won't take much abuse. I bought it used eight years ago. I'm trying to baby it along for a couple more years until I save up enough money for a good down payment.'' She shot him a droll look. ''Chances are, I won't have much of a trade-in.''

He settled back into the seat with a slight frown on his face. Some men couldn't stand to be the passenger in a car, and she wondered if he was bothered by having a woman in control. On the heels of that thought came her answer. She'd been in control last night, at least at first, when control had still been possible. *He* had encouraged it.

Slow heat suffused her at the memory. No. He wasn't a man who would be threatened by a woman in the driver's seat, neither literally nor figuratively. He was too sure of himself, too secure in his own masculinity. She sneaked a glance at him. His head was cocked, as if he were silently cataloging the assortment of creaks and rattles her car was making.

Her palms grew slippery on the steering wheel, and her breathing quickened. The closer they got to her condo, the greater her anticipation. Fragments of their time together last night flicked across her mind, and the images were hotly provocative. She remembered his face when the bra had slipped off her arms, his eyes glittering and intent. She could feel again the weight of his body crushing hers and the roughness of his hairy legs between her smooth ones. She remembered the slickness of his body against hers in the shower as the water had sluiced over them. The way he'd taken her hand in his and carried it down his body, and his harshly indrawn breath when her fingers had closed around him.

She chanced another glance at him. His eyes were narrowed, his nostrils flared, and she knew intuitively that he was remembering, too. His attention was focused on her with that single-minded concentration he was capable of, even when he'd been making love to her. She knew he was acutely aware of the path her thoughts had taken, and she was too aroused to be shy about the realization. She wanted him again; she wanted his weight and heat inside her, his hips pounding into hers and his arms around her afterward. Seeing her need reflected on his face sent her heart leaping, her mouth trembling.

Tearing her gaze away from him, she forced herself to watch the road. He didn't say anything. Neither did she. But the awareness grew with each instant, until the sexual tension in the car was suffocating.

Relief rushed up in her when she pulled the car into the space in front of her condo. He followed her up to the door, and when her shaking hands were unable to make the key work in the lock, he silently took it from her and opened the door. She hadn't taken two steps inside before she was turning to him, and he was crowding her against the wall, one foot sending the door swinging closed.

Their mouths ate each other, their tongues doing battle. He shoved a hand in her hair and held her mouth under his. Impatiently, she pulled the T-shirt loose from his jeans, sliding her hands up his torso with a low purr of pleasure. His hand moved to her breast, fingers closing on her nipple, and she arched her back, pressing closer. He parted her legs with one of his and moved close between them, rubbing his hips against her. He was rock hard, and the feel of his arousal made everything inside her go soft and weak.

Her mouth was freed when his lips nipped a line up the column of her throat. Breathlessly she murmured, "I thought about you today. About us."

She could hear the satisfaction in his voice, could feel it. "About us?"

"Yes." The word was a moan as he chose that time to bathe the hollow of her throat with his tongue. She moistened her lips, trying to regain her scattered thoughts. "I decided it would be ridiculous to deny what's between us."

He smiled against the skin below her ear, then took the lobe in his teeth. "Good girl."

She shuddered beneath his marauding lips, and her fingers skimmed over the layers of muscle on his chest to clutch at his heavy shoulders. The floor tipped crazily, and she leaned into him to steady herself. His mouth found hers again and she took time to savor, aware of just how easy it would be to drown in his kiss. Recklessly, she let herself do just that.

Every pulse in her body throbbed like a wound. She could feel his heart rocketing beneath her palm. When he released her lips, her head fell back dreamily, and she dragged his shirt up out of her way. She'd always thought decisions through carefully, but she couldn't recall ever having been quite so pleased with one she'd made. Tangling her fingers in the mat of hair that bisected his torso, she pressed a kiss above his nipple, sending a jolt through him.

She rubbed her cheek against his chest. "It's hard to keep my head around you." Her reaction to him was completely unprecedented. She wanted to touch. The taste she'd had of him had only whetted an appetite that should have terrified her. But right now she found it exhilarating. She turned her head, letting her teeth scrape his nipple, and one of his hands splayed across her hips, drawing her closer to the cradle of his.

"I think I like it when you lose your head." He released the catch on her bra, and she filled his palm, heat against heat. The sensations were excruciatingly exquisite, and need threatened to swallow her.

"I have it all worked out." She was panting now, her head resting against the wall weakly. Both of his hands were full, and his fingers, those clever fingers, were busy. She paused a moment to absorb the sensation of being trapped between the unyielding surface of the wall at her back and the large, hard body before her. Some traps were made to be enjoyed.

"We can have this," she murmured, going up on tiptoe to drag her lips over his chin. Catching his bottom lip in her teeth, she worried it gently for a moment before setting it free. "It can be enough. We can make it be enough."

The stillness came over him gradually, as if her words took time to register. "What are you saying?"

"No demands," she assured him, certain he would be relieved. "No strings." She let her hands glide over the smooth skin on his sides to the sleek expanse of his back. Her fingers danced up his spine, then stroked down each individual vertebra. "Just…this." The tips of her fingers caught in his waistband, and she exerted enough pressure to urge him closer to her. Leaning forward, she ran her tongue across his collarbone, drinking in his taste.

His fingers cupped her shoulders, and he forced a slight distance between them. "You're not the kind of woman to suggest—just what the hell are you suggesting, anyway?"

The dizzying heat that had spiraled up so rapidly was dissipating. Not vanishing, she reflected. That would be impossible this close to him. But ebbing enough for her to think a little clearer. Enough for her to read the carefully blank expression on his face and to wonder at it. The touch on her shoulders turned caressing, as if his fingers had a mind of their own. She was quite sure that without the hum of excitement still so vibrant in her blood, she'd never have had the courage to meet his gaze and answer. "I'm suggesting what we both want. An affair." She gave a little shrug. "Or whatever it's called these days." The intriguing muscles beneath her palms went tense, and she massaged them soothingly. "A mutually satisfying physical relationship." She was proud of the way the term rolled off her tongue. She didn't have the experience to know exactly how it was supposed to be referred to, but she was certain that he'd recognize it. Accept it.

"And what if I want demands?" he asked. Something in his voice had her observing him cautiously. His face wasn't blank now. It was set and hard. His eyes held a narrow pinpoint of light, that gleamed dangerously.

"You're the last person I expected to complicate this, Michael."

He took a deep breath and released her, thrusting a hand through his hair and turning half away. A part of her mourned the loss, even as another part was grateful to be released from his piercing regard.

"And you're the last person I expected to simplify it," he muttered. When he faced her again, he wore a baffled expression. "You don't want it like this, Kate."

One of her brows arched. "Are you telling me what I want?"

He had the sense to deny it. "Of course not. But it's not what I want. There was a time when I wasn't exactly discriminating when it came to women."

The admission, although it didn't come as a surprise, still made her want to punch him. "Do tell."

"I'm not proud of it, but the experience taught me a valuable lesson. A relationship like that leaves something missing. Mutual affection, trust, respect."

"Why do those things have to be missing?"

He blinked, as if her ingenuous question took him aback. "Because…" His voice stumbled for a moment. "Invariably one person wants more than the other, so one starts feeling guilty and backing away. The other one is hurt, angry and disillusioned."

Her lips curved, and she closed the distance he'd put between them. "You don't have to worry, Michael. I'm not going to get needy and start clinging."

His voice was bleak. "You aren't?"

She shook her head, smoothing her hands up the front of his shirt. "I'll admit that I don't have your…level of experience. But a no-strings relationship is exactly what *I* want, too."

His hands came up and caught hers. "There's no such thing as a no-strings relationship, Kate."

"Who says?"

He brought his face close to hers, close enough for her to see the muscle twitching in his jaw. "*I* say. Do you know why I stopped seeing a different woman every week?"

Her lips went flat. She wished he'd quit referring to them. The thought of those faceless, nameless women didn't exactly fill her with confidence. "Sheer physical exhaustion?"

His fingers tightened on hers. "I wasn't getting what I'd been searching for. Intimacy. That's what was missing from those relationships, Kate, and that's what I want from you. That's my demand, and it's a deal breaker."

She shook her hair back, her mind blank. This scene was

not going the way she'd envisioned it. She hadn't considered that, far from being relieved at her words, he'd be offended. He picked that moment to free her hands and press a warm kiss at the center of one of her palms, then closed the fingers on it gently, trapping the heat.

Her throat went dry, and her muscles turned to warm wax. "This isn't one of your business deals."

"Damn right. It's personal. Very personal," he added as he slowly urged her backward. It wasn't until she felt the wall at her shoulders that she was aware of moving. He placed his hands on the wall on either side of her face, effectively caging her. "And I'm clarifying the conditions."

"Fine," she managed to say as his lips cruised along her jawline. "But I have conditions of my own."

She flinched at the not-quite-gentle nip behind her ear, then shivered when his tongue soothed the spot.

"So you've said."

"We can't complicate this."

"Too late."

"It can't be." The licks of panic dancing in her stomach sounded in her voice, and his touch changed, growing impossibly gentle.

"There's nothing simple about this," he murmured, once again dropping a necklace of kisses across her throat. Because she was desperate to, she let herself believe that he was referring to their desire. "Or this." His lips captured hers in a slow, devastating kiss that lingered until every muscle in her body went weak. He deepened the kiss by degrees, each instant just a whisper warmer. By the time he lifted his mouth, she would have slid down the wall without his support.

"Michael." Her voice was thready, and she tangled her fingers in his hair. Only moments ago the passion had been a cauldron of churning emotion, threatening to overflow. It had changed to an aching tenderness so exquisite that she could weep.

His lips brushed over hers, once, twice and again. "Negotiations are over. This deal is closed."

"I don't see how both of us are going to get—" She fisted

her hands on his shirt to hold his mouth steady on hers, but after the soul-satisfying kiss, she broke away ''—what we want.''

It was gratifying to note that his breathing wasn't quite steady. ''Who's the expert deal maker here?''

Her neck arched beneath his mouth, thought fading in the face of the slow, lovely drift into sweetness. ''You are.''

''Then you'll just have to trust me.''

She was dimly aware that the issue remained unresolved. His lips sipped the hollow at the base of her throat and attempts at logic shattered. Her fingers tightened in his hair, urging his mouth back to hers. The heated pressure of his lips had thoughts fading, priorities shifting. Her last conscious thought was that he was right about one thing. There was certainly nothing simple about this.

Chapter 12

Two days. Michael could feel the headache throb at his temples as if to mark the passing of each slow second. It had been two days since he'd left Kate sleeping, still tangled in the pool of bedcovers. Sleep hadn't been as accommodating for him that night. He'd lain next to her, cradling her close, but his mind had refused to succumb to slumber. The passion had been sated for the moment, freeing him to deal with the more troubling emotions that had persisted in colliding beneath the surface. He wasn't an expert at self-analysis, but there had been one feeling that had been pretty easy to identify. Sheer, unadulterated panic.

He sent his gaze across the table and nodded soberly as Jake Winslow talked leverage buyouts and stock options with Hummels and his attorney, but his mind was occupied with far more serious matters. He could still feel the cold fist of fear that had gripped his insides when she'd made her little speech, laid out her terms. *Keep it simple.* Her phrase had slapped him neatly across the face, making a mockery of his carefully laid plans. He could never before remember being so far off base when estimating a woman.

He'd had entire business deals go sour and never come close to the helpless terror that her words had inspired. He'd made love to her over and over that night, as if his touch could wipe away her words. Even as he'd held her close, he'd been unable to shake the feeling that she was slipping away from him. With each passing moment it seemed the distance between them grew, until he'd freed himself from the intimate hold and left the bed at dawn, sweating and shaking.

Derek was talking now. Michael tuned in to the conversation long enough to ascertain that his vice president was pointing out Hummels's lack of options. Derek loved this part of the job, loved going in for the kill. Michael wished vaguely that he could whip up even a portion of the other man's enthusiasm. It wasn't like him to display such a lack of interest in a deal he'd worked so hard putting together. But, he thought gloomily, he'd never before had anything this important vying for his attention.

It was bitterly ironic that his conversation with Kate had reduced their relationship to a deal, complete with conditions to be met. She'd had only one term, really. *Keep it simple.* He rubbed an absent hand over his throbbing temple and contemplated the phrase again with baffled amazement. He, of all people, should be comfortable negotiating terms. He'd planned her seduction and wooing with all the corporate stealth of which he'd been capable. But to hear her refer to it that way had washed his vision with waves of red.

There was more between them than sex, and she was deliberately blinding herself to it. Voices around him rose as Hummels argued a point vehemently with Derek. Michael didn't even make an attempt to focus on the words. He'd come up smack against a truth and was still reeling from the impact.

There was more here than sex. He'd never denied that himself. But identifying just exactly what that "more" encompassed was a bit like opening a door without knowing what stood on the other side. He thought hard, then gave that mental door a cautious push. He liked Kate, had from the first. All right, her looks had caught his eye at the start, and then he'd reacted strongly to her concerns about Chloe, but he respected her, too. She was smart and funny, and she loved kids. That wall of reserve came down when she was around Chloe, and something about watching the two of them together made his throat go tight.

Deciding the process hadn't been too painful, he gave that mental door another shove. He knew her well enough to know that they wanted the same things…warmth, intimacy, family. They could find it together, if she'd just let him get close enough. He worried about her. That car she drove was a death trap, although he'd known better than to give her his opinion. The thought of her on the freeways in it, with its list of ailments, made his blood go cold. And she didn't have enough security at her condo to suit him. He frowned fiercely. Dammit, he cared about her. He wasn't a cold-blooded idiot. He wouldn't have decided to marry her if he was. Maybe it was even more than caring. Maybe it was…

The thought remained unfinished, and he backed away from it with a speed that, had it been physical, would have sent him stumbling. Cautiously, he skirted the idea, mentally examining it from the edges. Caring. That was a safe emotion he could admit to comfortably, and he felt that for Kate, in abundance. She cared about him, too, no matter what she'd said the last time they'd been together. She was simply too fastidious to have slept with him otherwise.

Feeling a little cheered, he scrutinized the realization, vaguely aware that the voices around him had calmed once again. So she cared about him, she had to, but she wasn't at ease with the feeling. Maybe she hadn't even yet admitted it to herself. She had a neat, tidy little mind and liked to keep things orderly. Admitting him into her life, into her trust, would upset that order, and she would naturally fight that.

The only way to get her to admit her true feelings for him was to make her trust him, which she didn't yet. She wouldn't let herself. He pondered the problem. Before Kate would trust him, he'd have to convince her of how much he cared. But how to do that? He'd been relying on his background in the corporate world to plan the relationship thus far, and trust simply wasn't a quality he'd ever needed to generate in the businesses he was taking over.

Suddenly he snapped his fingers, delighted with the idea that came to him. The men at the table stopped talking and looked at him expectantly.

"Gentlemen," he said, rising. "Let's take a break. I've got some arrangements to make."

The sunglasses shielded her eyes from the worst of the sun's glare, but it was the perfection of the day that threatened to blind her. Temperatures hovered in the low eighties, the sky was cloudless, and the warm blue water of the pool sparkled against white tiles. Kate sighed contentedly.

"Miss Rose, Miss Rose, watch this! Watch me, Miss Rose!"

Chloe did a somersault off the low diving board, and a tiny tidal wave threatened to capsize Kate's water mattress. She didn't release her breath until she saw the little imp's head break the surface again and Chloe began to dog-paddle toward her.

She clapped dutifully. "Very good, Chloe. You're getting better all the time."

The little girl reached the mattress and took hold of the edge. "I'm getting hot. Can I take this off?"

"No," Kate said quickly. "The life jacket stays on or we have to leave the pool area."

"That's what my dad always says," Chloe sighed. She slanted a glance up to Kate. "Did he tell you to make me wear it?"

"Yes, he did, and he's right. It's not safe for you to be around the water without one."

But Chloe's mind had already fixed on another topic. "This was a good idea Daddy had, wasn't it? For you to come swimming with me at our house."

Kate slid her sunglasses to the top of her head and turned to smile at the child. "It was an excellent idea."

"I'm a good swimmer, aren't I? Daddy's been teaching me."

"You're a very good swimmer, but even good swimmers need life jackets until they're bigger."

Chloe appeared lost in thought. Cocking her head, she asked, "Am I going to see you more this summer, Miss Rose?"

Suddenly feeling on shakier ground, Kate said cautiously, "Yes…you'll see me sometimes."

The little girl beamed. "Good. I already knew I would."

Kate arched a brow. "You did, did you?"

Nodding enthusiastically, Chloe said, "Uh-huh. 'Cuz Daddy promised me I would, but it had to be a secret. Oh!" She clapped one hand over her mouth, then giggled. Her eyes twinkled with amusement. "I wasn't supposed to tell anyone."

Kate couldn't prevent a wry smile. "You want me to tell you a secret? Sometimes your daddy isn't as sneaky as he thinks he is."

Chloe beamed. "I knew he would keep his promise. He says daddies always keep their promises, especially to their little girls."

The words, simply spoken, threatened to shatter Kate's heart. Whatever Michael's accomplishments in the business world, she reflected, emotion clogging her throat, whatever pinnacles he achieved, nothing would equal what he had accomplished with his daughter. He'd managed to raise her in an atmosphere that assured her of his love and acceptance. Surely that was a feat to be proud of.

"All daddies don't keep their promises, though, Miss Rose."

Shock held Kate silent for a moment as she stared at the child. Seven-year-old wisdom shone in Chloe's eyes.

"That's what Amy Wiltsie says, 'cuz her daddy always says he'll come and get her on Saturdays, but he never does. He always gets too busy. People shouldn't make promises if they're not going to keep them, right, Miss Rose?"

Kate blinked and said slowly, "No. People shouldn't make promises they can't keep."

Chloe chattered on. "Daddy says a promise is like a present, and you can't give it to a person and then take it back. That would be mean. Do you think that's why Amy's daddy breaks his promises, Miss Rose? Because he's mean?''

Kate took a deep breath and released it unsteadily. She wouldn't be nervous at the thought of facing four of her professors for her oral graduate exams, she thought. The experience couldn't possibly be as emotionally draining as a conversation with a first-grader. "No," she said finally. "He probably doesn't do it to be mean. He's probably just…" She glanced at the little girl, who appeared to be hanging on to her every word. She didn't think she was equipped to explain adult selfishness to a seven-year-old, and there was no reason to do so. Chloe would never have to deal with it, not from her father. "He probably just isn't as smart about some things as your daddy is."

Chloe released the side of the mattress and paddled around it, sending up steady splashes. "I'm going to have two daddies now."

Used to the child's penchant for bouncing from subject to subject, Kate followed her train of thought seamlessly. "You mean when your mother gets married."

The little girl nodded. "He won't be my real daddy, though. Mommy says I can call him Jeffrey." She wrinkled her nose. "That's a funny name."

Feeling on uncertain ground, Kate asked, "So you met Jeffrey at your mother's house the other day?"

Chloe took a huge breath, plunged her face in the water and came up sputtering a few seconds later. She was nodding her head even as she struggled to wipe the water from her eyes. "Uh-huh. He has white hair, but Mommy says he's not old, he's premature."

Kate battled to withhold a laugh. "You mean he's prematurely gray?"

Shrugging, Chloe said, "I guess. He had a ring on his little finger that was sparkly red, and he was wearing a monkey suit."

Even applying all her powers of translation, Kate still

couldn't grasp Chloe's meaning. Suspiciously, she asked, "Chloe, did you...I mean, are you sure?"

The little girl nodded. "It had a black coat and a little black tie and tiny black buttons. His shirt had folds in it."

This time Kate did laugh. "That's called a tuxedo, honey."

"A tucks—what?"

"A tuxedo. Men wear them when they get really dressed up."

"That's not what Daddy calls them," Chloe said stubbornly. "He said they're monkey suits and that he has to wear one when he's going to a zoo with other men."

Torn between exasperation and amusement, Kate muttered, "Sometimes your daddy is too funny for his own good." Because Chloe looked unconvinced, she changed the subject. "Your mother and her...Jeffrey...must have been going somewhere very fancy."

Chloe bobbed her head in agreement. "They went to a 'gagement party, 'cuz they're gonna get married. They musta got in love, right, Miss Rose? Amy Wiltsie says you gotta get in love and then you get married."

Amy Wiltsie, it appeared, was an authority on any number of subjects. "That's the way it's usually done," Kate replied weakly when it became clear that Chloe was waiting for a response. She couldn't tell the child that she was hardly an expert on the subject. There had been no love to observe between her parents, only a worn sense of obligation.

A memory sliced across her mind as clear as the summer day. She'd been just as curious about the concept of love and marriage as Chloe, but she hadn't been a little girl. She'd been fourteen or so, and it had been during her Romeo-and-Juliet stage. She'd been caught up in the sheer romance of the story and had startled her mother by asking her if she had been hopelessly in love with Papa when they'd gotten married. The dull astonishment on her mother's face had made more of an impression than her answer.

Wherever do you get such nonsense, girl? You better forget your silly ideas. Marriage is lots of hard work.

Something had made the teenage Kate persist, a notion,

however vain, that her father must once have had some heroic qualities for her mother to have married him. Her mother had looked discomfited at her tenacity before answering her dismissively. *Your papa ain't a bad man. He works steady, don't drink much, and he's never laid a hand to me.*

The memory left her with the same mingled regret and shock she'd felt that day. Even at fourteen she'd known that there had to be more to marriage than anything her mother had experienced. With the brash certainty of youth she'd vowed to herself never to settle for less than love. Only with the onset of adulthood did she begin to have doubts about being able to recognize it if it was offered to her.

Blessedly, Chloe interrupted her depressing thoughts. She heaved herself up onto the mattress, nearly toppling Kate off in the process. "I'm never gonna get in love."

A small smile crossed Kate's lips. "You're not, huh?"

Chloe shook her head, her hair spraying water drops. "Uh-uh. Boys are gross! One time at recess Tommy Sherman in second grade ate a worm."

Kate was fascinated in spite of herself. "You're kidding!"

"No, I'm not," Chloe said dramatically. "It was so sick. And he said the next time it rained he was going to do it again, so I was really glad it didn't rain anymore before school got out."

The two looked at each other and then started laughing. Suddenly, the warmth returned to the day for Kate, and the chill of her memories subsided. She leaned closer to Chloe and murmured, "You know what? I'll bet Tommy's stomach was even gladder that it didn't rain." Mirthfully, they let the giggles take over until they were both hanging on to the mattress, helpless with laughter.

It was almost eight-thirty by the time Kate got close to home, and her energy was fading as fast as the daylight. Keeping pace with Chloe was an exhausting feat, but she'd enjoyed every moment of the day. After spending the entire afternoon swimming, they'd made tacos and pudding, Chloe's choice, for supper. Then Chloe had insisted that they visit the stable. Kate had, however, withstood the little girl's wheedling pleas for horseback riding. Hank hadn't seemed to be in the vicinity, and Kate knew nothing about horses except that the big one, Diablo, made her especially nervous. She'd managed to coax Chloe into a bike ride instead, using Michael's bike to accompany the little girl up and down the long drive.

When she'd left the house, Chloe had been in bed but not asleep. Kate, though, was weary enough to drop where she stood. She'd left the little girl in Mrs. Martin's care and headed home.

She guided the car into a parking space near her condo and turned off the ignition with a satisfied sigh. She'd had a vain hope that Michael might be able to get away from his meeting and join them, even though on the phone this morning he'd told her that his meeting would run until late.

As she got out of the car and slammed the door, her thoughts were still preoccupied with Michael. It seemed too long since she'd last seen him, and despite her reassurances to herself that a little time apart was for the best, she couldn't deny the truth.

She missed him. She missed his crazy humor and that glint in his eye that told her he was teasing. She missed the way he felt about his family, unabashedly proud and protective. And she missed his strong arms, his mouth on hers.... Sternly she reined in her thoughts. Thinking along those lines could only get her in trouble. And it wouldn't do to let him know just how much of a hold he already had on her. She knew him too well. Give the man an inch and he'd take a light year. She'd meant it when she'd told him they needed to keep their relationship simple, although she was truthful enough to admit that she wasn't quite sure how to accomplish that. There wasn't anything simple about Michael Friday. But one thing she was sure of. Simplicity could only be assisted by distance. So these meetings of his were really a blessing in disguise.

Engrossed in her thoughts, she was halfway up her walk before she noticed the man crouched on her porch. She stopped abruptly, shock congealing into wariness. As if already aware of her presence, the man turned to look at her over his shoulder.

"Evening, ma'am. I'm just about done here, and then I'll be out of your way."

"Done?" Kate repeated cautiously, watching him with a careful eye. Her mind registered the khaki uniform he was wearing and the tool belt around his waist. Some of the tension seeped from her muscles, but she didn't take a step closer.

"With your door, ma'am. The boss wanted us out of here by six at the latest, but we ran into a little glitch. It's all taken care of, though."

The boss. Of course. She released a breath. The landlord must have decided finally, after months of fielding her complaints, to fix her doorbell. She hadn't thought it would be a difficult task, but she'd have to take this workman's word for it.

The man put away the screwdriver he'd been wielding and stood up. It was only then that Kate noted what he'd been working on.

"There must be some mistake," she said.

He looked at her quizzically.

She gestured toward the door. It had been replaced with a stout, obviously expensive one. "I asked him for a new doorbell, not a new door."

Looking puzzled, the man scratched his balding head and glanced back at the doors and then at her. "A doorbell? No, ma'am. He didn't mention a doorbell."

Kate sighed. Apparently there was some mix-up, one that was going to take a phone call to her landlord to resolve. No doubt the work had been done on the wrong condo. A slow grin spread over her face. Her landlord wouldn't be pleased, but she would end up with a new front door. That should more than make up for this misunderstanding.

"Could I see your work order?" she asked politely.

The man squinted at her. "Don't have a work order,

ma'am. Just got our orders from the boss and came right over here.''

At that moment, her front door opened and two other men, also in uniform, came out of her condo carrying some windows. Kate stared hard. *Her windows.*

"What should we do with these?''

"Put 'em in the van.''

Kate's gaze swung to the parking lot, finding the oversize van the man was referring to. As she read the logo on the side, comprehension dawned slowly. And with it came simmering temper.

Dodging the men, she stalked up the front steps into her condo, stopping short in amazement once she got inside. Slowly, she moved in farther, her gaze swinging from side to side. All the windows were new and had thick glass with tiny, almost indiscernible wires tracing through it. She strode into the kitchen and found that window replaced, as well. In addition, a new back door had been added, one with a sturdy dead bolt. Swinging around, she walked back through the condo. Two of the men were tidying up and gathering their tools. The man she'd first encountered stood just inside the front door, watching her placidly.

"If you'd just come over here, ma'am, I'll show you how to work the alarm system and the new door locks. Then we'll get out of your way.'' With a sense of resignation she followed his gaze to the box that had been installed inside her foyer wall. Lights blinked from within its confines like tiny red eyes.

The anger bubbled over and threatened to scald her with its intensity. Michael had done this. Without her knowledge, without her consent, he'd seen fit to make this decision for her. She took a deep breath and released it slowly, wishing she could exhale the fury as easily.

"Get rid of it,'' she told the man flatly.

His face was blank with astonishment. "Ma'am?''

She waved a hand around the condo. "The windows, the doors, the…alarm thingee, all of it. Get rid of it. I didn't order it and I don't want it.''

The worker shot a glance at the two other men, who raised their eyebrows and looked away, clearly agreeing that the woman was a clown short of a circus. Seeing no help in that direction, the man looked back at Kate helplessly. "Ma'am, the boss said—"

"I don't care what he said." Her voice was level, but the words were measured. "This is my home, not Michael Friday's, and he had no right—" Abruptly she cut herself off and jammed her hand in her hair with disgust. It was no use arguing with this poor man. He had only been carrying out orders, after all. Michael's orders. She'd reserved the brunt of her fury for the man who deserved it. Anger traced its tentacles throughout her muscles and stiffened her spine. She smiled grimly. She'd have plenty to say to Michael when she saw him.

"See, the thing is, ma'am, we couldn't undo this if we wanted to. I'm afraid the doors were damaged when we removed them. We didn't see much use being careful when we were just going to haul them away."

"All right." Kate gave him a tight smile that did nothing to reassure him. "I understand. And you people probably want to be getting home."

Her abrupt reversal had him shooting another look at the two men and then back again. Cautious relief filled his voice. "Yes, ma'am."

Stoically Kate watched as he demonstrated the locks. Then, at his urging, she gave him a list of numbers to set the alarm with. He wrote the numbers down on a tablet and handed it to her.

"You might want to keep this in a safe place, at least until you have it memorized."

She watched as they took their leave with almost comical haste and then shut the door, the new front door, after them. She leaned her forehead against its smooth surface. Damn him. Her throat knotted with tears, tears she refused to shed. She wasn't going to cry, not over a man. She'd known from the first that Michael wore power and control as comfortably as he wore those battered tennis shoes. She wasn't disappointed, not really, because she hadn't hoped, hadn't started to believe...

She whirled away from the door and away from the little inner voice calling her a liar. She reached for the anger, stoked it, preferring its heat to the numbing pain. So he was as adept at wielding that control over the lives of others as he was over unsuspecting companies. She'd let herself ignore that quality of his, overlook it in the face of his other traits, which she'd found infinitely more endearing. It was better that she find out now, rather than later, after she'd reached a point of no return with him.

But just what point would that be? a small voice inside jeered. And how far past it had she already gone?

With a flash of movement she hurled the tablet across the room, wishing she could cast away her doubts and resentments as easily.

Michael couldn't prevent an idiotic grin from tilting his lips. Anticipation had been building in him since the moment he'd heard Kate's voice on the phone. It had been a welcome change from the constant haggling that had taken place in his office the past few days. When Kate had told him she wanted to see him no matter what time he finished that evening, expectancy had begun to ride him hard. It had taken another two hours before he'd been able to bring the meeting to a close, and he hadn't even winced at the hour they'd set to begin tomorrow. All he cared about was the fact that he would see her. He glanced at the luminous numbers on his car's in-dash clock. In another few minutes.

He'd made a point of talking to her daily, but hurried phone calls were scant satisfaction. The hours he'd been keeping had prevented him from spending any time with her, time he needed to ensure that the bond they'd forged remained strong. She might not be willing to admit it yet, but the fact that she'd insisted on seeing him tonight was surely a good sign.

He pulled up in front of her condo unit and shut off the ignition. She hadn't given any clue about her state of mind, had, in fact, sounded a little distant on the phone. But it had been easy enough to figure out why she was so anxious to see him when she'd said there was something she had to say to him. In person.

The grin spread wider, and he jogged jauntily toward her door. If Kate wanted to thank him for the work he'd ordered done on her condo, he didn't mind a bit doing it in person. As he pounded on the new door, he examined it with a critical eye. His men had done as he requested and installed a sturdy model. He had no doubt that all his instructions had been followed to the letter. That was, after all, what he paid his employees for.

He could hear her on the other side of the door, unlocking the dead bolt. The sound filled him with quiet satisfaction. He'd rest a little easier knowing that her home was more secure. No system was burglarproof of course, but thieves were notoriously lazy. If a job was too difficult, most went on to easier pickings.

The door swung inward then, and he let his senses drown in Kate. Her long hair was left down and just a little wild, the way he liked it, the way that sent his imagination rolling. There was nothing the least suggestive about her shorts and top, but her long slim legs didn't need any fancy adornment to set his mouth watering. He stepped inside and inhaled the light, inherently sexy fragrance that was Kate. He lowered his head for a kiss and found himself embracing empty space. She was already moving into the living room.

He paused for an instant, then turned to shut the door. The security system caught his eye and he spent a few moments inspecting it. It was a top-of-the-line model manufactured by a branch of his company, and he didn't think any others on the market could match it. He strolled about the condo, checking the windows and, finally, the back door. He turned back to Kate, who was watching him expressionlessly, and grinned.

"Well, what do you think?" He approached her eagerly, feeling like a kid at Christmas, waiting for approval of the gift he'd chosen.

"It…was certainly a surprise."

His grin faltered a little, and he watched her more closely.

She didn't seem overcome with gratitude. In fact, he was having a hard time reading just what she *was* feeling.

"I hope you didn't mind my suggestion to spend the day with Chloe," he said more tentatively, and thought, hoped, he saw a slight softening.

"I always enjoy spending time with Chloe."

Relief flickered. She was probably just tired. Spending a day with his daughter would exhaust anyone. The little squirt had more than enough energy for everyone. "I'm sure she loved it, too. And I needed a way to lure you away from your apartment for the day."

She nodded. "Well, your 'lure' was certainly effective. Would you mind explaining, though, just how the workers got inside?"

Something in that cool, collected manner of hers finally registered. This was not a woman who was ready to cover him with kisses for the little surprise he'd arranged. Feeling his way carefully, he said, "Well, I kind of told them…" He broke off when her eyes flashed, then finished the sentence in a mumble. "Where you kept the extra key."

"I see." She offered him a brilliant smile, one that was frighteningly detached. "I guess I should be glad you didn't choose to tell the neighborhood cat burglar."

"Cat burglars usually climb in through windows," he explained helpfully. He thought—no, he was sure he saw her back teeth clench.

"I don't suppose it occurred to you, Michael, when you were arranging this little 'surprise,' that I don't own this condo. My rental agreement stipulates that I cannot make permanent changes to this unit without express permission from the owner."

"Oh, I got permission," Michael replied. "You don't have to worry about that. Your landlord was overjoyed when I explained what I was going to have done." And why shouldn't he have been? he thought smugly. This day's work hadn't come cheaply, and the materials would stay the property of the landlord once Kate moved out. The man had had nothing to lose and a state-of-the-art security system to gain.

She looked at him then. Her eyes were distant, the smile too bright, with strain at the edges. "Well, aren't I lucky? It seems you've thought of everything. But then, you're used to that, aren't you, Michael? Planning sneak maneuvers, take-overs…it all must provide plenty of experience for trying to run other people's lives. After all, if you know what's best for a company, you must know what's best for everyone else, right?"

He blinked. "You're mad," he said, a note of wonderment entering his tone.

Her teeth came together with a snap, and she stalked toward him, fairly radiating temper. Her hands slapped against his chest. "Brilliant deduction," she said through gritted teeth, giving him a shove. The fact that she didn't even sway him seemed to remove the lid on her simmering emotions, allowing them full boil.

"What in God's name were you thinking?" she said, her voice rising. "This—" she waved a hand around her condo "—had to have cost hundreds." Something in his eyes must have alerted her, and she stared hard at him. Aghast, she whispered, "Thousands. Oh, God." Sinking to the rocking chair, she pressed a hand to her stomach. "Do you know how long it will take me to pay that much money back?"

He scowled and took a step toward her. "Kate…"

She held up a hand to stop him. "Don't you dare—don't you even suggest that I accept this from you."

Wisely, he stopped where he was, but she couldn't keep him from explaining. "I worry about you. I just wanted to make your place a little safer, that's all."

"No," she corrected him caustically, "what you wanted was to make decisions for me, to control me."

Astonishment threatened to render him speechless. "Where did you get that idea? Honey, you're way off base."

Her head shot up, and her eyes flashed. "Oh, am I? Am I really? Let's recount what happened here. *You* think—" the inflection she gave the word made his eyes narrow "—that I could use more security. I tell you that should I wish such measures, I'll take care of them myself." Her chin rose challengingly. "Do you remember that particular conversation?"

He jammed his hands into his pockets, hard, and remained stubbornly silent.

"So, knowing that I don't choose to make those changes to my apartment at this time, you get the brilliant idea of doing it for me. After all, what do I know about what I want, anyway? Surely Michael Friday, the terror of the corporate world, is the best judge of what I need." She cocked her head at a challenging angle. "Isn't that about it?"

This conversation was so far removed from the one he'd thought he would be having with her that his mind was having difficulty making the adjustment. Her words were like small, sharp knives slicing at him. He still wasn't exactly sure how his intentions had gone so awry. All he knew was that each word she uttered was another stone in the wall she was building between them. The knowledge made his chest go tight. His first inclination was to tear down that wall, shatter her defenses in whatever way possible. He used all his willpower to keep his muscles relaxed, his voice even.

"You're wrong."

The simple words seemed to ignite her temper further. "Oh, am I? Am I really?"

Her disbelieving tone stirred the embers of his own temper. He strode over to where she was seated and bent down, shoving his face close to hers. "Yes, you are. I never gave a thought to 'controlling' you."

Her chin tilted up and their faces were so close they were almost touching. Glare for glare, temper for temper, she matched him. "Then what do you call all this?"

"I call it trying to keep you safe." Each word was bit out with measured precision. "I call it showing you that I care."

That last word scored a direct hit. It showed in her eyes, the way they widened. Doubt flickered across her face, and her voice was a little less combative when she spoke again.

"This wasn't the way to show it."

He straightened and dragged a hand through his hair. "You're telling me."

"C'mon, Michael, you have to admit it's not exactly hearts and flowers. I mean, a home security system?" Her voice tapered off a little when he fixed her with a steely look. "It's not the normal way most men would go about convincing someone, a woman, that they—"

"Care?" he finished for her grimly. "But I'm not most men, am I, Kate? I'll tell you what kind of man I am. The kind who wants to protect those he cares about. The kind who worries about their safety."

He saw the recognition in her eyes and knew she was remembering him telling her as much. But because stubbornness and doubt still showed on her face and because they fed the stream of anger he was trying to hold in check, he didn't let her off the hook. Not yet.

Turning half away from her, he said levelly, "But I can see how you reached the conclusion you did."

"You can?"

He ignored the cautious hope threading her voice and nodded. "Certainly. You placed a very different interpretation on my actions."

"Yes, I did."

"Taken in the worst possible light, I'll admit you could interpret my actions as controlling." He paused to read the agreement on her face before adding, "If you'll admit that I could interpret your actions as trying to use me."

"Use you?" She bounced out of the chair and approached him. While he watched blandly, her eyes started shooting blue sparks as her temper flared again. She raked him up and down with her gaze. "I'll admit that you'd make a handy doorstop, but just how else do you figure I could use you?"

He crossed his arms across his chest and met her scowl for scowl. "For sex."

"Sex!" Mouth hanging open, she stared at him in silent astonishment. When she regained her power of speech, she seemed capable of only a sputter. "You...you...brainless... egomaniacal...big...jerk! If I wanted someone on call for sex, what makes you think I'd mess with you? There are plenty of men willing to fulfill that role who aren't half as irritating as you are!'' She thrust her hand in her hair, turning away from him in disbelief. She must have sensed his slight move toward her, because her elbow shot out and caught him in the stomach. He released a slight whoosh of air.

''As if I were that shallow, that casual...that...that...''

His hands caught her stiff shoulders and turned her gently around to face him. ''I know,'' he said simply.

Nonplussed, she stared at him, as if wondering if he was trying to drive her crazy. ''You know?''

He nodded, feeling a bit more cheerful. ''Sure I know. You're not the type of woman interested in only a physical relationship. You'd have to really care about a man before you'd get involved with him.''

''That's right,'' she agreed, but was stopped short by the beatific smile that spread across his face. He'd boxed her neatly into a corner, and for an instant she looked hunted.

''I accept that,'' he said softly, reaching for her, relieved when she didn't try to avoid his touch. Kneading her shoulders with gentle fingers, he continued, ''And I want you to accept that I care about you, too. Maybe this hang-up I have about safety and security for those I care about is just paranoia. But that's what motivated me, Kate.'' He tipped her chin up with one crooked finger. ''Caring, not control.''

Her gaze met his for an instant, then skittered away. She moistened her lips, and when she spoke, she was careful not to look at him. ''This isn't what I meant by keeping it simple, Michael.''

His thumbs rubbed some of the knots out of her shoulders. ''I told you it couldn't be simple.'' But she was still and tense before him, and a cold premonition pierced him even before she spoke again.

She ducked from beneath his touch slowly, with an awkward movement very different from her usual grace. She seemed to pace aimlessly in the small apartment, but when she came to a stop, the length of the sofa was between them.

His eyes narrowed. That distance wasn't lost on him.

''I need some time.'' She rubbed a weary hand across her

forehead, and if her words hadn't struck him with bolts of terror, he'd have felt sorry for her. She looked almost forlorn standing there. "This isn't...it isn't working out the way I thought it could." She dropped her hand, and her eyes looked haunted. "I have to figure this out. Just please...please, Michael, give me some time."

She was slipping away from him. Everything inside him wanted to lunge for her, to hold on tight, to prevent her from vanishing from his life. He stayed where he was, his hands fisted at his sides. "You don't need time. You need to face up to your feelings." That brought some emotion to her face, to her voice. And he thought he'd much rather be faced with her annoyance than her detachment.

"Oh, so now you're an expert on my feelings, as well?" she said caustically. "Does that expertise come from the corporate world? Can you take over someone's thoughts and feelings as easily as you take over a company?"

His mouth flattened and he swallowed a retort, swallowed the anger and fear that threatened to swamp him. Anger and fear wouldn't get through the wall she put between them, it would only add another brick to it. "Shutting me out won't solve anything."

She heaved a huge breath and pushed her hair back from her face. He clenched fingers that itched to follow suit. "I'll be the judge of that," she said somewhat shakily. "I want you to leave now, and I'll let you know if...when I want to see you again."

He caught her verbal slip. The fear was back, but it was doing battle with pride, and losing. "If that's what you want." He'd survived rejection before, and with very little effort would again. Probably. If it left a deep and ragged void in him this time, it would be easy enough to fill. He had Chloe, he had his work, he had... He refused to believe that was emptiness already seeping in. This shot all his plans to hell and back, and maybe that was why he felt as if a vise were squeezing his chest. But that didn't mean he was going to beg.

Without another word he turned away and walked to the

door. His hands were unsteady as they reached for the knob. The sound of the door closing behind him shouldn't have sounded so final. So bleak.

And it shouldn't have filled him with a sick certainty that he'd just lost something he could never hope to replace.

Chapter 13

Michael drove like an automaton, his sports car eating up the freeway. It was easier not to think, not to feel. But he knew reaction was only minutes away. Reality wasn't kind enough to allow numbness to remain permanently.

He roared off an exit ramp, his headlights slicing through the darkness. He drove the car expertly, trying to direct all his awareness into an appreciation for its speed and handling. When he reached the canopied, winding roads of Great Falls, he reluctantly slowed down. He wasn't interested in wrapping his Jag around one of the huge trees hovering at the roadside.

Feeling was already returning, seeping through his determined resistance. And with it came thought. Both had refused to stay banished for long.

He'd lost her.

The knowledge hammered at the base of his skull in painful dissonance. A roaring in his ears accompanied the certainty, and his gut felt hollow. Somehow, some way, his actions had conspired against him in the most baffling manner and driven a wedge between them. A wedge, hell, he thought bitterly. More like a damn fortress.

The darkness of the night mirrored his soul. Moonlight slivered through the treetops, offering only miserly glimpses of silver. It was for the best. If he tried hard enough, long enough, he'd be able to convince himself of that. He didn't have the time to spare away from Chloe, from the business to try to get a clue on just how Kate's mind worked. If she couldn't accept the fact that someone cared about her, that was her problem.

But right now it was feeling a lot like he was the one with the problem. The air in the car seemed to shrink and go stale. Taking each curve and dip of the shadowy road with unconscious ease, he hit the buttons to lower the electric windows. The balmy night air rushed into the confines of the vehicle but failed to relieve his strangled lungs.

He hauled in a giant breath. Okay, so forgetting his plans for a relationship with Kate Rose wasn't going to be easy. But he'd faced disappointment before, hadn't he? He was a master at weighing the odds and cutting his losses when they didn't stack up favorably. There was no reason for this situation to be any different. He'd clouded it with emotions, always dangerous. But he was through with those emotions now, ready to lock them away, and he hoped like hell he never had to deal with them again.

Lord, it was stifling in here. His hand went to the tie he'd loosened hours ago, yanking it free from his shirt. His fingers tripped over themselves working a couple more shirt buttons open. The task didn't relieve the suffocating grip on his lungs. He was lucky this thing with Kate had ended before he'd gotten in any deeper. He'd always hated to walk away from a situation he'd invested heavily in. This wasn't business, of course, but a personal relationship followed the same rules, didn't it? And he really didn't have that much invested in Kate. After all, it wasn't as if he were in lo—

His fingers froze on the wheel. A creature of the night scampered across the road in front of him and froze there for an instant, reflecting his own immobility. When it raced to safety, his half-formed errant thought did the same.

He shifted his foot to the brake and the powerful car responded, tires squealing as he slowed rapidly. There was no more than a foot at each side of the road separating it from the woods, but there were plenty of private drives winding through the trees to houses set well back. He pulled into the first one he saw and just sat for a moment, trying to get his breath. But that seemed impossible.

Opening his door, he stumbled out of the car and leaned weakly against it. The heat that enveloped him left a sheen on his skin, a fine tremor in his limbs. He dropped his hands to his knees and panted raggedly. He'd never experienced an anxiety attack, and since many would swear he didn't possess nerves, he had never expected to. But something gripped him right now and was threatening to rob him of every reasonable response.

Get ahold of yourself, he ordered mentally, his breath coming in huge gulps. The thing to do in a crisis was focus. Focus. He forced his lungs to work more rhythmically by sheer, fierce will. He pushed feelings aside; they screwed everything up, anyway. If this was, in fact, a business deal, before he'd cut his losses he'd tally up pros and cons and weigh them both carefully.

Yeah. The breath billowed out of him in one long stream of air. Already the mental ledger was flipping open in his head, eager for the application of logic and cool, calculated reason. Kate or no Kate? Which represented the greater risk?

She was intriguing, yes. She'd intrigued him from the start. Chalk one up for the pro side of the ledger. But intriguing was just a stone's throw from maddening, wasn't it? The woman threw him more curves than the Orioles's starting pitcher. Confusing definitely settled on the con side.

The businesslike tallying was soothing, and he straightened weakly, leaning against the car. On the pro side he'd definitely have to add gorgeous. Sexy. Loved kids. Got along great with Chloe. And Chloe thought Kate was wonderful, as well. But Kate sure didn't trust easily and was prickly as an irritated porcupine about her independence. Add those to the opposite side.

He ran a hand through his hair, feeling a measure of normalcy returning. This was where he'd erred to begin with, when he'd strayed too far from profit-and-loss analysis. Personal relationships should function more like those in business, he reflected. It made everything far more practical and eliminated hormone-laden decision making. Not that hormones weren't important in a personal relationship; his sure responded each time he was near Kate. Another positive. And he genuinely liked her. Respected her. Cared about her. He circled around that admission, deemed it safe. He even cared...deeply. He only wished she was as straightforward about her emotions, he thought self-righteously. If she confronted them head-on, as he had, maybe she'd stop throwing up roadblocks every time he got too close.

It didn't take a rocket scientist to figure out that he still had far more to gain by proceeding with his plans regarding Kate than by bowing out. And if he was truthful with himself, it was what he wanted. He wanted to marry her. He wanted to settle into a life with her, one that would be rich and fulfilling for both of them. He wanted to make a family with her and Chloe. That hadn't changed.

Ice-edged panic glided up his spine and curved painfully across his heart. After the scene tonight, she was lost to him as surely as if she'd been removed from this planet. She might have seemed confused, but she'd left no room for doubt as to what she'd wanted. Him gone. If he'd brought about that response by telling her he cared about her, he would terrify her if he mentioned marriage.

He swallowed hard as the nerves threatened to punch through him again. All he had to do was stick to his original plan. Marriage would come at the culmination of a relationship filled with mutual affection, respect, trust and damn good sex. It would happen, if he didn't allow himself to go haywire with emotion.

Air trickled back into his lungs, and with it came resolve. He'd messed up tonight, primarily because he didn't understand Kate well enough yet to predict how his actions would affect her. His first mistake had been in not forcing her to tell him what was behind her fierce need for independence. His second mistake had been leaving her in the first place. Determination had him turning to get back in the car.

He switched on the ignition and backed out of the driveway, heading for the city. He wouldn't make the same error twice tonight. And this time, he vowed, he was going to show a measure of the finesse he was capable of. Somehow he'd make her understand. And accept.

He reached for his car phone and dialed her number. Impatiently, he waited through five rings before she answered. Not bothering with a greeting, he said shortly, "It's me. Don't hang up. I'm coming over again, and I want to talk to you." Her weary protest had his lips firming. "I'll be there, Kate. And you'll either open the door, or I'll shout what I have to say for the whole neighborhood to hear." The crashing of the receiver in his ear signaled her displeasure. He flipped the phone off and pressed more firmly on the accelerator. He had about twenty minutes to come up with a way to persuade her to give him another chance. He kept the gnawing fear at bay by refusing to contemplate failure.

The single light above her porch was glowing, and a relieved breath escaped him at the sight. She was up, and she was going to let him in. That was a start. He hadn't relished playing this scene out for the entertainment of her neighbors.

He bounded out of the car and up her walk, wiping his palms on his pant legs. Hesitating on her porch, he took a moment to marshall his arguments, but the door swung open, robbing him of that small advantage.

Kate glared at him with sullen defiance. His gaze feasted on her hungrily. She had obviously showered; her hair was still half-wet and drying in riotous curls down her back. She was barefoot and clad in a white terry cloth robe. She backed away to let him enter, then turned and walked into the living room, sinking onto the couch.

Michael paused awkwardly before following her. Somehow, in the face of her stubborn silence, his carefully rehearsed persuasiveness was fading away. He battled to hang on to the unnatural calm that had settled over him on the way here. If he gave in to the pendulum of panic and despair that had enveloped him on the way home, he was lost.

"Thanks for seeing me."

Her brow arched. "Well, you didn't leave me with much of a choice, did you?"

He swallowed around the knot in his throat. This wasn't starting out promisingly. "No," he admitted. "It was important that I see you again tonight. Too important to wait."

Her eyes flashed, and he knew he'd misjudged the depth of her resentment. "Important to whom? Ah, yes. To Michael. The only one whose wishes count."

Because he couldn't think of anything else to do with them, he thrust his hands into his pockets. "Believe me, Kate, I didn't come here to make you uncomfortable."

"No, I don't believe you did," she said coolly. After the barest of pauses, she added, "I think you came because I was right earlier."

He eyed her blankly.

"When I said you needed to be in control. That's what this is about, Michael, and you can deny it all you want. It doesn't make the truth go away." She shot from the couch like a tightly coiled spring to pace in the small area of the room. "You call and say you're coming, so naturally I'm expected to let you in. That's the way you planned it, isn't it?" Her eyes were sheets of blue lightning. "You're very good at getting your way."

"Control seems to be a big issue with you." It took effort to keep his voice even. "Why don't you tell me what's behind that? Or should I be asking who's behind it?"

Her expression froze and she stopped in her tracks, her eyes huge and haunted. For an instant he thought she would crumple, and his muscles bunched, ready to spring to her aid. Then slowly, visibly, she straightened and tucked that momentary weakness back out of sight. "My father used power in lieu of emotion." Her voice was void of inflection. "He dictated everything we ate, where we went, how we wore our hair, how we spent our time. We could barely breathe in that house without checking with him first. Going away to college was the first decision I ever made on my own, and he's never forgiven me for doing so without his permission. I'm not allowed to spend time alone with my youngest siblings. He's afraid they'll pick up notions of independence the way you pick up a virus. I think I understand the reason he is the way he is. But that doesn't mean I respect him.''

The last words sounded as though they had been ripped out of her, leaving a jagged wake of pain. He was sure they had. He knew too well that resentment could be a double-edged sword. The need to comfort, to explain was instinctive.

''My actions were motivated with the emotion your father lacked. Caring, Kate. Not control. Maybe that doesn't make it okay, but I'd like to think if you'd ever shared any of this with me before that I would have acted differently.''

She just stared at him, those deep blue eyes giving no hint of her thoughts. Desperation leaked in through the cracks of the careful shore of confidence he'd rebuilt on the way over. ''All I'm asking is that you trust me, just a little. Just enough to give me the benefit of the doubt when I say I would never do anything to hurt you. Enough to believe me when I say I don't want to control you or make you unhappy. Hell, I want to marry you.''

He watched the shocked dismay flood across her face with chagrin, and if he could have reached his own butt, he'd have kicked it. Blurting it out like that wasn't the wisest move he'd ever made, but he was rapidly finding that wisdom wasn't always a conscious choice. So much for well-laid plans.

Kate actually swayed under the impact of his words, and her face went as white as the terry cloth. She brushed at the hair that tumbled over her shoulder with a hand that trembled visibly. Her reaction did nothing to relieve the tightness in his chest.

''Marriage,'' she echoed bleakly. The hollow shock in her eyes had talons of fear clawing through his gut, piercing deep. She shook her head slightly, as if to clear it, and reached a blind, searching hand behind her for the sofa. She dropped onto it as if her legs had suddenly given out. ''Michael, this isn't what I meant by keeping it simple. Marriage." She took a deep breath and released it. "This isn't simple at all."

Because he couldn't stand the distance between them for another instant, he crossed the room and sank down beside her. "God knows I've messed this up," he murmured, as much to himself as to her. He reached down for her hand and measured his palm against hers. "Just tell me you'll think about it. Think about us. We could have it all, Kate." He linked their fingers, watched her intently as her gaze slowly rose to his. "We could be a family. You, me, Chloe and as many more kids as you want." Her eyes flickered at his words, and he allowed himself to take hope from the tiny sign of emotion. "I told you I cared about you, and I know you feel the same way about me." Still she was silent, and he urged, "You do, don't you?"

She nodded jerkily without releasing his gaze. Relief slid like a balm over his nerves. His free hand rubbed soothingly up her arm, then cruised down again in a repetitive, rhythmic motion. "What do you say we let the past stay there. In the past. The present is ours, yours and mine. I'll give you all the time you need to decide what you want in your future. No pressure, no strings."

She shook her head wearily. "No pressure? What do you call this?"

He released her only to pull her closer, turning her so that her shoulders rested against his torso. In a gesture evocative of comfort rather than desire, he folded his arms around her and hugged her to him. Resting his cheek on the top of her head, he rocked them both slowly.

"Let's not worry about labels," he murmured into her hair. "Let's just concentrate on each other."

Michael rose from the table as Jake started replacing papers in folders. "I've got everything I need," the lawyer said. "I'll get together with Hummels and his attorney myself tomorrow."

"Make sure he understands this is my final offer," Michael said.

Jake placed the files in his leather briefcase and snapped the lock shut. "It shouldn't be much longer. I could tell we had him intrigued when you suggested putting him in charge of research with a generous budget."

"We were right all along."

Jake nodded. "He's definitely got some project in his head that he's dying to get financing for. And it must be expensive if he couldn't even count on the cash from marketing the microchip to finance it. He's still trying to create a loophole, wanting us to sign off on any future projects he's the sole creator of."

Michael snorted. "Fat chance. The music has stopped, but he's still dancing. You can let him know that he has until 5:00 p.m. today to agree. The offer goes down by a million each additional day he delays."

Jake grinned wolfishly. "I'll tell him." As he left the office, he passed Carla Patrie on her way in.

Michael sighed and looked at his watch. He was determined that today would be his last in the office for a while. But taking care of loose ends had already cost him most of the day. His frustration only partially stemmed from that fact, however. It had been too damn long since he'd heard from Kate, approximately fifty-eight hours and counting, as a matter of fact. When he'd left her at dawn the other morning, she'd avoided his eyes but had promised to contact him later. He'd agreed, noting the relief flickering across her face when he hadn't argued.

He'd promised her some time without pressure. And there was too much at stake for him to push, even a little. But that didn't make the waiting any easier. And although he'd felt a measure of confidence return at the way she'd allowed him to hold her throughout the night, the panic and fear were merely held in check for the moment. Kate hadn't given him any indication of what her response to his proposal would be. He didn't dare take her answer for granted.

"Don't scowl so, Michael, this really won't take long," Carla said. She strolled to the table with a studied grace. Her bright red suit was perfectly matched by the polish on her long nails. Her black hair was cut so it just barely grazed her shoulders. When she passed him, she trailed an expensive, musky perfume that was designed to raise a man's blood pressure.

It left Michael unmoved. It couldn't compare to the punch-in-the-gut scent Kate wore, one that had more to do with her own essence than any manufactured aroma. There was nothing about Carla that could compare to Kate in any way. Carla was savvy and tough, and she exuded ambition and brains. He'd hired her for the second quality, forgiven her for the first. She dropped the sheaf of papers she was holding on the table.

"What's this?" he asked.

"I've finalized the plans for the most comprehensive marketing strategy this company has ever seen," she said smugly.

"For the home computer security system Derek completed?"

"None other. That little system, Michael, is about to take programming America by storm. I mean, I've planned the works. Television, radio, software magazine advertising…not to mention hiring Jerome Livingston, the Madison Avenue advertising guru."

As he quickly scanned the outline she'd placed before him, his eyebrows climbed. "This plan of yours is going to take our budget by storm, too."

"You have to be willing to invest in advertising your project if you want to get maximum return."

"Have you run these numbers by Dennison in accounting?" he questioned.

She shook her head impatiently. "The man has no vision, Michael."

"He's not supposed to have vision," he answered wryly. "He's a numbers man." He listened as she gave her pitch again, then read through the papers more carefully. Finally he halted her in the midst of her spiel. "Go see Dennison. Tell him I'll authorize a ten percent higher advertising budget on this project. Anything over that, and I mean a penny over, will have to be approved by me personally."

Carla looked triumphant as she gathered the papers together. "Smart move, Michael. We're going to make you rich." She stacked the papers into a pile and then tapped them with a flaming nail. "Actually, I've got a suggestion that will save you some money."

Michael cocked a brow. "Do tell."

She leaned forward, crossing her leg and showing a smooth expanse of thigh. "The open house we have planned to coincide with the marketing blitz? Rather than spending a mint on renting a place with the right atmosphere, why don't you consider having it at your home?"

He blinked. "At my place?"

Carla pressed her advantage. "Sure, why not? I hear it's fabulous, and with all the newspaper and software magazine execs invited, it will give the publicity a more personal angle."

"I realize you've never seen my home, Carla, or you'd never have suggested this."

She frowned at his lack of enthusiasm. "No, I haven't, but from what I've heard, it's certainly spacious enough."

"Oh, space is one thing it has plenty of," he agreed ironically. "The thing that's missing is furniture." When she looked blank, he continued. "It doesn't have any. Or not much."

Carla shrugged. "Well, that's not a problem. You've got three weeks before the open house is scheduled. Get a decorator."

"Why is this so important to you?" he quizzed. Carla didn't reply, but her fingernail tapped faster. A slow smile crossed his face. "You couldn't book a place for the open house, is that it?"

Raising her chin, she snapped, "We're on a tight schedule, Michael, and it is the wedding season. All the appropriate places were taken months ago. If you hadn't stonewalled me for so long about setting a date for the program's completion—"

His hand went to his chest in a gesture of innocence. "You're going to blame this on me?"

"It's not as if I couldn't find *something,*" she said smoothly, "but why settle for less than what we need when the perfect solution is right in front of us? Really, Michael, you couldn't get better publicity if you tried."

He looked at her, mulling the idea over. He'd tightened security at the house even more when he started working on FORAY there. With the additional precautions he'd taken, he was actually in a better position to do as Carla asked.

"I could give you the names of some interior design firms who are very reputable. And it sounds like it's past time for you to contract with one of them, anyway."

Resigned, Michael heaved a breath. "Just how desperate are you?"

Carla composed her features and lifted her chin. "Very," she admitted after a long minute. "The only places that would be available are either too small or so far in the suburbs that half the invited guests wouldn't come. The longer we wait for something to become free, the more expensive this whole thing becomes."

"We could go ahead with the marketing plan and drop the open house idea," he suggested hopefully.

That nail began tapping again, mirroring the frustration on Carla's face. "And risk a drastic reduction in preliminary sales."

He gave up. Rising, he muttered, "Fine. We'll do it at my place."

Carla smiled with satisfaction and rose, as well. "Good idea. I'll get you a list of firms that might be able to help you get the house ready."

"No thanks," he muttered. "You've already done enough."

He propped his hips against the corner of the table as she left the office and scrubbed both hands over his face, wondering just what the hell he'd let himself in for. It looked as though he were going to have to break down and hire one of those damn interior designers he'd avoided so scrupulously in the past.

Dropping his hands, he scowled at the thought. As if he

didn't have enough to do, now he was going to have to embroil himself in discussions with some long-haired, ponytailed moron about furnishings in ice-cream colors whose names he couldn't even bring himself to pronounce. He consoled himself with the thought that if he hated the results, he could always have the whole works hauled away and start over.

His intercom sounded. "You have a visitor, Mr. Friday." Bernie's voice wasn't quite as surly as usual. The next moment he knew why.

"Daddy, it's me!"

Michael's morose mood dropped away when he heard his daughter squeal enthusiastically into the intercom.

"Me who?" he asked, pretending to be mystified.

"Me Chloe! You know me!"

"Oh, Miss Friday, is that you? Please come in. I've been expecting you."

"He's expecting me," she announced to the occupants of the outer office.

Trask's voice sounded then. "Chloe, let up on the button."

The voices abruptly went silent and then Chloe was bursting through his door, hurtling toward her father. Michael caught her in his arms and swung her around until the room was filled with her giggles. When she was out of breath, he settled her on one hip. "So, shortstuff, where have you been?"

"I just got done with my first tumbling lesson and I asked Trask if we could stop here to see you and he said yes but if you were busy we had to go home but I knew you wouldn't be busy," she said, the words all running together.

"I'm almost done for the day. I'm just waiting for a call from Jake," Michael said to Trask. He turned his attention back to his daughter. "Did you learn anything at gymnastics today?"

She nodded enthusiastically. "I'll show you." She wiggled down from his arms and squatted on the floor, doing a series of somersaults across the room.

Michael and Trask clapped dutifully. Chloe beamed at them. "I already knew how to do a somersault, that's baby stuff, but now I can do a whole bunch of them all in a row. I could have done more but you have too much furniture in here, Daddy.''

''You did just fine,'' Michael assured her.

''And guess what Trask signed me up for this afternoon?''

Michael raised his eyebrows at Trask, who appeared to be looking anywhere except at his employer.

''T-ball!''

''T-ball?'' repeated Michael blankly.

''It's baseball, sir, for little ones. They hit the ball off a stand…'' Trask's voice trailed off and he shrugged. ''They were signing up at the rec center and she seemed interested. I thought—''

''You going to be a ballplayer, champ?'' Michael asked his daughter.

She nodded enthusiastically. ''We have a practice on Saturday. Can I go, Daddy, please, please, please?''

''Well,'' said Michael amusedly, ''since Trask thinks it's a good idea, I guess I have to agree, don't I?''

''See, Trask?'' Chloe said triumphantly. ''I told you it would be okay with Daddy.''

''Your schedule is going to be so busy you won't even be able to squeeze me in.''

She giggled. ''I can't squeeze you into anything, Daddy. You're too big. You wouldn't even fit under my bed.''

While Chloe practiced her somersaults, Michael ran the open house idea past Trask. ''What do you think?''

''We could minimize the security risks. With the extra help we hired, there shouldn't be any problems. I think you're forgetting something, though.'' When Michael raised his brows, he reminded him, ''The house is pretty empty. How are you going to get it ready in—'' He looked inquiringly at Michael.

''Three weeks.''

''In three weeks?''

''I'll think of something,'' he said, and then glared at the doubtful look on Trask's face.

Chloe picked that moment to somersault across the room

and landed at her father's feet. Bouncing up, she hugged his leg and demanded, "Come home, Daddy. It's lonely there without you."

He ruffled her long blond hair. "Well, guess what, short-stuff? It's lonely *here* without *you.*" He looked at Trask. "I'm not going to be more than a couple hours. Why don't you two head home and plan something to eat tonight. I'll be home in time for dinner."

"And then you'll stay home," insisted Chloe.

"And then I'll stay home."

"And tomorrow you'll take me to T-ball."

"And tomorrow I'll take you to T-ball," he repeated obediently.

"Then we'll go home and cook up a wonderful sa-prise for you, Daddy. You're gonna love it. Come, Trask," she said with a queenly air. Then she ruined the effect by practicing her somersaults all the way out the door.

Still smiling, Michael crossed to his desk and dropped down into his chair. Resignedly, he reached for the phone book, flipping to the yellow pages. The number of decorating firms listed, he discovered, filled more than a dozen pages. He scanned the names, but his mind was already wandering.

It wasn't some fancy design outfit he wanted to call, it was Kate. The telephone, only inches away, beckoned temptingly. Just one call, he mentally justified to himself. Only one. A few minutes spent talking to her to find out whether she was all right. Whether she'd been thinking about him as much as he had her.

He forgot his desultory search in the phone book and leaned back in his chair. The knot in his gut seemed a permanent fixture, caused by uncertainty. He needed to know what she was thinking, what she was deciding. Their future depended on her decision, and because it did, he couldn't call her. He'd promised Kate time without pressure. He hadn't realized how difficult it was going to be to live up to that promise, but he was going to do so if it killed him. Which it seemed to be doing, in torturous, bloodless increments.

His intercom sounded, and he slapped his palm against it,

turning it off. He didn't want to see anyone else at his office. There was only one person he wanted to see, *needed* to see, and that one person was denied to him, at least for now.

His office door opened then, and when he looked up, he thought for a moment that his imagination had obligingly conjured up the woman who had filled his mind.

"Kate," he breathed. She looked every bit the vision he'd first thought her. Her hair was piled on top of her head, probably in deference to the heat outside. She was wearing a one-piece black short outfit that ended several inches above her knees, with matching sandals. He decided she could wear sackcloth and look as if she'd just stepped off a runway.

"Hello, Michael."

She shut the door in back of her, and the motion finally snapped him out of his self-induced reverie. He rose from his chair and rounded his desk, stopping to lean against its corner. She was here, as if he'd summoned her by the fierce need inside him, and suddenly anxiety was crowding aside his pleasure at the sight of her. His mouth went dry and his palms became clammy.

"I was at the library all day, but when I called your house, no one answered. I took the chance of catching you here." When he didn't answer, her gaze finally settled on him. "I hope that's all right."

"Yes." The word had to be forced from his throat, so he cleared it and tried again. "I've been wanting to see you. Talk to you."

"You didn't call, though."

"You asked for time."

She nodded and fiddled with a tendril of hair that had refused to stay restrained. It framed her jaw in a soft spiral. It finally occurred to him then that she matched him for nervousness. He couldn't for the life of him decide whether or not that was a good sign.

When he spoke there was none of the gut-wrenching anxiety he felt, none of the need, only mild curiosity in his voice. "You needed time, you said, without pressure, to think about us. What did you decide, Kate?"

His question hung suspended in the air between them, an invisible challenge. Almost as soon as it left his mouth, he wanted to call it back. If she was here to tell him it was over, he was in no hurry to hear the words. But the uncertainty he'd been living with was as vicious as any ending could be, and he was not a man to endure either patiently.

She left her position at the door and moved into the room, skirting his desk to move toward the long table where they'd sat at their first meeting. Trailing her fingers over the backs of the chairs, she finally responded to his question. "I've decided that I'm a coward."

He shook his head. "No."

One corner of her mouth curled wryly. "Oh, yes. It's far easier to push you away than to decide what I really want."

The air in the room was suddenly in short supply. "Are you through pushing?"

Her gaze met his for the first time since she'd entered the room. "Yes."

He closed his eyes for a second, relief welling up inside him, so sharp that it threatened to choke him.

"I don't know if it's fair to you," she continued in a low voice. "I'm nowhere close to accepting your proposal. I don't know what my decision will be or when it will come."

He could look beyond her doubts and see the confusion in her eyes, and the protectiveness bubbled up inside him, demanding a release. "Take all the time you need." He wanted to wipe that worry from her lovely face, so he let one corner of his mouth quirk up. "I promised you no pressure, remember? You're in control. You're top dog. Head honcho. Chief banana. Do with me as you will."

Her expression lightened a fraction. "Don't be a jerk, Michael."

With mock seriousness he replied, "I'll try very hard not to be, Kate." He savored her sudden smile and the accompanying kick in the chest it brought him.

She walked toward him and curled her fingers around his. Settling his hips more comfortably against the desk, he drew her slowly to him and rested his forehead against hers. "I've missed you," he murmured.

Her eyes squeezed shut. "Me, too."

He reached out with his free hand, skimming the back of his knuckles along her delicate jawline. He found the exquisitely soft skin below her ear and traced a fingertip there. "We'll take it as slow as you want," he murmured, and meant it. "You'll get all the time you need, but not distance." His arms closed around her then, and he was grateful when she leaned into them willingly. "I can't stand one more hour wondering when I'm going to see you again."

Her head tilted up so that she could meet his eyes. He fancied that he could read a slight lessening of doubt in them. "I can't give you any guarantees."

His answer was spoken against her lips. "Life's a series of risks." And then his mouth sank onto hers. Relief, hope and need tangled inside him. He let himself drown in the pleasure of touching her, letting her taste, her smell, the incredible softness of her skin combine into an explosion of sensations that stripped his mind clean. The need for her was instant, and their time apart had it honed as sharp as a knife.

When she tore her mouth from his, his lips followed demandingly. But her words stopped him. "There's one more thing."

He took a deep breath and consciously loosened his hold. "More conditions, Kate?"

"You might think so."

Because he didn't trust his hands not to fist, he released her to grasp the edge of the desk in back of him. "Okay, let's have them."

She fumbled with her purse, and he took great satisfaction in noting that her hands were inclined to tremble. But that small measure of satisfaction was wiped away when he saw what she was taking out and handing him.

A check. He read the amount but didn't reach for it. His gaze met hers, and he observed the determination there.

"Take it. There will be one every month until I've paid you back for those improvements you made at my condo."

Temper threatened to shred the earlier vows he'd made about patience. "Why would you pay for security measures you never wanted in the first place?"

Her eyes were clear and her gaze steady. "My house, Michael. My responsibility."

Responsibility. He'd learned the hard way how she felt about it, how she felt about maintaining control over her own life. The thought of her having to strain her budget to pay him back for his stupid blunder made his jaw tighten. She would insist that he accept it because she wouldn't be obligated to anyone. Another thought occurred to him then, and he flicked the check with one finger. "Maybe this won't be necessary."

"It's very necessary…" she started tartly, and he laid his fingers against her lips.

"What I'm thinking is that we can sort of trade services."

Her eyes above his hand narrowed suspiciously. He smiled at her, slow and engaging. God, she was lovely. "I kind of got myself in a bind today, and I could use some help."

She pushed his hand away. "I'm not much good at corporate takeovers."

"But you're great at decorating." Quickly he told her about the upcoming open house.

"Michael, that's only three weeks away. How are you ever going to find a firm that can get things ready that…oh, no." She put a hand up to ward off his wheedling smile. "You can't possibly expect me to—I don't know anything about decorating a house!"

"There really wouldn't be that much to do," he said, trying to convince her. "The rooms are painted, the floors are ready, I mainly just need furniture. We'd concentrate on the downstairs rooms that the people would see."

"But these things take time. Ordering furniture, having things upholstered…"

"I've found that if you wave enough money, vendors are willing to do the impossible." He leaned forward to place a kiss on her lips, stemming her next protest. "Do you know how much money I was prepared to flush for a designer?

Knowing that I'd probably hate what he or she came up with? This is a chance for you to wipe out your ridiculous notion of owing me and help me make my house into a real home while you're at it.''

The thought appealed to her, he could tell as he watched the emotions flit across her expressive face. Pressing his advantage, he murmured, ''I already know that I like what you've done to your condo, and it would give us some time to spend together. You could take me to see the pieces you're considering.'' His arms slid around her waist, drawing her to stand between his legs. His lips went to her neck.

''I suppose we could get a few rooms done in time,'' she mused. ''But it's going to be time-consuming. And you'll have to tell me what you like.''

''Okay.'' His lips cruised up to her ear, and he whispered several colorful suggestions.

''Michael!'' The hue in her cheeks deepened and she brought her palms up to press against his chest. ''I meant your taste in furniture, not your lurid fantasies.''

''You should be more specific.''

''And you should be caged.''

''That sounds fun, too,'' he said agreeably. He nibbled at her neck until the shudders started in her. Then he brought her closer and swept one hand up inside the loose pant leg of her shorts. His fingers explored, and then he touched silk encasing firm, rounded flesh, and he wanted.

He'd spent his life wanting. As a child his wants had been simpler—a better place to live, enough food on the table and more money for his mother. As he'd matured, they'd changed, as well. A home, money, a family and the ability to protect those he cared about.

He was used to the wanting, but the craving was new. It clawed a deep, ragged furrow through him, twisting aside any attempt to harness it. It was the craving for one woman, this woman, and he knew nothing could ever tame it, and no one but she could slake it. It should have been frightening, but instead, bursts of exhilaration dragged in its wake.

He heeded the last semblance of sanity still swirling in his head and tore away from her, striding across the room to lock the door before returning to Kate.

"Nosy secretary," he said by way of explanation, and crowded her against the desk.

Her hands went around his neck without urging, one hand sliding to tangle in his hair. He debated searching for the pins that held the mass of curls on top of her head, but instead he lost himself in the smooth white curve of luscious neck the hairstyle bared.

The need reared up in him, raging and fierce. He went still in her embrace, struggling to control it. There had been too much at stake here today, too many emotions racing beneath the surface, colliding and careening inside him. Control was necessary, because without it his emotions would consume him, consume them both.

Kate's mouth found his and made a mockery of his struggle. Her mouth was avid and heated, and his tongue stabbed its satiny warmth. The kiss was long, deep and wet, and long before it was over he'd forgotten the need for control.

Impatient hands tugged the shirt from his jeans, and his body jolted as they skated up his sides, a long, sensuous glide. He pulled the shirt over his head, and the feel of her hands on his chest triggered the urgency he'd tried, and failed, to suppress. Every clutch of her hand, every gliding caress stripped away layers of manners and carefully cultivated civility, leaving exposed someone he didn't even recognize.

With his hands beneath her hips, he lifted Kate to the edge of his desk, then pressed her knees apart and stepped between them. There was something raging inside him, the craving, the need for her. If he'd seen even the tiniest bit of hesitation on her face, perhaps he could have slowed, could have pulled away. But her expression was fierce, her hold on him more so.

Her fingers found every curve and hollow on his chest and shoulders, and her mouth followed in their wake. He heard her moan, a low, urgent demand of need, and the sound snapped whatever slight hold he had on the civilized. He found her mouth with his and devoured it, even as one hand found a silky thigh and followed it to heat.

He swallowed her gasp of pleasure and let the weight of his body absorb some of her shudders. With the tips of his fingers he flirted with the lace-edged panties, knuckles rubbing against the dampened silk. Her body twisted under his touch, straining upward. Deliberately he stilled, lifting his mouth from hers, waiting for her eyes to flutter open. Then his fingers delved further, burying themselves in the fire he'd ignited, and he watched her eyes unfocus.

He caught her cry in his mouth, pressed closer to her as her hips bucked frantically against his probing hand. His vision grayed, and he shook his head to clear it. He wanted to watch Kate, see her lose herself in pleasure, watch her face as the sensations carried her up to the precipice. With one deft, sure motion, he sent her hurtling over the edge and greedily drank her cry of release. Then he drove her up again.

With shaking, clumsy hands, he unbuttoned her clothes, baring the scraps of lace she wore beneath. He pushed the fabric down her creamy shoulders, following its path with his mouth. With more urgency than finesse he removed the garment from her, and it pooled, forgotten, at their feet.

The filmy undergarments were meant to entice, but he was past teasing. Her bra was released and pushed away, and his mouth closed urgently on her breast. He lingered there, drowning in the taste and smell and softness of her. The flavor of her skin was hotly exotic, and he could dimly hear the dazed whimpers that caught in the back of her throat, while her heart rocketed beneath his lips.

There was sheer animal pleasure in the scrape of her nails on his shoulders, the twist of her fingers in his hair as she sought to bring him closer, as her body strained and shuddered against his greedy mouth. Kaleidoscopic colors burst behind his eyelids, and her hands dropped to the waistband of his jeans.

Gritting his teeth, he warred with her fingers to release the button. He could feel every tooth of the zipper as it raked down his aching length. Covering her hand with his, he dispensed of the task quickly. Kate helped him push the jeans over his hips, her hands staying to cup and caress while he extracted a foil packet from the pocket and kicked the jeans away.

He moved to protect her, fiercely resenting the need to do so. Lowering her back to the desktop, he arranged her legs around his hips, opening her to him. Then he levered himself on top of her and ruthlessly drove up inside her, burying himself to the hilt. *Not yet,* the craving whispered inside the chambers of his mind. *More. Much more.*

He stopped, hauling in great breaths to relieve his strangled lungs. But Kate wasn't willing to wait. Her body surged up beneath him, agile and quick, taking him deeper, harder, faster. Her hands found his, and their fingers interlaced as she rocked them both to madness. He could feel the tightening at the base of his shaft, recognize the mist that swam before his eyes as he raced with her to the culmination. He had one final thought right before he followed her to climax.

It wasn't enough. It would never be enough.

Awareness returned in slow increments. Her soft breathing against his cheek was still not quite steady. His greater weight was holding her pinned beneath him against the unyielding surface of the desk. He propped more of his weight on his elbows, unwilling even yet to leave her. Her nipples were still hard, stabbing lightly at his chest, and incredibly, he could feel his sex stir within her again. Reluctantly, aware of the inadequacy of the protection with each passing moment, he withdrew from her. He caught her by the elbows and helped her up so that she stood between his parted thighs.

He loved that look on her face. Languorous and dreamy, she didn't appear quite ready to rejoin the world. He bent and nuzzled her neck, then kissed her, a sweet, warm kiss that tasted uniquely of Kate. She rubbed her cheek against his chest and kept him close with her arms looped around his waist.

"Honestly, Michael." Her voice wanted to be scandalized but still sounded drugged. "On your desk?"

All that creamy, smooth skin was too much temptation to pass up. "I wouldn't consider desecrating it by using it as a desk again," he assured her, worshiping the lines and curves of her shoulders with his mouth. "After what just happened here, I'm going to turn it into a shrine."

Chapter 14

They'd pulled it off, Kate thought, looking around Michael's house with pride. There had been times during the last three weeks when she would have given up, but no obstacle had been insurmountable when faced with Michael's determination.

And money, she added wryly, because it had been money, incredible amounts of it, that had convinced salesclerks to arrange speedy delivery and tempted custom upholsterers to work quickly. It had been a frenzied time. She'd shopped during the day and studied at night. Now, with her exams finally behind her, and the visible signs of this success before her, she had every right to feel smug.

They'd made a good team. Because he'd said he liked what she'd done with her condo, she'd haunted antique stores, bringing him pictures of pieces and ideas for their placement in his house. Then he'd accompanied her to the stores to buy the pieces he'd decided on. He hadn't been picky, almost always deferring to her judgment. Then there had been reproduction furniture stores to haunt for furniture with similar styles that would be sturdy enough for someone of Michael's size. The end result had been rooms where old and new mingled harmoniously. It looked, finally, like a home.

Longing welled up at the thought. It was Michael's home, and Chloe's. The fact that it could be hers, as well, sent her heart into a fast skitter. She'd been too busy to think about their relationship over the last few weeks, or so she told herself. But the temptation had been there, curling through her consciousness like smoke under a door.

She could marry Michael Friday. Sometimes the idea sent giddy streamers of pleasure cascading inside her. Everything she'd ever wanted was right here; all she had to do was reach out and take it. A home, a family, Michael and Chloe. Almost everything she'd ever hoped for.

And then the doubts would crowd in, layered with paralyzing fear. She'd promised herself that she wouldn't settle, as her mother had, for anything less than love. That word had been glaringly absent from Michael's vocabulary, and she knew the omission wasn't accidental. He was too honest to promise something he couldn't deliver. Strange how that knowledge could be so shattering, even when her own feelings were a hopeless tangle.

Kate walked with a quiet whisper of movement to one of the marble-topped walnut tables she and Michael had picked out. With one finger she made a minuscule adjustment to the frivolous snuffbox sitting there. Michael had spotted it on the way out of one of the antique shops and bought it on impulse. When he'd tried to present it to her, she'd laughed him off, declining.

She didn't want to take anything from him, not with his proposal between them, still unanswered. Somehow, accepting gifts from him would romanticize his offer, which could only lead to disillusionment. She wouldn't allow herself to mistake what he was proposing merely to fill a void inside herself that she'd carried all her life. If she decided to marry Michael Friday, it would be with her eyes wide open. It was the condition of her heart that was still undetermined.

The noise filtering from the kitchen was a quiet, well-ordered bustle. She'd been told politely but firmly the one time she'd inquired that her help wasn't needed. That left her with way too much time on her hands, and after the frantic pace of the last three weeks, the time weighed heavily. It was much too easy to think, to feel. And because she was afraid to examine her feelings, she did a coward's turn. Intending to look for Chloe, she plowed straight into Michael's chest.

"Absolutely fantastic," he murmured, sliding his hands up her arms to cup her shoulders.

"The house looks great, doesn't it?"

He bent down to press his mouth against the exquisitely sensitive skin behind her ear. "I wasn't talking about the house."

Pleasure shimmied down her spine, turning into a shudder when he brushed his lips along her jawline, pausing a fraction above her mouth to whisper, "What do you say we blow off this upcoming exercise in boredom and go upstairs to try out that walnut four-poster with the feather ticking you talked me into buying?"

Her head jerked back and she stared at him. "You mean the Victorian bedroom set? You bought it?"

He nodded slowly, a heated gleam in his eye.

"I didn't know you were interested in it!" she exclaimed. "I thought you wanted to concentrate your purchases for the downstairs, where the party would be." In her excitement, the words began to tumble over themselves. "Did the pieces survive the shipping all right? How do they look? Do you remember the shop where we saw all the antique lace? The bed would be perfect draped in—"

He covered her mouth with his, and the rest of the words slid down her throat. After a thorough kiss, he lifted his lips to mutter aggrievedly, "It's a major blow to my ego to suspect that the bed tempts you more than I do."

"Oh, I don't know, Friday," she purred, stroking a hand down his tie, then shooting him a glance from beneath her lashes. "I'm beginning to think the only adornment that piece needs is you, stretched out on top of it."

"And the only adornment I need is *you*, stretched out on top of *me*."

She straightened his tie and brushed a tiny piece of lint off his lapel. "You have a dirty, predictable mind. I'm beginning to admire that about you."

"Oh, yeah?" His eyes lit up and he took a step closer, ignoring the waiters who were setting up tables around them. "Tell me more. What else do you like about me?"

His question had emotion clogging inexplicably in her chest. Everything, she could have answered. Every little thing. The way he moved. The way he smiled, quick and teasing, or with a slow, wicked curve of his lips. His gentleness with his daughter. The way he could make Kate's skin heat without even a touch. The way he looked at her as though she were the only woman in the world, making her wish…dangerous things.

He traced a fingertip down the line of her throat. "Go ahead. Don't be afraid to stroke my ego. You'll find I have a high tolerance for sweet nothings."

She released a shaky laugh and stepped back. "I better not. I don't want you to go into insulin shock."

There was a satisfied quirk to his lips when he vowed, "Later." And watched the pulse in her throat throb at his promise. "Where's Chloe? Is she ready?"

"I haven't seen her since I left her with you," she said. The little girl had literally been dancing with anticipation earlier while Kate had patiently worked with her hair and helped her into the frilly blue dress they'd bought for the occasion.

"I brought her downstairs with me," Michael said, his gaze scanning the room. "She said she wanted to find Trask to show him her dress."

A huge clatter sounded from the kitchen then, and their eyes met. "Chloe," they said simultaneously. They reached the kitchen door as a very annoyed caterer pushed it open and ushered her out of the room. Chloe's eyes were suspiciously bright, and her bottom lip quivered.

"I didn't mean to get in the way," she told them in a small voice. "I couldn't find Trask and I thought he might be in there."

Michael scooped her up and hugged her tight. "Don't

worry about it, bug. We have plenty of food. And wait until Trask gets a load of your new dress." He waggled his eyebrows, making her giggle. "It's going to knock him out."

"There he is!" she exclaimed, spotting him as he entered the house with a group of men. "Let me down, Daddy."

Michael set her on her feet and she took off across the room. He watched her indulgently, then looked at Kate. "Think she'll ever learn to get somewhere by walking?"

She smiled, following the direction of his gaze, and watched Chloe pirouette for Trask and the men he had in tow like a princess before her court. Something about that group of men hanging so close to Trask had the smile fading from Kate's lips. "Michael, who are those people with Trask?"

"Security."

She looked at him sharply, but his face was as bland as his voice. "You hired them for tonight?"

"I hired them before school was out," he informed her. "The bidding for the NASA contract was competitive, and I didn't see any reason to take chances."

She looked at the men again, more carefully this time. All were dressed unobtrusively in dark suits. If Michael hadn't told her differently, she might have guessed that the first guests had arrived. "You did take a chance, though, didn't you?" she asked slowly. "All this…" She waved a hand around the room. "Why would you agree to have the open house here if you're worried about keeping FORAY secure?"

He took her hand and squeezed it comfortingly. "I minimized the risks," he said, then brought her hand to his lips and nipped at her knuckles. "Took a few precautions." His grin was broad and a little wolfish. "Don't worry. I always plan for every contingency."

Although she didn't have a great deal of experience with business parties, Kate thought this one appeared to be a success. Guests had started trickling in a few hours ago, and right now the house was full, with people spilling out onto the terrace. The French doors were left open, letting in the balmy summer air. She had the fanciful idea that even the weather hadn't dared not cooperate with Michael.

She'd stayed by his side for a time, enjoying the possessive arm he'd kept around her waist as much as she'd enjoyed watching him work the groups he was talking to. He was a master of subtlety. When talking to a woman with closely shorn hair and a sleek white dress, he'd paused as if to ponder her question about the exploding boundaries of computers.

"It's an exhilarating time, with technology developing so fast, but it does make it more difficult to protect sensitive or private information. Good security is going to become even more necessary."

In other words, Kate had thought as they'd joined another cluster of guests, you're going to need the programs designed by Michael's company.

He'd introduced her to so many people that her head was spinning with names after only a few minutes. When his attention had been demanded by some magazine reporters, Kate had taken the chance to slip away. She preferred being an observer, moving through the crowds unnoticed, letting the snippets of conversation fragment into a verbal collage.

"The man's a bloody genius." This was said admiringly from a fortyish man watching a computer display of the software Michael was marketing.

"A shrewd businessman can pay the finest minds to do his thinking for him." Kate looked curiously at the woman with improbably gold hair, wondering what she was talking about. The balding man next to her snorted. "A shrewd businessman better *be* the finest mind, otherwise—"

"Try this mushroom crepe. Isn't it to die for? Who do you think—"

"He's ruthless but honorable. A damn near lethal combination."

Kate caught sight of Chloe in the crowd, which had grown considerably since the open house had begun. She made her way toward her. The little girl seemed to be in her element, skipping from one group to the next. As Kate watched, she sidled up to a waitress with a tray and took a wrapped artichoke heart and bit into it. Her mouth screwed up comically, and the next moment she had her napkin to her mouth getting rid of it. Kate almost laughed out loud.

When Chloe wandered into the next room, Kate was jolted to see a man dressed in a dark suit move surreptitiously in the same direction. She stopped, staring hard at him. Though she couldn't be certain, she suspected that it was one of the nondescript gentlemen she had asked Michael about earlier. He moved nonchalantly through the crowd, never approaching Chloe, but always keeping her in his sight. Michael might be convinced that having the open house here presented no risks, but as he'd said, he'd taken precautions.

"Do I note your fine hand in all this?"

Kate was so accustomed to moving silently through the mass of people unnoticed that at first she didn't respond. Then, when the hand touched her arm, her eyes jerked to meet Derek's.

He gestured toward the room. "Michael's creativity runs to leveraged buyouts and software design. And I know how he feels about decorating firms. So, unless Trask suddenly developed a real knack for furnishings, you're the brains behind his home's face-lift."

She gave a slight shrug. "I just made some suggestions."

He took a sip of his drink, his glittering, pale blue eyes fixed on her above the rim of the glass. "Well, you've got a gift for it. If you ever want a career change, you certainly have another area of talent."

She shook her head. "I can't imagine tiring of teaching."

He cocked his head, surveying her with such concentration that she grew uneasy.

"Do I have all my teeth?" she asked somewhat tartly.

"What?" His gaze jerked up to meet hers. At her expression, he grinned. "Sorry. I was just thinking." In the stubborn silence that followed, he inquired, "Don't you want to know what about?"

Kate clutched the stem of her wineglass more tightly in her hand and shook her head. "I don't think so."

Unabashed, Derek offered, "If you made most of the suggestions for this place, you'd be pretty comfortable here. Surrounded by things you liked, things you picked out with Michael.'' His grin widened when her eyes narrowed. ''Hey.'' He gestured with his glass. ''It only occurred to me that maybe things between you two were getting serious. Most couples pick out china patterns before furniture, but Michael has always been a little unconventional.''

Shock straightened her spine. ''I never—I haven't—'' Impatiently she shook her head. ''Go away,'' she said clearly.

''So that's how it is,'' he murmured, and then began to chortle. ''Oh, this is rich. Don't tell me Michael managed to choose the one woman in the world not anxious to wrestle him down and pin him to the marital mat.'' He shook with silent laughter.

Rather than throwing it at him, Kate swallowed some of her champagne, then contemplated the bubbles in the glass. ''I'm so glad you find us amusing.''

With effort, Derek sobered. ''No, not at all. Michael and Chloe are two of my favorite people. I knew what he needed, even before he did. I'm just glad he found it.''

She cocked her head at him. ''Somehow I don't see you as someone who celebrates happily-ever-afters.''

''They're fine.'' He grinned. ''For other people. But if Michael succeeds in convincing you to marry him, well—'' he toasted her with his drink ''—that's one more reason for me to envy him.''

Kate watched Derek melt away in the crowd before shaking her head in bemusement. The man made an unlikely cupid, but he did seem to think highly of Michael and Chloe.

Chloe. Her head snapped up and she scanned the crowd. It had been several minutes since she'd last seen the little girl. Automatically, she began moving through the throngs of people. The man Michael had following her wouldn't necessarily be able to head her off before she could find mischief. Kate felt a lot better when she was able to keep Chloe in sight.

Pushing the kitchen door open, she peeked inside. Chloe was sitting on the counter, humming and kicking her feet. The caterers worked around her, paying her no attention.

"Miss Rose!" The little girl's face lit up.

Kate crossed over to the counter. "What are you doing—hiding out?"

She nodded. "Don't tell Daddy, but his party is kinda boring. Do you think I should show everyone how I can whistle?"

"I don't think that would be a good idea," Kate said. The little girl's shoulders slumped.

"When will this be over?" she wanted to know.

"I'm not sure. Maybe an hour or so."

Chloe swung her feet harder and leaned back on her hands, staring at the ceiling morosely. "That's forever."

"I know this isn't much fun for you, but I'll bet your dad is real proud of the way you're acting so grown-up tonight."

Chloe's eyes brightened. "I am?"

Kate nodded.

"I haven't been doing somersaults or anything in the house," Chloe assured her. "There's no room with all the people around, anyway. And when I don't like the food, I just spit it out in a napkin."

Hiding a smile, Kate said, "That's very mature."

Chloe nodded happily. "I guess I will go back for a while. I like those little cheeseball things. And those puffy white thingees with the meat in the middle."

Laughing, Kate accompanied her from the room with the admonishment, "Better take it easy on the snacks, kiddo."

Chloe skipped away while Kate looked around for Michael. Her eyes immediately honed in on his large, broad form. He looked up then, caught her gaze on him and smiled. It really wasn't fair, she mused, that all he had to do was look at her to make her blood turn molten, her limbs go soft and weak. She thought she could read impatience and polite boredom in the civilized manner with which he was listening to the man beside him.

She watched him excuse himself and make his way over to her, stopping to greet people and flash that charming grin. Men seemed to like him, admire him. And the women…he had an even more predictable effect on them, she thought wryly as she watched the furtive looks that followed him.

"Hi." He came to a stop beside her and looped an arm around her waist. "Are you bored to tears yet?"

She shook her head. "I'm afraid Chloe is, though. I just brought her back from the kitchen."

He frowned and looked over her head in search of his daughter. "Maybe I should tell her it would be okay to go to her room and play."

"Yes, I'm sure the security man you've had following her around all night would be grateful for the rest."

He stiffened, then shot a look at her bland face. "Can't get anything past you, can I?" he murmured. "I didn't think it would hurt anything. You know how fast the little sprite can disappear."

"I felt better knowing someone else had an eye on her, too," she admitted, and he relaxed.

"Chloe's not the only one who's bored," he said in a low tone. He lowered his face, his gaze heated and intent. "What do you say you and I disappear somewhere and neck?"

She pretended to consider it. "I don't think so," she finally said. "Trask and I just returned from the storage closet, and I've already reapplied my lipstick."

He stifled a laugh. "I'd believe that if he was running for his life across the lawn instead of circling the crowd the way he is."

She punched him lightly on the arm. "Are you saying I'm frightening?"

"I'm saying that Trask would have a heart attack if a woman propositioned him, and he'd die a thousand deaths before he actually spoke to one of his own free will. Why, I remember one time when he…"

Kate missed the rest of his sentence. She was staring past him in shocked recognition. He followed the direction of her gaze and his features hardened abruptly.

"You've got to give the arrogant bastard credit, don't you? He does have style."

Something in his tone diverted her attention from the silver-haired man twining through the crowd toward them. "Did you know he was coming?"

"He wasn't invited, if that's what you mean. But they paged me from the gate. I told them to go ahead and let him in." His mouth crooked with something that bore no resemblance to humor. "I'd rather be able to see him than to have to defend myself from a sneak attack."

Kate eyed him carefully. His choice of words made it sound as if he were preparing for war. Which, she supposed he was. Another battle in a never-ending string of skirmishes where no clear victor emerged. "What do you suppose he wants here?"

Michael lifted a shoulder. "He wants to do what Jonathan Friday does best, I imagine," he said grimly. "Spread a little misery around."

"Well, Michael, it seems you've done it again." Jonathan nodded to the display nearby featuring the new home security system. "A nice little program, actually. You're going retail with it, I assume."

Michael inclined his head slightly.

"Of course. Should do quite well, too." He raised his glass of champagne in Kate's direction. "Miss Rose, isn't it? So pleasant to see you again." Her lack of response didn't seem to faze him in the least. "And that—" he turned slightly to indicate Chloe across the room "—must be my granddaughter."

Kate quietly slipped her hand in Michael's and laced her fingers with his in an unconscious sign of support. His body was rigid, the muscles taut, and the air about him became lethally charged. "She's not *your* anything." His voice was smooth and cool as silk, but the flame in his eyes would caution the more wary. "Blood doesn't mean everything. You taught me that."

The man raised his eyebrows in amusement. "I wonder if the courts would agree with you. Some interesting test cases these days on grandparents' rights, don't you think?" He let his words sink in before turning and strolling away.

"Unbelievable," Michael said in a low voice. His still,

careful control was more telling than a shout. The tension was all but coming off him in waves. As she watched, he tucked that awesome fury back into the mental pocket where he kept it. Kate wondered if he knew how close to the surface it lingered.

Her fingers tightened in his. When he brought their clasped hands to his lips to kiss her knuckles, she released a breath she hadn't been aware of holding. "And here I was thinking these things were dull."

He slanted a look at her. "Stick with me, kid," he said wryly. "I'll liven up your life."

Looking away, she saw Jonathan on the other side of the room with one of Michael's security men close by. "Why don't I find Chloe and take her upstairs."

Michael gave her a grateful look. "Would you? I'd feel better knowing Jonathan couldn't get within ten yards of her."

Nodding, she turned and went in search of the little girl. She finally spotted the tips of small blue kid shoes peeping out from beneath one of the tables that had been set up in the dining room. Kate bent down and lifted the edge of the tablecloth out of the way. "Pretty good hiding place, Chloe. I almost couldn't find you."

The little girl nodded but didn't respond. She was unusually quiet and pale.

Kate peered anxiously at her. "Chloe, are you feeling all right?"

"My stomach is doing cartwheels," she confided in a thin voice. "I don't like Daddy's party."

Kate held out her hand, and Chloe wiggled slowly out from beneath the table. Her heavy-lidded eyes and pinched mouth were more telling than her words. "I think you must have overdone it on the appetizers, honey. You don't look too good."

She felt the little girl's clammy forehead, then lifted her in her arms. "You and I are going to go upstairs and get you ready for bed, how's that?" When Chloe nodded listlessly, Kate felt a small pang of alarm. She knew the child well enough to know that bedtime usually didn't come without a battle.

Upstairs she helped Chloe change into her pajamas and brush her teeth, and then, when her condition worsened abruptly, she held her head while she was sick. Afterward Kate put her to bed and stayed beside her while she slept.

It was a couple of hours before Michael appeared at her side. "She's asleep?" he murmured, kneeling beside the bed. "How'd you manage that?"

Kate pushed back the blond strands from Chloe's face. "She didn't feel well." At Michael's instant alarm, she said soothingly, "A stomachache, I think. She was sampling the food pretty freely, and some of the hors d'oeuvres were rich."

"Does she have a fever?" Michael's hand went to his daughter's forehead, relief crossing his features when he felt her coolness.

"No, but she was sick once already. You might want to have something nearby in case she wakes in the night and feels ill again."

"If she wakes up, I'll be here."

Kate's heart turned over. Her hand went to his shoulder and massaged soothingly. "I know you're concerned, but it isn't necessary for you to wait up all night."

"Oh, it'll be okay. I can bring a rocker in here, maybe catch a few winks." His gaze caught hers then, and his expression was charmingly rueful. "You think I'm nuts, don't you?"

Her lips wanted to tremble, so she pressed them together and shook her head. That sweetness could still take her unaware, slip under her defenses and stir everything soft inside her. "Couldn't you just use the monitor?" she asked unsteadily, indicating the one that sat on Chloe's dresser.

"Yeah. Yeah, you're right. At least, that's why I bought it. I can turn it on and hear her from my room."

"That will save you a stiff neck."

"I just hate this, you know?" he whispered. Their voices were pitched low to avoid waking the sleeping child. "Every time she's sick I get such a helpless feeling. Maybe it's even worse with her, because she's normally so darn active that seeing her lying still scares the hell out of me. I guess I'm just a typical overreactive parent.''

''Not typical,'' Kate contradicted softly. Her voice was filled with the emotion that was gripping her heart. ''Never typical.''

His hazel gaze met her blue one, and he brought her hand to his mouth and pressed a soft kiss there. ''This isn't exactly the ending to the evening I had planned.''

She smiled and gave in to an impulse to run the back of her hand along his jaw. He'd shaved before the party and his skin was still smooth, a hard, sensual glide. ''There will be other evenings.''

He caught her hand in his, trapping it against his cheek. ''You can count on it.''

''Michael.''

Both pairs of eyes jerked to the doorway, where Trask stood. He gestured with the cordless phone he held and, with an eye on the sleeping child, tried to pitch his voice lower. It came out a gravelly rumble. ''You better take this. Trouble at the company.''

With a quick glance at Kate, Michael rose, taking the phone and stepping out into the hallway. Kate had time to do no more than raise her eyebrows questioningly at Trask before Michael was back. He gestured to both of them, and they followed him out of the room.

''That was the fire department,'' he said without preamble. ''There's been an explosion at our office complex.''

Chapter 15

Michael raised a hand, squelching their questions. "I don't have any details, but we have to get down there right away." Then he stopped and looked worriedly toward his daughter's door. "Someone needs to stay with Chloe."

"I'll do it," Kate said. "You go ahead. I'll plan to stay the night."

Relief lit his eyes. "Thank you," he muttered, brushing a kiss across her forehead. He showed her how to work the monitor, then led her to a bedroom down the hallway. He stood there a moment, looking torn. "I'm going to take some of the men with me, but I'll leave one in the house and one outside."

"We'll be all right here," Kate murmured. When he reached for her, she went into his arms and laid her head against his chest. "Be sure and call me when you know something."

He gave her a quick, hard hug and turned to leave the room.

When he got to the door, she said, "Michael? Please be careful." He exchanged a long, level look with her before turning away toward Trask. She could hear the urgent tones of the men as they hurried down the hall.

She looked at the bedroom that was to be hers for the night, and an unwilling smile tugged at her lips. This was the room where Michael had put the antique bedroom set that she'd told him about. Walking over to the dresser with its oval mirror and ornate knobs, she trailed a hand over its smooth, glossy surface. He'd done more than just buy the set, she noted. Despite his protests that he was incapable of doing so, he'd managed to furnish the entire room. Against one wall was a wardrobe with burled walnut on the doors. On either side of the bed were tables with scrolled legs, on top of which sat matching lamps with leaded shades. She crossed to one of them and with a finger sent the shade's beaded fringe dancing.

The bed was piled high with pillows. He hadn't draped it in romantic lace. Instead it was covered with an antique quilt. When she recognized the pattern, her eyes misted. The colors in the wedding ring design were muted by time, but age gave a richness to its beauty. The symbolism of the pattern was unmistakable, the pairs of entwining circles constant and infinite. Just as a pair of lives entwined. Just as hearts did.

Taking a deep breath, she turned away jerkily, seeking a distraction. She'd need something to sleep in. She didn't relish the thought of wearing her lingerie to bed, especially since she might need to rise and go to Chloe. After a moment's thought, she went in search of Michael's room and found it, located across the hall from his daughter's.

He'd spared no attention for his own bedroom. As Chloe had told her once, it was empty, save for a bed. A huge one, she noted, before tearing her fascinated gaze away. There was nothing in the space that spoke of Michael, no stamp of his personality. She went toward the closet and opened it, revealing an endless expanse of suits and shelving. It was from one of the shelves that she plucked a T-shirt to wear.

She checked on Chloe before returning to her room. The little girl hadn't changed position and seemed to be sleeping soundly. Although her cheeks were a little flushed, her skin was cool, and Kate was satisfied that her diagnosis had been correct. An upset stomach caused by too much unfamiliar, rich food had probably caused Chloe's discomfort. Chances were she'd be back to her turbocharged self by morning.

Kate undressed, draping her clothes across the foot of the bed. As she slipped the T-shirt over her head, she fancied she could smell Michael's scent on the soft, worn cotton.

Pulling the bedcovers back, she slipped beneath them. The feather mattress was heavenly, the pillows soft. It was the kind of bed that could make going to sleep an exercise in decadence. But slumber didn't lure her. Worry teased at her mind; she wouldn't sleep until Michael came home safely.

It was ridiculous, really. There would be police and fire-fighters present at the scene. They would prevent any bystanders from getting hurt. She moved restlessly, the sound a murmur of cotton against cotton. Surely he wouldn't be foolish enough to try to enter the building.

She frowned in the darkness of the room, wishing she knew a little more about his holdings. In a company that dealt with software security, she couldn't imagine what would cause an explosion. She wondered if Michael had any clue, then berated herself for not asking him before he'd left. Not that his answer would have made the hours pass any easier.

She'd never been one to enjoy waiting, although it seemed as though she'd spent most of her life doing so. But waiting for her parents to change, for life to be different when she was a child couldn't compare to the worry-filled hours she had ahead of her tonight. The darkness had a way of mutating anxieties into full-fledged nightmares. Lurid imagination made a distressing companion at this time of night.

She twisted against the sheets in a restless, frustrated movement. What if Michael was injured tonight? A cold blade of fear accompanied the thought. Knowing him, he'd be right in the thick of things. When something of his was threatened, he went into a whole different mode. The idea of him hurt, maybe bleeding, made her sick and shaky inside. She wanted him back here, safe. She wanted to see him quirk the half-irritating, half-endearing grin and hear him wisecrack about her concern. She wanted to feel his arms around her and know that he was going to be all right. She wanted…him.

She jackknifed upright in bed to relieve her strangled lungs. The thought of life without Michael left her heart barren, her soul bereft. What was this, then, if not love? How odd that the emotion she'd searched for all her life should have been so difficult to identify. So frightening to feel.

Because she was more than frightened…she was terrified. She couldn't imagine giving up what she had with Michael and Chloe, turning her back on her newly discovered love for him. She'd always been a sensible, practical person. By no means could she be called a risk taker. But now she was contemplating taking the biggest risk she could imagine by offering a lifetime of her love to a man who wouldn't, couldn't promise the same.

The minutes dragged by too sluggishly to count toward hours. Left only with her worries and doubts, she found the big old bed excruciatingly lonely. Twice when Chloe made a sigh or a whimper in her sleep, Kate got up and padded soundlessly to the little girl's room to check on her. Both times found her still asleep, her breathing steady.

After she checked on Chloe the second time, she was loath to return to her bedroom. She decided to go downstairs to the family room and avail herself of one of the books that lined the shelves there. Though reading might be as difficult to concentrate on as sleep, it would help pass the time until he was back.

The house was dark, but since Chloe's door was open, she didn't want to turn on the hallway light. She picked her way carefully down the stairs. If she could find the light switches downstairs, she just might go to the kitchen for a glass of milk to bring back up with her. And it wouldn't hurt to have a plate of crackers and some flat ginger ale ready in case Chloe woke up and needed something to settle her stomach.

At the bottom of the stairs she kept a hand to the wall to guide her way and then turned into the hallway. If possible, it seemed darker there, and her fingers went on a blind search for the light switch. Before she found it, her bare toes met something immovable.

Kate stifled a gasp. Only her hand supporting her on the wall saved her from toppling over the crumpled figure on the floor in front of her. Her heart lodged in her throat. For an instant she just stood still, focusing on moving air in and out of her lungs again. Then she bent down and touched the person's shoulder gingerly. It was a man, that much she could tell. Though his features were difficult to discern in the darkness, she thought it was one of the security people who worked for Michael.

Her movement brought him to his back, and her fingers searched for the pulse below his jaw. It was thready but discernible, and relief filled her. She rose, intent on finding a light, any light, then rubbed her fingers curiously. They were wet and sticky with a substance she couldn't identify.

Dread curled in the pit of her stomach, and with it came certainty. It was blood, the man's blood, but she'd do him no good until she could see his wound. She didn't know the house well enough to remember where the nearest light switch or telephone were, but the kitchen was straight ahead, at the top of the hallway. If she could turn on the light there, enough would spill into the darkened hallway to aid her search.

She stepped over the man cautiously and hurried toward the kitchen. Forgotten was the book she'd meant to select. She moved past the door to the family room without giving it a thought. But once she'd walked past the next closed door, she stopped in her tracks as if yanked by an invisible chain.

Kate didn't breathe for a moment, straining all her senses in an attempt to convince herself that she was imagining things. But she wasn't. The sounds she'd heard were real. Real enough to have the blood congealing in her veins.

Someone was in the den.

She looked at the closed door out of the corner of her eye, as if even by moving her head she would alert the prowler to her presence. The noises were muffled but distinct. The tapping sounds could have been made by a pen against a desktop.

Or by fingers on a computer keyboard.

Fear trickled down Kate's spine. Without conscious thought she began backing up, slowly. She didn't want to take the chance of going to the kitchen now. If she was discovered, the only other way out of that room was a door to the outside. And she wasn't going to leave Chloe in the house unprotected.

She gave one desperate thought to the man Michael had said would be on security outside before dismissing it. She had no idea where to find him, and there was no telling what kind of shape he would be in. She could only imagine that the intruder would have had to go past him to get into the house.

No, her best bet was to get upstairs. Surely she would find a phone there, either in Michael's room or perhaps in Trask's. She could dial 911 and get the police here, preferably before the prowler found what he was looking for in Michael's den.

Fingers touched the back of one of her heels, and a scream tore up Kate's throat. In her distress, she'd nearly backed up over the poor security guard. Clapping a hand to her mouth, she muffled all but a thread of sound and stopped for a moment, praying it would go unnoticed. She was unable to hear anything over her hammering heartbeat. Her breathing seemed unnaturally loud as she strained her ears to listen for the sounds coming from the den that had alerted her to begin with.

She was too far away to hear them, she prayed, and made herself turn around. Taking great care, she stepped over the body sprawled in the hallway and hurried as fast as she dared to the staircase.

The first tread under her foot felt like the road to freedom. Odd, but she hadn't noticed the way some of the steps creaked when she'd been on her way down the stairs. She was halfway up now, and the air was getting a little easier to draw into her lungs. Only a few more yards. She wondered where the phone might be kept in Michael's room, assuming he had one there. She hadn't noticed a table or stand for it.

A hand on the back of her shirt jerked her off balance, and terror clawed up her throat, shredding her voice. She grabbed wildly for the banister, her other hand making a fist and swinging out. It encountered a body, close, very close, behind her. Then an arm snaked around her throat, and her grip was torn away from the railing.

A gloved hand was slapped across her mouth and she bit down, heard the muffled curse. Her elbow jabbed out frantically, and she brought a leg back for a swift backward kick. The damage it did was probably minuscule, but her desperation lent a wildness to her actions that made her difficult to contain. The arm around her throat tightened cruelly, and her struggles weakened as her oxygen supply was inexorably cut off. Colors swam before her eyes and her knees went watery. When she was yanked around and forced to start down the stairs, the pressure around her throat was loosened just a little.

She had to keep Chloe safe, she thought dimly. And Michael. Would the intruder still be here when Michael got home? Her thoughts came slow, as if she were drugged, but she recognized the need to protect. She used the very real weakness in her limbs to her advantage and went suddenly, totally limp, pulling her attacker off balance. One arm released her and she used up the rest of her dwindling strength to give a mighty pull away.

She had only an instant to savor her freedom. She felt, rather than saw, the black-clad arm coming toward her and took an automatic step back. Her foot touched air and she teetered, arms circling frantically. Then, as if in slow motion, she lost the battle with gravity and toppled down the rest of the stairs.

Michael pushed open the hospital door and saw Kate sitting upright on the examining table. His eyes slid closed. Panic and relief ricocheted inside him. She was conscious, thank God. They'd told him that she hadn't been when she'd been found. And then he opened his eyes and stared fiercely, cataloging her injuries.

She couldn't prevent an occasional wince as the doctor wrapped her ribs. His gaze traveled her form, saw the bandage wrapped around her ankle and the bruise marring one cheekbone and felt rage. Hot and quick it boiled, scalding him with its intensity.

"Come on in." Her voice was strained, her smile wobbly, but her eyes were welcoming. "There aren't any needles in sight."

He closed the distance between them and stood at her side, out of the way of the doctor's deft movements. Reaching for one of her hands, he brought it to his cheek and held it there.

"How's Chloe?"

"She's fine," he assured her. He forced a deliberately neutral tone to his voice. "Never even woke up. Still no sign of fever, either."

"Thank goodness. I was afraid…" The breath shuddered out of her then, and he pressed a kiss to her hand, then meshed her fingers with his.

"There was a man on the floor," she murmured. "He was hurt."

"Harmon. One of my security guards," he explained tersely. "He's here, too. I'll check on him in a few minutes."

The doctor finished and stepped back. "Well, that should do it. You're going to have a whale of a headache for a while, and we'd like to keep you overnight for observation."

"No," Kate said.

"Yes," Michael contradicted immediately. "We're not taking any chances with you." He'd already put her at risk that night in a way he never could have foreseen, and for that, a nasty demon of guilt would eat away at him for a very long time. He traced her delicate jawline with his fingertip. "Don't fight with me on this, baby. I'm too worried about you."

"I'll line up a nurse to come and take you to your room," the doctor said, and left.

Kate gave a sigh and then winced again as her ribs protested. "There was a prowler in your den."

"I know." His fingers tightened in hers. "It was a setup, start to finish. This wasn't just any prowler. He was at the open house tonight and hid himself inside until after dark. The explosion was just a decoy. He'd prearranged it with a rigged car left in the parking lot. It was a ruse to get us out of the house, giving him free access. Quincy, the guard I had stationed outside, spotted him leaving. He alerted the police, but rather than following him, Quincy decided to check the house." A deed, Michael thought grimly, that would earn the man a hefty bonus. "He found you and Harmon and called for an ambulance, as well."

Disappointment laced Kate's voice. "So the intruder hasn't been caught?"

He hesitated, then said slowly, "He's not in custody yet."

"Damn," she said tiredly. "I never even saw his face. I had just a glimpse of him right before I fell, but he was wearing a face mask." Her gaze lifted to his and her eyes widened. "He was after FORAY, wasn't he? Oh, Michael, all your work isn't ruined, is it?"

"Shh." He lowered his face to her hair, careful not to jar her. "Don't worry about it, baby. I told you I'd taken precautions. We'd switched my computer in the den with the one Trask keeps in his room. All my files, all my notes are safely locked up in the basement. And—" he brushed his lips across the silky, tangled strands "—I've got a security camera mounted in the wall above my desk."

"Where?" Her surprise was obvious. "I've never noticed it."

He almost smiled and brought her hand up to nip at her knuckles. "That's because I'm good at my job. Not that you were looking for one. Luckily for us," he said, sobering, "neither was our intruder. At least, he didn't look in the right place. And when he didn't find any cameras, he felt safe enough to push his mask up out of the way while he worked on breaking the code on the computer." He saw the question in her eyes and couldn't quite hide the bitterness in his answer. "It was my father."

Her hand came up and cupped his jaw. "Michael, I'm sorry."

His gut twisted, one violent churn. "Yeah, so am I. Sorry that you were in danger because of me, sorry I couldn't protect you from him. But most of all I'm sorry that I didn't destroy that bastard completely the first time, and avoided this situation altogether."

He turned away from her, regret and fury a tight knot in his throat.

"Don't you dare blame yourself for this, Michael."

The vehemence in her voice had his gaze jerking to meet hers. "Jonathan Friday has been making his own choices for a long time. Yes, some of those choices affected you, but you're not responsible for them, and you shouldn't feel guilty for *his* actions."

He gave a grim laugh. "This time I'm going to take him down for good. Corporate espionage, breaking and entering, assault and battery—he's going to find prison a far cry from the country clubs he's used to." And even his father's hatred would find it difficult to reach beyond the prison walls and threaten anyone Michael cared about. The knowledge banked his rage slightly. Only slightly.

"Don't do it."

He stared hard at her, sure he'd misunderstood her meaning. "Don't do what?"

She hesitated, and he could see the exhaustion working on her, watched her attempt to hold it at bay.

"Where's that nurse?" he muttered, starting for the door.

"Don't try to destroy your father again." Her words followed him, stopping him in midstride.

"Kate." His shoulders were tense, his spine as inflexible as his will. "You don't know what you're asking."

"I do," she said softly. "I know how guilty you're feeling right now. A guilt like that will work on you, make you want to strike back at the one who tried to hurt you and yours. But you can't hurt him without hurting yourself."

He turned to her then, the resentment bubbling inside him. "If you think I'm going to let him walk away from this when you could have been killed tonight, then you don't know me very well.''

"I know what it is to want to protect, Michael. I felt that need tonight, for both you and Chloe.'' She was swaying a little on the table and gripped its edge tightly to steady herself. But there was no hint of weakness in her voice. "Think about it, Michael. You don't have to go to the police. You've got the film from the camera. That's your leverage over him. He'll know that it would take only a whisper from you about the events of this evening to ruin him.''

He stared at her stonily, refusing to acknowledge the truth of her words. "You don't know him, Kate. If I have the tape and don't use it, he won't see it as restraint. He'll see it as me being a sucker.''

"Who cares?'' Her voice was starting to rise. "You're a smart guy, you can figure a way to use the film to get what you want. But you don't have to put your father in prison to do it.''

"You're wasting your pity on Jonathan Friday," he said flatly.

"I don't care about him," she retorted, "I care about *you*. Hatred can be its own kind of poison, and you've seen what it's done to your father. Don't let it eat away at you, as well." Her tone softened, the sincerity unmistakable. "You're not like him. You couldn't send your own flesh and blood to prison without regrets. If you deny that, you're lying to yourself. Don't you see?''

As if pulled by the strength of her gaze, he turned to look at her.

"To do battle with him, you have to get down to his level. Every time you do, he reels you in a little further. Show him you're a better man than he is. Walk away. That would be your greatest triumph over him.''

The silence echoed, grew. She must have seen his answer on his face, because she made one last plea. "I'm not asking that you do it for me or for Chloe. I think you need to do this...for yourself.''

He swallowed convulsively and looked away. He clenched

his hands reflexively at his sides, and his voice was bleak when he answered.

"I can't promise you that."

The door to her bedroom opened, revealing a mellow wedge of light. Kate tried to move to her back in the deep mattress, but her bruised ribs hampered her speed.

"I'm awake, so don't you dare go away."

Michael padded into the room, barefoot and shirtless. He leaned one arm against a walnut post at the base of the bed.

"You should be resting," he chided. "The doctor wouldn't have let you come home with me if he knew you weren't going to sleep."

"That's all I've done," she muttered. "Is Chloe down yet?"

He nodded. "Out like a light. Fetching and carrying for you all day must have worn her out."

She smiled. The little girl's concern had been heartwarming, and her ideas for entertaining Kate had been creative, to say the least.

She held out a hand to him, and after a moment's hesitation, he walked over and sat down gingerly on the edge of the mattress, watching her face closely for any signs of pain.

Determined not to show any, she stroked the back of his hand. "Have you been avoiding me?"

"Not a chance of that, honey. But I had some things to take care of today."

Her attention focused on her fingers as they traced invisible patterns on his skin. "And?"

"And..." he repeated, then waited for her gaze to meet his. "I went to Jonathan with a copy of the film."

Her breath caught in her throat, and cautious hope bloomed inside her.

"The look on his face when he saw himself breaking into my computer was worth the price of a ticket," he said wryly. "But then he reverted to type."

"What did you decide?"

His hand twisted up to grip hers. "We came to a mutual

understanding. He's decided it's time to retire, and sunny California is beckoning him. I thought putting a full continent between us would be wise." He paused for a moment, his expression pensive. "You know, I've spent a lifetime trying to avoid becoming like my father. It occurred to me that if I took the old bastard down, I'd be falling with him."

She bit her lip, her heart suddenly full. "You made the right decision."

"Jonathan's hatred consumed him until he had room for nothing else in his life." His shoulders lifted. "I have more. Much more."

He reached out his free hand to toy with the ends of her hair. "Chloe said she made sure you took your pain pills today. Where does it hurt the most?"

She caught his hand in hers and carried it to her heart. "Right here."

His fingers caressed her lightly. "Remind me to kiss it and make it better."

"I don't think you could help with that," she murmured, her gaze dropping from his. "I needed to work some things through for myself, and I've done plenty of thinking in the last couple days."

His fingers stilled, and his face grew serious. "Before you start, there's something I need to tell you."

She shook her head. Her thoughts had become too compelling to deny expressing them any longer. "Please...let me finish. I have some regrets in my life, Michael. I don't want you to become one of them."

His voice was carefully blank. "What exactly does that mean?"

She bit her lip, trying to explain something she'd never had to put into words before. "When I was a child, it was never the poverty of money in my house that hurt me, it was the poverty of emotion. I grew up promising myself I'd have more."

"You can have more."

She heard the banked urgency in his voice, and she slid a hand down his arm in an automatic effort to soothe. "I was so worried when you went to investigate the explosion. So afraid you'd get yourself hurt.'' Her touch grew more absent as she sorted through her tangled emotions, smoothed them out one by one. ''I miss you when you're not around. You make me angry, you make me laugh...you make me burn.'' His arm jerked a little then, but she didn't notice. Her senses were turned inward. ''My life is fuller than I ever dreamed possible, and that scares me so much.'' She swallowed around the lump in her throat and forced herself to continue. ''I have so much to lose now, and it makes me wonder how much bigger that void in my life would be if you decided not to be in it.''

''You aren't going to have to worry about that.''

She squeezed her eyes tightly shut for an instant. ''I can't bear to think of a future without you in it. You're all I think about, all I want.'' She opened her eyes and lifted her gaze slowly to his.

His mouth was crooked in that engaging half smile, his eyes intent. ''I think I know what you're trying to say. Sometimes looking at me makes you feel like you've been sucker punched, right?''

She blinked. ''Hardly eloquent, but I imagine...yes.''

He nodded. ''Do you feel like you're falling off the edge of a cliff when we kiss?''

She took a deep breath, released it. Some of the tight, panicked emotion went with it. ''Another experience I don't have firsthand knowledge of...but falling? Yes.''

''Do you get all hollow and empty when we're apart? Does the thought of not ending up together make you feel like a horse kicked you square in the chest?'' He wasn't waiting for her answers now, he was just letting the words pour out in a torrent, as if some sort of personal reservoir had burst. ''I don't have a medical degree, but I think I can diagnose your affliction. Unless we've both caught the same strain of a weird virus, I'd say we're in love.''

''Yes, that's what I've been trying to tell...'' Her voice trailed to a stop as her heart careened to her throat. *''We're?''*

His smile was lopsided. "As in you and me. You can't imagine how relieved I am that I'm not in this deal alone."

The sudden joy quaking inside her spilled into her voice. "Is that what this is? A deal?"

He nodded. "The biggest. In fact, I'm going to have to take back the proposal I made a while ago."

For an instant, Kate's happiness threatened to plummet to somewhere in the vicinity of her stomach. "You are?"

"It was shortsighted. I think I can make you a better offer."

She settled herself more comfortably against the pillows and smiled slowly. "Offer away."

"What I'm thinking about is a lifetime merger. No escape clauses."

"None wanted."

He took her hand in his, raised it to his mouth and nipped at her knuckles. "That's good. Of course, the terms are generous. You get half of everything of mine, except my heart. That goes to you, one hundred percent."

She reached out her free hand and cupped his hard jaw. "How about a mutual trade?"

"I was hoping you'd suggest that. In fact, that was going to be one of my demands. As a concession, in the event of more children, the labor contract will be negotiable."

Laughter bubbled up. "Watch the terms you put on the table, champ. I've seen your reaction to needles and blood."

His grin was wicked. "This is called a sweetheart deal. We both get what we want. And all this is accompanied with the unprecedented offer of your lifetime use of my body. Of course, that would be a reciprocal agreement."

She slid her hand to the back of his neck and urged his head down. "That would be *my* demand."

He whispered against her lips, "I was hoping you'd say that." Then his lips parted hers and the kiss shimmered through her like a promise. Slow. Deep. Devastatingly thorough. When he lifted his mouth from hers, Kate opened her eyes, sure she saw a reflection of her own dreams in his.

"I love you, Michael." Certainty threaded through the

drugged sound of her voice. It had taken her a long time to identify it, to accept it, but there was no denying the genuine emotion coursing within her.

His face was still close to hers, so she saw the feeling cross his face. "I'm glad. Because I love you, too. It took me a while before I let my heart catch up with my head, but when I did, it was a hell of a collision. Remind me to tell you sometime about my first and—God willing—only panic attack."

That sounded intriguing. "What?"

His kiss was quick and hard. "Later. Right now, you need rest."

Her protest slid down her throat when he rose from the bed and shucked his jeans, then crossed to the door to shut it.

He looked good painted with moonlight, she thought achingly. The light splintering through the darkness of the room adorned muscle and sinew with a patchwork of silver. Rounding the bed, he climbed in beside her and helped her to her side so that her back was nestled against his chest. Taking great care not to jar her other ankle, he stretched his legs out, and his hand went to her hip, caressing gently.

"Michael." The word was a whisper of sound in the night. "I'm still not tired."

His voice was a low rumble in her ear. "You need to sleep."

In answer, she took his hand in hers and brought it to her mouth, worrying the pad of one finger with her teeth.

His breathing faltered. "I'm not sure that this is what the doctor ordered."

"A good CEO," she said, pressing a kiss to his palm, "makes rules rather than follows them."

"Excellent point." Her hair was lifted out of the way so that he could string a trail of kisses from her nape to her ear. He took the lobe in his lips and scraped it lightly with his teeth. She shuddered, her legs moving restlessly.

She turned her head so that her mouth could find his. Her lips clung, moist and hungry, urging him to take more. There was pleasure to be savored in the rock-hard body pressed tightly against hers, in the faint tremors that hinted of a desire kept tightly under control.

His lips moved to her shoulder and he slid his hand up under the edge of the T-shirt she was wearing. His fingers closed on her nipple and his touch scorched a path to her womb. She whimpered, wiggling closer to him, and he seemed to understand her urgency. He ran his hand down the center of her body and cupped her.

When the first explosion rocked her, her back stiffened, shudders breaking over her in waves. Then he was lifting her uninjured leg so that it was braced against the mattress. She felt the blunt tip of his sex probing her, and she gave a murmur of satisfied pleasure, one that quickly turned to a gasp as he slid deeply inside her.

"Don't move," he murmured in her ear. His hands were stroking over her breasts, her stomach. "I don't want you to hurt your ribs. Just let me…" He drew his length partially out of her slick, wet femininity before sinking back in.

Her breath came in whimpers, and she pressed back against him, silently demanding.

He kept his hand on her stomach to anchor her to him, his hips rocking gently against her bottom, his shaft within her pulsing in rhythm to the aftershocks that gripped her. His powerful hips moved lazily, purposefully against hers. She could feel him deep inside, the length of him touching off tiny pinpoints of pleasure until all her senses, all her nerves seemed centered at the point where they joined.

Their position was at once frustrating and exciting. She couldn't see him, couldn't touch him. All she could do was feel and ride each bright sensation he created to its pinnacle.

His hand drifted downward, burrowing in the moist tangle of hair between her thighs. He parted her with his fingers, unerringly finding the tight bundle of nerves hidden between the soft folds. It was exquisitely sensitive, and she whimpered, trying to move against him.

His hard body against hers kept her immobile. "Easy," he breathed in her ear, his voice strained. "Let me, baby. Just…easy now…"

His control slipped, unveiling a measure of desperation. His movements grew faster, deeper. She rocked against him and his fingers clenched her hips, driving hard. That was all it took to hurl them both to completion.

Chapter 16

It took bullying, cajoling and the shameless use of wiles she hadn't known she'd possessed, but Kate managed to convince Michael to allow her to have breakfast downstairs the next morning. Unexpectedly, it had been Trask who'd proven her ally. When he'd brought Chloe to her bedroom, he'd overheard part of the argument.

"I don't see the harm," he'd shocked them both by saying. When the two of them had looked at him, he'd turned a deep, dark red. "Can't hurt," he'd mumbled. Chloe had gleefully agreed.

So Kate found herself stretched out on the couch in the family room with a lightweight quilt spread over her and too many pillows at her back. But the scrambled eggs and toast Trask made tasted like heaven in her new location, and they indulged in an informal picnic. Chloe was ecstatic at the idea of being allowed to eat in a room other than the kitchen, although Michael warned her repeatedly not to expect it to happen again.

It was a relaxing time, with Michael sitting on the floor next to her, her hand between both of his, fussing over how little she ate. Chloe distracted them by doing a cartwheel she'd been practicing in gymnastics, barely missing hitting her head on the edge of an end table. Trask distracted her with her markers and paper and she busily began drawing.

"Enjoy it," Michael advised Kate wryly as they watched the little girl bent over her paper in concentration. "The times she's actually as quiet as this are few and far between."

"I think I'll manage."

His face grew more serious. "I've been thinking about the coming school year. I thought maybe we could wait until the first conference and listen to what Chloe's new teacher has to say about her progress. If she hasn't improved any, I'll be willing to discuss medication then."

Her fingers laced with his, and it took very little urging for him to lean closer for her kiss. "Chloe Friday," she uttered softly, "is very lucky to have you watching out for her."

His eyes lit up. "What about Kate Rose? Is she lucky, too?"

Her brow rested against his. "Very."

"I'm glad you feel that way. Because I arranged a little surprise for you."

Her sudden suspicion must have shown on her face because he started talking faster. "I thought it was time to introduce myself to your family."

The introduction of that subject hit her like a fast curveball. "My family? Why?" He should have saved the angelic look. It didn't settle well on that rough-hewn face. At any rate, she was too familiar with his tactics to buy it.

"I just wanted to introduce myself. After all, they're going to be my in-laws. I called your oldest brother, and he had your father call me back yesterday."

Suddenly all the simple happiness was leached from the day. Her voice was as flat when she inquired, "And?"

"I introduced myself. He was…impressed. I think he approves of me."

"I'll bet," she muttered. Her father's approval would correlate closely with his idea of Michael's success. He would be dazzled if he guessed even a fraction of Michael's worth. Money would sway him in a way emotion never would.

"The surprise, though, will be here next week. Actually, we'll bring them here in five days."

It took a moment for her brain to click onto his meaning. Even when it did, she was afraid to let herself believe it. "Them?"

His face was as hopeful as a little boy's when he replied, "Your brothers and sisters. From something you said once, I thought you'd like to have them visit, alone, so after we talked awhile, I ran it by your father. He was a little reluctant at first, but when I told him how much room I had..." His words were choked off when she threw her arms around his neck and hugged tight. "I'm hoping your reaction means you like this surprise better than my last one."

Her breath hitched in her throat, and she nodded furiously. Loosening her arms, she looked at him with every ounce of the love she felt squeezing her heart. "You couldn't have given me anything I'd value more."

His hand went to her hair, pushed it away from her face, then cupped her jaw lightly. "I'm glad, honey. And I'm hoping this will be the first of many visits they make here. Heck, we have enough bedrooms. They could each have their own. Of course, that means we're going to have to go furniture shopping again."

Her smile only trembled a little. Leave it to Michael to think of family, to understand how much this time with her brothers and sisters meant to her. She moved her head slightly, pressed a kiss to his palm and watched his eyes go lambent.

"Ahem."

They looked at Chloe, who stood up and approached them with her paper in her hand. "I'm done with my plans and now I will show them to you. No whispering, please," she intoned when Michael turned to grin at Kate. "I will need your eyes and ears up here. Remember, our ears and our mouths can't work at the same time."

"Oh, Lord," Kate muttered as her own words in the classroom came back to haunt her. Michael's shoulders shook silently.

Chloe peered at both of them until she was assured of their attention and then went on. "You know Mommy is getting married again." She frowned. "She kept it a sa-prise for a very, very long time, and I don't think that was very nice, 'cuz I didn't get to help plan anything, not even my dress." Her face showed her displeasure with that lapse.

"What'd you do, sweetheart, design your own dress?" asked Michael indulgently.

"No, Daddy, I planned your wedding. Here you are in your nicest clothes." She held up a picture of Michael in his jeans and a bright yellow T-shirt. "And here is your bride." They looked at the picture of a barefoot woman in a long white gown.

"Uh...do you have someone in mind for that position, bug?" Michael wanted to know.

"Da-a-d. Just look at the picture." She shook it impatiently. "It's Miss Rose, of course. She can be your happy bride and you can get married tomorrow and live happily ever after and get me a puppy."

"Pretty slick the way she worked that last part in, don't you think?" he asked Kate.

She nodded, bemused.

"Of course, first you gotta get in love." Chloe peered at them anxiously. "You're not supposed to have a wedding without getting in love." She chewed on her bottom lip for a moment, then beamed at them. "Maybe you can get married Saturday, after cartoons."

"Well, first of all, squirt," Michael tried to tell her, "weddings take lots of time to plan. You can't just decide to get married in a few days."

Her bottom lip jutted out. "I did lots of planning," she informed them. "We still have some food from your boring party and people could eat that. And then we could all go on a hommeymoon to Disneyland."

Trask gave a sound suspiciously like a snort of laughter,

but it was impossible to be sure because his face was buried in his hand.

"This is fair," Chloe reminded them. "I didn't get to pick Mommy's new husband, so I should get to pick your new wife, Daddy." She watched them both anxiously. "It's very fair."

Michael grinned up at Kate. "How about it, Miss Rose? Is this the most romantic offer you've ever had, or what?"

Kate caught Chloe's earnest hazel gaze and her eyes began to pool. Here was everything she'd lacked in her life, and she had almost been afraid to accept it. But these two had seeped under her defenses, filled a void she'd never had a name for. Now there was only one possible answer.

"Your chief negotiator makes a persuasive case, but she left out some important conditions," she said shakily.

Michael's brows rose. "Deal breakers?"

"Absolutely."

"Better lay your terms on the table then."

She tilted her head, pretended to consider. "My demands are simple, really. A lifetime contract with the CEO, with equal interest in the young negotiator over there."

His hazel eyes glinted as he gave a slow nod. "Done." And to the delight of the onlookers, the sweetheart deal was sealed with a kiss.

* * * * *